American Fever

American Fever

Dur e Aziz Amna

SCEPTRE

First published in Great Britain in 2022 by Sceptre
An imprint of Hodder & Stoughton
An Hachette UK company

1

A CIP catalogue record for this title is available from the British Library

Hardback ISBN 9781529393354
Trade Paperback ISBN 9781529393361
eBook ISBN 9781529393378

Typeset in Sabon MT by Manipal Technologies Limited

Printed and bound in Great Britain by Clays Ltd, Elcograf S.p.A.

Hodder & Stoughton policy is to use papers that are natural, renewable
and recyclable products and made from wood grown in sustainable forests.
The logging and manufacturing processes are expected to conform to
the environmental regulations of the country of origin.

Hodder & Stoughton Ltd
Carmelite House
50 Victoria Embankment
London EC4Y 0DZ

www.sceptrebooks.co.uk

For Ammi and Abbu

Raat yoon dil mein teri khoyi hui yaad aayi
Jaise veerane mein chupke se bahar aa jaye
Jaise sehraon mein hole se chale baad-e-naseem
Jaise beemar ko bevajah qarar aa jaye

Faiz Ahmed Faiz, *Nuskha Hae Wafa*

Intimacy . . . be it of hatred or of love, can be defined as confident, quasi-immediate translation.

George Steiner, *After Babel*

Kujh shehr de lok vi zalam san
Kujh sanoon maran da shauq vi si

Munir Niazi, *Safar Di Raat*

January

By God, I had planned to keep it to myself and God. But then the sheets speckle red. Blood, like pomegranate jewels, spots the pillowcase.

It's the night of Kelly's wedding. The Pacific Northwest has received a flurry of snow, and as I get out of bed to gargle away the metal from my mouth, I wonder how the drops of red will look on the pristine white of the patio. I wonder if the blood means the disease is now severe, even lethal. Mostly, I wonder how much of this is America's doing.

*

In the morning, I go out to the living room, where Kelly and Ethan are nursing their coffees, clearly hungover. I tell Kelly she has to take me to the doctor. She still has mascara on from last night.

'Can this wait, Hira?'

I shake my head, tell her it must be today, and my host mother's face sets into annoyance, which is doubly unfortunate because she and I shared a tender moment last night, the kind of thing that has become a rarity of late. This must not be how she and Ethan planned to spend the first morning of their marriage, but I can't drive and she is the adult in charge, so this is how it has to be.

In the car ride to the doctor's, I try to make conversation, telling her I had a great time attending my first American

1

wedding. Kelly loves it when I posit myself as a virgin to America, so that cheers her up a bit. I also mention that I spoke with Ali on the phone after the party.

'So are you two dating now?'

'He lives in New York. I'm going back to Pakistan in five months.'

'Yes, but life is long,' she says. 'And you're smart. I'll be shocked if you don't find your way back to America.'

'You're assuming I want to.'

See, that's my problem. Kelly's doing me a favor by driving me around the day after her wedding. Why can't I keep my mouth shut?

'Well,' she says, frowning. 'They do say it's the land of opportunity.'

Kelly lives in rural Oregon, where the state of opportunity is such that I haven't been able to find an afterschool job in five months. But it's 2011, America is still king of the world, the cool guy's in the White House, and Kelly can't comprehend the rest of the world not clamoring for these shores.

'I just hope you see your own potential,' she continues. 'If you remain in Pakistan, I'll always worry about your safety.'

Again, it's 2011, and Americans are worried about everyone else's safety, sated in the knowledge that their nook of the world is far safer than elsewhere, although don't tell them why that might be. History is what happens in other places. America transcends it. This will all change, but at the time I can merely nod.

'Leaving home isn't easy,' I say, offering my own banality in response to hers.

'And you've already done it at such a young age,' she replies, upbeat, as we take the Eugene exit. 'Mark my words, you'll be back in no time. My mother tells me that the first time she returned to Hamburg, she cried every morning for California.'

2

'Did you ever ask her how many times she's cried for Hamburg?'

Kelly sighs. I am so bloody difficult.

'She is much happier here.'

I pinch back my tongue and change the subject to the honeymoon. Kelly and Ethan are leaving for Hawaii next week.

But I don't buy it, that thing she says about her mother. Of course, one can be happy anywhere – certain zip codes help and yet none are necessary – but it is Kelly's certainty that irks me. Her mother must have done what many emigrants do – create neat narratives for their children, flimsy accounts of one-way movement they then begin to internalize. A lie told often enough becomes the truth. And perhaps these accounts are not lies but simply omissions that elide over how home is forever that other place, the first one to drive you to despair, the lover you took before learning to externalize the deeds of the world. It is the sole landscape of dreams, the only place that will ever convince you that its failings, its bounties, its excesses, and caresses are all your own. After all, where does it end and you begin?

*

The doctor is a lean man with suspiciously white teeth who asks me to repeat my name.

'I want to get it right,' he insists, and I smile as if I haven't heard that a hundred times already. I tell him about the cough that sits like a nail in my throat, the fever that comes and goes, the fatigue that burrows into my body each afternoon. He nods.

'How long have you had the cough?'

'Three months.'

He raises his eyebrows.

'And you're just seeing someone now?'

'I thought it was a winter cold.'

He shakes his head in disappointment, typing away at his computer.

'Also,' I begin, because it is no longer a thing I can keep to myself and God. 'I coughed up blood last night.'

The doctor swivels in his chair to face me.

'Blood?'

Kelly looks up from her phone.

'You didn't tell me that, Hira.'

'I just saw it this morning.'

'Do you have night chills?' the doctor asks.

'Yes.'

'Productive cough?'

'Productive?'

'Is there phlegm?'

'Yes.'

He glances down at my file.

'It says here you are from . . . Pakistan?'

I nod.

'How long have you been in America?'

'Five months.'

'Were you sick while you were in Pakistan?'

Not exactly, is the answer.

'No,' I tell the doctor, my eyes falling to the faint scar on my arm.

He writes down some tests, looking grim. I take the elevator to the lab, where the nurse asks me to cough vigorously into a tube. Then she ties a tourniquet around my arm and feels for a promising vein. I look away towards the window, which overlooks low-lying buildings flanked by fir. Spencer Butte sits in the distance under a blanket of snow. When I arrived in Oregon last summer, evenings would linger forever, the sky full of pink promise even at dinnertime. Now, it is not

4

yet four but the sun has already grown meek, leaving behind the unmistakable blue of dusk. Perhaps this is the only thing common between here and home – the cruelty of a January evening.

'The nurse will call tomorrow. Let's hope for the best,' the doctor says when I return to his office, looking very much like he is hoping for no such thing.

Kelly is quiet in the car. I wonder if I should call Ali when I get home. What will he say? That I shouldn't assume the worst, let the tests come back, it might not be what I think it is – the sort of stuff people say to buy time to react to someone else's misery.

As for my parents, I decide I'll wait till the next day. After the nurse has called and confirmed what I already sense is true, and I have thanked her and she has hung up, I will not put down the receiver but instead dial that +92 home. And I will tell my parents, with the certainty of iron, that I'm terribly sick, and it's their fault.

I

I had wanted to go. Of course, I had wanted to go. Not desperately, passionately, like the Hollywood foreigner's yearning for America, like the Third Worlder's slobbering. Mostly, I had wanted to leave. At sixteen, I was tired of limits, aghast that life could be so small. Tired of those same girls I had known all my life, girls who called their periods their 'visitors,' girls who opened their legs to a waxing lady each month so they would have no hair 'down there' by the time they got married, girls who wore their piety and innocence like goddamn medals to be polished every night before bedtime.

I got along with them just fine, was even voted class monitor once. And there were days, winter days when we all stood together inside the 11CT classroom because it alone had a gas heater that worked, pulled at the sleeves of our royal blue uniform coats, and rubbed each other's frozen fingers. We begged Rasheed Chacha at the gate to let us buy Kashmiri chai from the cart outside, and he'd tell us no, hadn't he been over this, he couldn't let us roam outside. Please, Chacha, what did it take of you, we'd say, and if the day was especially cold, he'd shake his head and let us go, knowing we'd bring back a cup for him. Those among us who didn't get money for the canteen shared a cup with a friend. 'Tum piyo, nahi yar, tum lo,' we insisted, offering each other the prize at the bottom. Pinkened almonds and pistachios. These were the days I didn't want to leave, when I wished to stay forever in that huddle of silly girls, who only sought of the world reasons to laugh or to cry, who were always looking to fall in love, who didn't know, didn't desire to know, how powerful and clever and beautiful they were, who had already decided on the low, petty ceilings of their limits.

There were such days, but by the end, they were getting far and few between.

*

It was the end of May, the day of the last school exam. I stood in front of the mirror, wiping beads of sweat off my chest. I liked how my stomach looked in the early mornings – a concave lowland, before it swelled with the caretaker Aliya's ghee-laden parathay that turned the entire kitchen redolent with burnt animal fat.

My room was already bright – I had left the windows open at night when the air was cooler. The sun carpeted the floor, forming pools of light by the bed. Science textbooks and sheets of loose-leaf paper, filled with answers to all possible exam questions, were strewn on the floor. During the night, when the fan whirred above, the sheets flapped in the breeze, forcing me to stumble around in the dark for makeshift paperweights. Several mornings in the past month, I had woken up to find odd objects on the floor: a severely dog-eared *Jane Eyre*, a tattered copy of O Level Biology Past Papers, and once, my dusty copy of the Quran.

After drying off the sweat, I twisted my hair into a braid. My uniform hung by the door, its blue faded from years of daily wear. Putting on the kameez, the school logo embroidered on its front pocket, I thought back to the email Ammi and Abbu had gotten last September.

Ammi and Abbu had collectively decided to send me to a girls-only school – Abbu because he thought co-ed was corrosive to adolescent morality, and Ammi because she said girls grew up bolder, louder, and uncaged when not in the shadow of men. Reading the email, they both shook their heads, appalled. I wasn't the least bit surprised though. It was true that we were looser without boys; at school, we brayed, stomped, spat, and danced as if we were air. But the freedom was always tenuous, a throwaway clause in the overall contract. The hot breath of surveillance was always there.

I remembered the school trip four years ago, when we were so young, still on the brink of blood. A few of the girls had spotted an idle hose lying, snake-like, on the grass in Liaqat Bagh. It was hot, and we took turns drenching each other with the stream, shrieking as the water ran down our backs. Then the supervising teachers saw us.

'What do you think you're doing?' they screeched, circling like vultures. 'Do you realize that all the gardeners and cleaners can see through your slips?'

All the uncles in their Toyotas could see us too, but that wasn't the point.

One of the teachers, the spite of the entire world in her eyes, said, 'That's what they want, isn't it? They want to be mod squad. They want the entire world to see them.'

In a few years, that would be exactly what we'd want – in the short walk from school gate to car, in the leaked videos of Eid Milan parties where we danced to Himesh Reshammiya, after the one-second-too-long gazes we shared with tailors and ice cream vendors, we would move like currents in the Jhelum, writhe our backs because we knew the whole world was watching. But that day in the park was before all of that. All we had wanted then was the pleasure of cold water hitting our sweaty arms, the abandon of bodies smelling like the children that we were.

A week after the email was sent to our parents, we all stood in line as Mrs Saleem went around, measuring the distance between the edges of our kameez and our knees with a tape ruler. Several girls bent forward to shrink their torsos, the same way we stood in prayer, diffident and bowed even when upright. Rabia tugged at her shirt, trying to hide the fact that she'd taken her uniform to a tailor the day she got it and asked him to cut four inches off. Four inches, when every inch was political. The cloth clung to her body, dipping around her slender waist and blooming outward as it reached her hips. It ached the rest of us, how good she looked in it. That day, she got a strict warning from Mrs Saleem, after which the teacher turned to me. Seeing my long, baggy kameez, she nodded.

'Allah approves of this length, ma'am?' I asked.

She glared at me before moving to the next girl. Later, she took me aside.

'Arrogance is a terrible look,' she said. 'And trust me, our society does not forgive it in young ladies like yourself.'

It's one of the ways in which older women punish younger ones for what the world has done to them. *If it was this way for us*, they think, *why not for them as well*? Not for me, I knew.

'I'll see that for myself, ma'am,' I said, holding her gaze until she looked away.

*

Mrs Saleem was invigilating that day's exam, so I rushed down to breakfast after changing. I read only the front page of the paper, dark with the headline announcing that ninety-four Ahmadis had been killed in an attack in Lahore. I looked up at Abbu, the most single-minded diner I have ever met, who had just finished his toast and was meticulously picking at the crumbs with a sticky finger.

'Did you read this?' I asked, holding up the page, worrying how I would explain things like this in America. That's how sweetly young I was, that I thought Americans knew who Ahmadis were.

Abbu's forehead creased at the sight of the page.

'I can't talk about it,' he said, and shook his head. 'It's too painful.'

Ammi and Abbu did that often. Most news was too sad or too serious to be discussed with me and Faisal. The girls at school had little interest in newspapers – it was the age of newly liberalized TV channels churning out one drama serial after another. I ended up discussing most news articles with my twelve-year-old brother, hoping to indoctrinate him at an early age about the perils of a religiously monolithic country. He nodded along to my words, remembered names and dates, and once got in trouble with Abbu for referring to the local maulvi as an ullu ka patha.

On the way to school, the driver, Uncle Shafiq, drove though the cantonment with little interruption. We cruised past the women's university, St Paul's Church that had recently been painted a hideous pink, and the British period Flashman's Hotel. It was a once-beautiful building, constructed all on one floor so guests didn't have to climb a single stair. As we drove through the heart of the city, it got busier. Cars were starting to line up by Mall Plaza, where dozens of signs jostled for space on fading white walls.

Siddique Currency Exchange

Torab Money Mart: We Accept All Major Currencies
Euro International & Western Union

Five minutes from school, several cars waited at a green signal. A warden was managing traffic – his shrill whistle emanated in the distance.

'It's a route,' said Uncle Shafiq.

I slumped in the car seat. Politicians or top-brass army officers traveling through the city sometimes insisted that all traffic stop for them and their coterie of vehicles to pass through. Security reasons, they said. It started seven years ago, in 2003, when someone tried blowing up Musharraf on the Chaklala bridge. They didn't get him, but the rest of us were paying for it since, in fear and lost time.

'Some bastard's on his way,' Uncle Shafiq grumbled. I bit the inside of my mouth to hide my smile. With my parents in the car, Uncle Shafiq said little except to ask Abbu, 'Where to, saab?' Around Faisal and me, his words became looser, franker. Now, he turned the steering wheel this way and that, maneuvering through stalled vehicles, squeezing the car into any space he could find. Finally, we saw the cavalcade of military jeeps rush by, some with sirens twirling.

'They grabbed the land, and now they're after our streets,' I said, and Uncle Shafiq nodded with force. Finally, an adult who respected my views on the state of affairs.

I walked into the exam room a minute before it started. Mrs Saleem looked at me with arched eyebrows. 'Route tha, ma'am,' I said, knowing how rehearsed that sounded – it was 2010, that was Pindi's favorite excuse. I sat down in my assigned seat next to Rabia. The exam was O Level Urdu B, an absurdly easy module meant for second-generation speakers in Britain. We had all grown up in Urdu but when, after a year of slogging through Mir, Ghalib, and Altaf Fatima, we revolted against the harder Urdu Literature syllabus, the school acquiesced. Mrs Saleem, who had taught the literature class, was furious, and we thought that was the reason she hated us. Later, I would understand her heartbreak better – being a teacher who thought poetry and prose, Ludhianvi's 'Taj Mahal', *bazeecha-e-atfal hai*, Iqbal's 'Shikwa', all had something to give to her students, only for them to consider none of it worth their effort. But we were serious science students, many of us aiming for the Aga Khan or King Edward medical schools. No one had time for dead poets. And I suppose it was egalitarian, because the school didn't mandate English Literature either, and so it was quite possible to graduate from our high school not having read a single novel in either language. It was a travesty even Macaulay hadn't envisioned.

At ten, Mrs Saleem announced that we could open the leaflets. Scanning the paper, I felt the entire class breathe a sigh of relief. The questions were simple, many of them taken, without change, from previous exams.

Write a 150-word essay on the importance of friendship.

Write 200 words on the need for environmental conservation.

Rabia and I shook our heads at each other. Just how much we were being shortchanged in our education would become evident only in retrospect, but even then, the exam felt insultingly easy. By eleven, we were all done, shuffling in our chairs. I read through my answers twice, wondering whether to go out into the heat or keep sitting in the classroom, where they had recently installed air-conditioning. The remote control, still wrapped in plastic, rested in Mrs Saleem's hands; every now and then she pressed buttons to adjust the temperature on the dial. 22. 24. 23. 19. I looked out the window, where the sun pounded the concrete. Someone clicked her Picasso pen in and out until Mrs Saleem told her she'd take it away. Rabia exhaled loudly, then stood up and handed in her sheets of paper. After that, more girls got up. I took one last look at my answers and then put them on top of the pile on Mrs Saleem's desk. I almost gave her a smile, then remembered that I was done with her patronizing ways forever. Instead, I nodded and walked out, towards freedom, into a summer leading to America.

*

Some of us headed to the school canteen, with its steel walls painted over in Coca Cola red. Over the past four years, whenever I had money, I would leave Aliya's dry sandwiches uneaten in the lunchbox and pay twenty rupees for a piping-hot samosa set on a bed of chickpeas. Today, Rabia insisted it was her treat, telling the canteen lady to make generous plates for all five of us.

'Aunty, it's the last time we're eating your chaat. Full plates, please, not like the past four years.'

The older woman, a muslin scarf wrapped tightly around her head, wordlessly made the plates and put them on the metal counter.

'One hundred,' she said.

'You'll make us pay even today, Aunty?' Maryam asked, shaking her head. The woman started back blankly, and Maryam stifled a laugh. Rabia paid and we took our plates to an empty classroom, where the bulletin boards were plastered with exam schedules and verses from the Quran. Those verses were a hazard and a half – sometimes the fan shook them off the wall and they landed on the ground, making the teachers rush over to retrieve them while gasping, whispering to Allah for forgiveness. Some of the girls had adopted the performance too – it was pure, blustery performance – picking up the cardboard and kissing it repetitively to atone for the blasphemy of God's words touching the earth, when the real blasphemy was the assumption that God gave a damn.

13

'I'll miss this place,' Maryam said, as we sat down on the green metal chairs.

'We'll all be together next year too,' Rabia pointed out.

In the fall, most girls were moving to a newer building of the same school, where they would complete the last two years of high school. There was a rumor that the new place had slick whiteboards instead of the chalkboards that left us snowy each time we dusted them. It even had Wi-Fi. We had spent the past few years begging for access to the one computer with internet each time we had to research something for class. Knowledge was jealously guarded at the school, and even when we were allowed, the computer instructor kept her beady eyes on the screen. Did she really think we relied on a school computer to educate ourselves on the illicit, when there was the Oxford Dictionary, the Urban Dictionary, Choka and Chhaka dial-up cards, older sisters, gyno aunties, and most of all, our own sly little mouths, whispering about every god-damn thing under the sun?

'Well, almost all of us will be together,' Rabia continued, puncturing samosa crust with a fork. 'When are you leaving, Hira?'

'In two months, end of July,' I replied.

'You'll have a great time,' she said, her mouth curved in a smile that was half genuine at best. 'The States are so much fun.'

I had vacillated on what to call it ever since I got the acceptance letter – US, USA, or America. I had read that the latter offended South Americans; a columnist in the newspaper called the term 'provincial.' People like Rabia, who had visited several times, always called it 'the States.'

'It must be very expensive for your parents,' she noted. 'I'm surprised they can afford it.'

'It's fully funded.'

I had told her this before.

'Oh, nice. Where have they placed you?'

Rabia's family flew every summer to visit relatives in New York or London, returning each August with Times Square magnets and British biscuits in colorful metal tins. At home, Ammi now used one of those tins as a jewelry box.

'Oregon,' I said. 'It's a really pretty state on the West Coast.'

'Hmm, never heard of it.'

Rabia could knock the breath out of me with how deftly she turned the tide in conversations. Throughout that past month, with the exams coming up, she called me daily after school, asking for exam papers, comforting me by saying we would both do just fine. But we were young and hungry in a place full of young and hungry people, so anytime one of us did do fine – like when I got the US scholarship – it felt like a betrayal.

I didn't know this back then, but no one in the world would ever be as much like me as Rabia and the other girls I was leaving behind. No matter what we did or where we fled to, whether we had babies at twenty or became surgeons at thirty, we were all shaped by the dawn and dusk of the Potohar, its parched gullies and ridges, the tyranny of Pindi winters, chaat samosay, naan kabab, the gravel of the morning assembly loudspeaker, the acridity of the chemistry lab, but above all the knowledge that we were all in it together – that giddy, intractable project of not being an adult.

But right then, with Rabia making me feel small like she often did, I was eager to leave them all behind.

*

I had received the acceptance letter two months ago in March, when the air was still mild. The interview had gone well, mostly because the organizers put me and four other finalists in a room and asked us questions that required little besides common sense.

'What if someone invites you to jihad during your year abroad in America?'

We were dorky aspirants to the upper class and couldn't tell ass from elbow, New York from Nevada – no one was going to be inviting us to jihad. One of the applicants, perhaps to stand out, said he would try to reason with the person and hear his point of view. The rest of us gave each other looks of mixed horror and satisfaction, knowing we were down to four contenders. Only in retrospect did I see how odd it was of the interviewers, all middle-aged Islamabad professionals, to ask that question of sixteen-year-olds, to see exactly how we tripped over it.

The envelope had arrived all the way from D.C., the address of the US State Department printed on the top left.

'Must be important news,' the delivery man had said, amused, as I caught my breath. I waited until his motorbike took off to rip open the seam. My feet were bare against the dusty patio; it hadn't rained in a while.

15th March 2010

Dear Hira Amjad,

We are pleased to inform you that you have been selected to participate in a ten-month study exchange program in the United States of America. The program is fully funded by the Department of State and includes the cost of travel, housing, and a monthly stipend of $150. In the upcoming weeks, you will receive more information on host family placement from your Country Coordinator.

That next afternoon, my family went to Majeed Huts at Quaid-e-Azam University to celebrate. We ate dal fry and chicken pervezi. Abbu wiped his hands with leftover naan, and Ammi pinched her nose with disgust, digging inside her handbag for a paper napkin.

'Are you really going to let her go?' Faisal asked, and I thought that was bold of him. My parents preferred to talk around things and rarely about them. Ammi opened and closed her mouth. Abbu furrowed his forehead, the way he did when he was about to say something profound. I loved hearing Abbu say profound things – I even wrote them down in my notebook from time to time – but sometimes they served to obfuscate conversation and provide him a way out of clear answers.

Sure enough, he asked, 'Beta, don't you remember what Hazrat Muhammad said?'

We got so much Islam at school, at home, on TV, we pretty much only remembered what Hazrat Muhammad said.

'"Seek knowledge,"' Abbu quoted. '"Even if it takes you as far as China."'

Looking back, I can see how insufficient that explanation was, and I wonder if my parents themselves bought it. Yes, knowledge for the sake of knowledge was admirable. Yes, ours was a religion that encouraged exploration; Tariq didn't conquer Andalusia by staying home. But we were sitting on the campus where my father had arrived when he left the village, the place where he had become fluent in English and heard of Marx and student unions, but also where he had honed himself to apply for the civil service job that would be his way out of economic precarity, his passport to the rest of the country, the rest of the world. More than likely, it was that desire to move further up the rungs of class, the forever promise of progress, and the conviction that this progress equated to westward movement, that made my parents decide that sending their young daughter across two oceans was a good idea.

Not that they didn't have doubts. Once, I had overheard them in their bedroom.

'I keep thinking we'll lose her.'

It was Ammi, sounding almost embarrassed of herself. Emotions are a nuisance to my mother.

'She's so headstrong,' Abbu had replied. He had said that several times to my face, but always as a reprimand, not with the pride I then heard in his voice. 'Too strong, if anything. That country will do nothing to her.'

'Mrs Imtiaz called the other day,' Ammi continued, as if Abbu had not spoken. 'She said the road to America is one-way. Whoever goes there gets consumed by it.'

There was silence, long enough to tell me that the conversation had ended for the time being and would now percolate separately inside their minds. I could tell it wasn't the first time they were talking about it, and it wouldn't be the last. I tiptoed around them for the next few days, dreading that they would sit me down and tell me that they had changed their mind, putting an end to my big break, my adventure, before it began. But they stuck to their decision, arranging for my medical check-up and asking around for the best dollar exchange rates. Abbu even tried to get me a quicker appointment for the visa, knowing the Americans were notorious for unexplained delays, but the woman who picked up the phone snorted and hung up. It turned out the power of Pakistani civil servants did not extend to the thick, grey walls of Islamabad's most guarded embassy.

II

'So, have you talked to your host family yet?'

The girl was speaking to me. I shook my head word-lessly, trying to discourage conversation.

It was June, and all sixty selected students were on our way to Karachi for an orientation aimed at preparing us for America. Everyone from northern Punjab was on the same flight, including Zahra, who was now sitting next to me and detailing the hour-long conversation she had with her host mother the previous night. Her long purple earrings swayed as she talked.

'They live in New Jersey,' she said. 'Near New York.'

Another girl sitting in the middle aisle turned towards us, clearly impressed. Every family member of mine had asked how far Oregon was from New York, the one city they all knew of from the screaming headlines of 2001.

'The best thing is,' Zahra continued. 'They're Muslims.'

'Mashallah, so lucky!' The other girl joined in, unable to contain her envy. Her accent was that of the smaller Punjabi cities, a baby-pink scarf wrapped tightly around her head.

Two years before, I had taken on the scarf as well, a white one with crochet edges, pushing it down my temples to cover all wisps of hair before I went to school. Ammi covered her hair only in bazars flooded with men, flinging the dupatta off as soon as she got back to the car. Her contract with it was strictly social, the dupatta often thin and sheer. She draped it in what Faisal and I called the PTV style, after our favorite news-caster who covered her head just enough to follow guidelines

19

but not too much that she would be rendered unattractive for prime time. The first day I went down for breakfast wearing the scarf, Ammi stared but said nothing. At the end of the week, she came up to my room after I returned from school. I stood by the mirror, unclasping the safety pin that held the cloth together. I loved doing that, letting my hair fall out at the end of the day, surprising even myself with the cascade that hid below.

'Why have you started wearing that?' she asked.

I didn't have a great answer. The hijab was accruing some cachet at school. The sporty head girl wore it, and the Islamiyat teacher had taken to making us clap for every new hijabi in class. There were wider factors at play – the Farhat Hashmization of the new middle class, the commodification of trendy Islamic attire – but these weren't things my fourteen-year-old mind could grapple with.

'I want to be a good Muslim,' I told Ammi.

'There are more attractive ways of being a good Muslim,' she said.

Abbu, on the other hand, nodded with appreciation when he saw me in the scarf, because for months he had been pointing out every young family friend who covered her hair. 'Doesn't Ameer's daughter look so sweet in the scarf, Hira?' Ours was never a propaganda household. Ammi and Abbu parented in uneven ways, often sending out contradictory messages about faith and practice and leaving it to Faisal and me to reconcile them as we saw fit.

I wore the scarf for a few months before realizing I violently hated it, detested the way my face looked unanchored by hair, felt ashamed of proclaiming a kind of piety I did not possess. That summer, I joined an evening tuition center with Rabia. The class was co-ed and Rabia always arrived with kajal-lined eyes, her hair brushed into a halo around her head. She also laughed more, and loudly. One day, she called after tuition to tell me about the boy who had asked for her number after class, and I realized that would never happen to me. That killed me. Slowly, I started taking the scarf off, not wearing it to family parties at first, then abandoning it at school. Ammi got Aliya to put it away, but we didn't talk about it.

On the plane, I turned to look out the window as Zahra happily gave the other girl details of her host family, emigrants from India. They had moved from Hyderabad in the '80s and lived in a town called Edison. On the phone, she spoke with them in Urdu. I wondered what the point of traveling to America was if you were going to go live with a Muslim family that spoke Urdu. I hadn't communicated with my host family yet, but I knew enough about them to know all the ways they were different from me. White. Christian. American.

'They said they'll have biryani waiting for me in New Jersey,' Zahra laughed.

'You can get that when we land in Karachi,' I said.

The girl in the scarf stared at me with distaste.

*

We spent the next few days at a hotel near the port, built alongside an inlet of the Arabian Sea overrun by mangroves. The smell of salt pervaded the rooms. Each morning, we had breakfast and assembled in the meeting room to learn about the program, which had been set up within a year of September 2001, providing scholarships for high school students from Muslim countries to spend a year in the US. Mr Shahid, the program coordinator, handed out list after list, which we put into neat red folders. There was a list of things to bring, a list of niceties to learn, a list of things to avoid (political debate, tattoos, demanding a paratha for breakfast). He read the last one out loud and peppered in some cautionary tales: the kid who had woken up his host

21

mother before dawn so she could make sehri for his fast; the girl who had refused to clean her own bathroom, saying she never did that back home in Lahore.

'American moms,' he said, 'are not like Pakistani women. They have jobs, and they've volunteered to host you. For free – remember that none of these families are being compensated. You should be ready to look after yourselves and do chores.'

Chores were brought up frequently. Americans seemed to do a lot of chores: they mowed lawns, shoveled snow, did laundry each week. Later that day, we had to sit in a circle and say what our favorite and least favorite chores were, and no one came up with anything good. I was one of the few students there who had attended a private school, so my family was likely better off than theirs, but it seemed that all of us had grown up doing little except school and play. The washing and cooking and cleaning – we had our mothers for that, or the women our mothers hired. The whole point of our lives was to not become like them.

*

Mr Shahid had worked for non-profits in Karachi for many years before being offered the role of Country Coordinator by the Americans. He liked visiting D.C. twice a year for events but had no desire to move there.

'Life is more comfortable here,' he said over lunch the second day.

'Too many chores in America, sir?' Zahra replied, and he let out a loud laugh. He was sitting at our table, having taken a liking to me and Zahra. Middle-aged people have always been my key demographic.

'You people are young, you can adapt. I'm too old to move to another country. English mein baat karun to lagta hai jhoot bol raha hoon.'

I took out the notebook they had given us – a garish photograph of the Statue of Liberty on its slippery cover – and wrote down what he had said.

'Speaking in English feels like a lie.'

It was the kind of thing Abbu would say. Ammi's degree in Anglophone Literature and her job as assistant professor in English kept her fluent. Faisal and I went to English-medium schools, where we were encouraged to always speak in the language, although everyone knew it was social suicide to speak in anything but Urdu outside of a teacher's earshot – English was too snooty, Punjabi too oily. But it was different with Abbu. He and Mr Shahid were of the same milieu of men, raised and educated in humbler languages only to discover that unless you were a landowner or industrialist, the path to progress was paved with abcd's. Abbu had learned English only in his twenties, perusing *Peter and Jane* books for grammar while he dabbled in hashish and leftist politics at university. Not that this hindered his acerbic wit in that third language. When some French civil servants visiting Islamabad pointed out that Europeans had been the ones to bring many spices to the Subcontinent, Abbu listened with deference before adding, 'Yes, they brought them here and left them here.'

One afternoon, we got a rushed tour of Karachi's highlights: Frere Hall, where the air teased us with the scent of roasted corn on the cob; a museum that was once the summer home of a Hindu merchant; and Jinnah's mausoleum, where Zahra pointed out all the couples furtively holding hands.

The group had seamlessly sieved itself into gender-based factions, even though Mr Shahid encouraged us to mingle.

'In America, everything is co-ed,' he said.

I thought back to the dictum Abbu had pronounced when I was twelve and he found out I was hanging out daily with the neighbors' son. Boys are not friends, he had said. Classmates, yes. Husbands, yes. But not friends. It was clear that the other girls had gotten similar lessons, because – although none of us believed it, so many of the girls were constantly smiling at their phones and then putting them face-down on the table, likely talking to those boyfriends they'd dump as soon as they hit American turf – everyone knew to play the part. All the girls hung out together, waiting to walk down to the conference room in groups, sitting together in tight clusters at dinner. The boys did the same, but with the stretchy, loitering ease that they were allowed and we weren't.

In private, we made fun of the new lexicon we were being taught. 'Making the bed is your chore today,' Zahra would say to me. 'Will you go to Prom?' we asked each other. Americans called their mothers 'mom,' which embarrassed us, the vowel sounding drawn out and childish. None of us was poor, but neither were we the kind of rich who grew up calling their mother 'mom.' We had a word for kids who did that – *burgers*, foreign like the beef patties sold at McDonald's.

*

At the end of orientation, we had dinner at a restaurant by the sea. For what seemed like hours, we sat in two vans, girls in one, boys in the other. Buses hurtled past, weary faces looking out of windowless frames. Large ads screamed about the beauty of Lux-imbued skin and Pantene-treated hair. The driver, Shahzeb, snaked through thick evening traffic, sometimes honking, sometimes twisting the steering wheel with such force that all of us turned quiet to let him concentrate.

'He's not bad-looking,' Zahra whispered in English, looking at the back of Shahzeb's head. Shahzeb was what Ammi would call a 'proper driver,' the kind that kept the rearview mirror turned away while driving women around. From where I sat, I could see the veins running down his left hand that sat on the gearshift. He was no older than thirty, and painfully handsome.

'Shut up,' said Isra, scandalized.

'What?' Zahra's eyebrows were raised. 'Just because he's a driver means he can't be good-looking?'

'Sshh. What if he hears you? He'll get ideas.'

I had little patience for girls like Isra, who acted like it was only men who got ideas, as if they themselves had never thought of how it would be to touch them – drivers, school guards, gardeners – men we were always told to be wary of, men who often knew us better than our fathers did.

Soon, we were on a highway that looked out at the sea. On the other side stood apartment buildings taller than any I had ever seen.

'That's where the rich people live,' Isra pointed out.

'But it's so far from the city,' I said.

'Exactly,' she nodded. 'Gated and secure, no riff-raff.'

I looked at the buildings, plastered in white against an otherwise blank skyline. The apartments seemed surly and disassociated, unlike the house we rented in Pindi that was right off G.T. Road. Sometimes, when a vegetable hawker dragged his cart down the sidewalk, I could see his wares from our rooftop: hairy carrots, onions with cracked skins, turnips that appeared tie-died in purple and white.

'I would never want to live there,' I concluded.

'Yeah, right,' Isra replied. 'It's the best living in Karachi right now.'

She was clearly parroting something an adult had told her. No one our age used the term 'best living.'

'Do you know how unsafe this city is?' she continued. She was from Karachi and didn't let anyone forget that. 'You would be lucky to live far away from all that mess.'

Karachi was always burning; a donkey in Chakwal could tell you that. After Benazir was killed in 2007, all we heard

25

about for weeks was the rioting in the south. There was a beautiful shot of a Suzuki Mehran covered in flames that the news channels kept playing over and over.

'Uff, Karachi, cry me a river,' Zahra said, rolling her eyes. Isra opened, then closed her mouth. Four days of Zahra had taught everyone to steer clear of that tongue of hers before it neatly slit them into two.

Mr Shahid had reserved a long table on the balcony, from where we could make out the fishermen's blue boats, lit up with fluorescent bulbs. As we passed around the appetizers – fried prawns and masala fries – Zahra whispered, 'Usman likes you.'

Unlike most of the girls, Zahra had made friends with the boys in the program, once even sneaking out for ice cream with them after midnight. She had asked me to come along but I refused. We were not allowed to leave the hotel premises and I was so worried we would get caught and Abbu would find out and there would go America, my golden year, and there I would be, back with those schoolgirls I had just left. I regretted my decision as soon as she left. For what seemed like hours, I lay awake and imagined her roaming the streets of Karachi, making every boy feel like she was flirting with him. Now, I asked, 'How do you know he likes me?'

'He told me, yar. Do you think he's cute?'

I looked over at Usman, who was talking to Mr Shahid. He had a bowl cut and shy eyes; he looked just the kind of boy who would need someone else's help in asking a girl out. Did that mean I was the kind of girl who attracted such a boy?

I was beautiful – not in a way that stole someone's breath, but very few people were attractive that way. When family friends visited, the aunties always told Ammi she had a beautiful daughter, and perhaps they were saying it in that polite way people say such things, but I never thought to myself, *oh, she's lying.*

26

I grew up paying my body little attention. Pimples came and went, a few gray hairs turned up very early in my teens, a tooth chipped – these things I noticed, but could never get myself to agonize over. Ammi also never let me dwell too long on questions of beauty. She had grown up in a household where being a woman meant little, and there was nothing by way of feminine vanities that she wished to pass down to me. If she complimented me, it was on grades, nice manners, intelligence. When she got me my first bra three years ago, she wordlessly left it on my bed. I found it and gingerly put the plain brown garment on, fumbling with the fishhooks, standing on my toes to catch a reflection in the bathroom mirror. We didn't talk about it.

Later, in Oregon, my host mother would ask me, hesitating over each word, if I compared myself to the American girls around me, if I felt self-conscious in the face of Western beauty standards. I was mortified by her question, unsure how to respond without embarrassing her. What did my beauty have to do with American girls, what did my lineage have to do with theirs?

I was beautiful because my mother was beautiful. My mother, who could pause for a second by the mirror near the front door, smooth back her hair and put pink lipstick on, and then walk into any party. My mother, who turned the room slightly luminescent every time she smiled.

I turned to Zahra.

'You can tell Usman I'm not interested.'

III

'Hira beta, sending you away was not an easy decision for us.' We had just finished Sunday lunch. I settled back into the creaky dining chair, mentally prepared for the forthcoming sermon, knowing there would be a few before I left. Abbu was in the business of sermons – gorgeous, aphoristic incantations that went on too long.

'We want you to take advantage of every opportunity America gives you,' he continued. 'But at the same time, you cannot forget who you are. You have to represent yourself as a Pakistani, a Muslim, and a girl.'

Years later, I can better deconstruct the orthodoxy of these expectations, but even back then they rankled me. The last one was particularly itchy because it implied more exacting standards on all fronts – the bar for being a good Muslim and a good Pakistani seemed much higher if you also happened to be a girl. Ammi was nodding with encouragement. She had given me her own version of the lecture a few days ago, starting off with a long story about a girl she'd known in college who had sex with a married man, became pregnant, and had to give herself an abortion. 'So, don't do anything you'll be ashamed of,' Ammi had finished. The link between her story and its lesson for me was tenuous, but I was rendered wordless because Ammi had just said the word 'sex' to me. We had never discussed it before, but there she was, assuming I knew all about it, acknowledging that it was fine that I did. She said the word in an otherwise Urdu sentence, so the literal

28

pronouncement, 'They did sex,' hung in the air, and inside my head, for a while after.

'Yes, Abbu,' I replied now. 'Don't worry.'

'I'm not worried. I know my daughter will make us proud,' Abbu said. 'Also, another thing. Westerners are odd in many ways. They dress and do things differently.'

The previous year, Faisal and I had been reading the *Guinness Book of World Records* when we stumbled upon the world's most expensive bra. I had immediately clamped the book shut and sent him off, then later inspected the listing and its accompanying image. The model took up an entire glossy page, hip swung to one side, a star-studded blue bra tight against pale breasts. The year of publication was 1999, and the bra was called the Millennium Bra.

'You have to celebrate the best of American culture, and ignore the rest,' Ammi chimed in. 'Everyone has their own way of doing things.'

'For instance,' Abbu continued, not satisfied with Ammi's neutrality. 'Make sure you keep a water bottle as a lota. Westerners don't wash themselves after using the toilet.'

To think I was once that young, shocked into incredulity at the crusty American ass. My eyes grew wide. What did he mean – not wash themselves? What did they do, just stand up and carry on right after? Abbu nodded with some pleasure, seeing he finally had my full attention.

'It's true. In fact, some people say goray log smell a little strange sometimes . . .'

'Alright, enough,' Ammi cut him off. 'Why are you scaring her?'

She turned to me.

'No one smells. Your father has such strange ideas. Just keep a water bottle with you.'

*

29

The week before I left, we drove down south to Multan to see my grandparents. Most summers, Abbu rented tiny, isolated hill-houses up north for us to spend a week in, but there was no time that year. My parents preferred the Galiyat – Khairagali, Nathiagali, and so on – over the likes of Hunza and Chitral, remote valleys that were expensive to get to, favorites for Western tourists until 2001, after which they all stopped coming. The Galiyat, Abbu said, were more suitable for 'families like us,' which I took to mean families who could afford to rent vacation homes but drove up with groceries so they didn't pay mountain prices for onions.

The motorway was lined on both sides with eucalyptus trees. Further south, these were replaced by the low hills of Kallar Kahar, and then by fields of cotton. Flat-roofed houses sat by the banks of dry riverbeds. Men chatted under the shade of trees, away from the morning sun that was already beating down on the plains. We begged Ammi to turn the AC on. Mid-July was a time of high heat, the land looking out for the first rain.

This is a landscape that, through the repetition of countless trips, through the particular potency of childhood pilgrimage, has marked itself indelibly on my mind. Cotton in the summer. Rice paddies filled with water in the early winter. The sun setting into these paddies, into irrigation canals, into small lakes. Mud houses with deep blue doors. A horse standing by its trough. The arc of a woman's back as she threshes a bale of rice. The dignity of a lonely bicycle making its way down a country road. A motorcycle, parked under a tree. Next to the tree, a small graveyard.

As we pulled into the rest stop where people disembarked to pray and have lunch, Ammi insisted that Abbu park in the most remote corner of the lot, away from the Pir Wadhai buses and intercity wagons. It is perhaps hard to overstate how much my parents dislike being around other people. 'The worst thing about public spaces,' Abbu has always insisted, 'is the public.'

We got chai and sandwiches, returning to the car to eat them. 'People of all kinds,' Ammi said, grimacing, as she quickly walked past a crowd of men disembarking from a wagon to Talagang. Abbu shook his head, as if in pain. 'This place has become too awami over the years,' he acceded, with dismayed finality.

Ammi and Abbu said things like this a lot, and I took note each time, desperate with the hope that this vigilance would help me break the circuit, prevent me from turning into my parents. One of the exquisite delusions of adolescence – the self-chosen life. In time, many of us realize how lofty an accomplishment it would be, to be only as terrible as our parents.

Abbu didn't talk to me for days after I hit Aliya's daughter Farah during a game of country-country many years ago. He paid Farah's school fees each month and checked her annual report cards, making sure she was performing well and that Aliya hadn't pulled her out of school. Ammi said we treated Aliya and Uncle Shafiq better than other people treated domestic workers, but Aliya drank water in a separate steel cup and Uncle Shafiq was always served his lunch in chipped plastic plates that otherwise sat untouched in a corner of the kitchen. Once, I intentionally picked up the steel cup in front of Ammi, because she had just yelled at Aliya for burning the bhindi. Ammi didn't say anything as I gulped down the water but looked on with fear, as if I might drop dead.

As we neared Multan, the scenery changed to factories and crowded towns – the industrial heartland of Punjab. Young men and children idled outside storefronts advertising Ufone bundles and Dalda Oil. In the old part of the city, donkey-carts and rikshas competed for space on tiny streets. Fish for sale lay under the sun, their mouths agape in death. Men zoomed

31

by on motorbikes, balancing blue tanks of water and bunches of steels rods that teetered threateningly behind them. After nine hours on the road, the car finally pulled into the narrow porch of Ammi's old home.

The following day, I woke up to Faisal shuffling in bed next to me.

'Stop moving,' I mumbled. Seeing I was up, he wordlessly turned his back to me. Faisal was shooting up several inches in height, and he insisted Ammi or I massage him every morning because his back hurt.

'I'll miss these massages,' he said as I pressed my hand between his shoulder blades. 'Are you excited for America?'

'Of course,' I said, eyelids sticky with sleep.

'Nana Ji isn't happy you're going.'

I thought of my grandfather, with his bushy beard and kind eyes.

'Of course, he isn't. Nana Ji hasn't left Pakistan in his life.'

'He went to Makkah.'

'Doesn't count. Did he say something?'

'Yes, I heard him talking to Ammi last night.'

'What did he say?'

'That you're too young.'

'Right. Not because I'm a girl. If it was you, no one would care.'

'Probably not,' he said, getting up. 'Let's go wake Ammi up, I'm starving.'

While he went off, I picked up the cell phone my parents had finally let me use that summer. Zahra had sent me a message.

'Just saw this woman at Jinnah Super. What's your opinion on adjusting a bra in public? Yes, no?'

'No,' I replied. 'So tacky.'

I thought of venting to her about my grandfather, but then remembered that almost every girl at orientation had a similar

32

story. Some aunt, uncle, or cousin had approached their parents, telling them it was a terrible idea to send off a young girl to America for a year.

I felt nervous all day, wondering if Nana Ji would broach the subject again. Sure enough, after we were done with lunch and my father had gone off to read and nap – he always said he could take his in-laws in small doses – Nana Ji leaned back in his chair and said, 'I still don't understand why you're sending her away.'

My mother's face grew weary. I stayed still, so they weren't reminded that I was right there. Not that it mattered; adults think nothing of discussing children in front of them.

'Abbu, we've talked about this,' Ammi said. 'We have to do what's best for her.'

'How do you know it's best for her?'

How could it not be – the wide expanse of a new country, a year of immersion in English, freedom, freedom, freedom? Nana Ji beckoned at me to come sit with him. He put an arm around my shoulder, the starch of his white cotton kameez crisp against my skin. My grandparents' freshly laundered clothes always hung in a small storeroom in their house. As a child, I was fascinated by how stiff and enormous his clothes looked, hung alongside my grandmother's small ones. Whenever he put on his kameez after showering, I would hear the crackle of his arms breaking through the starch.

'My sweet child is going so far from us,' he said now, closing his eyes and rocking me side to side. I leaned against him. He smelled like he had all my childhood: of soap and cigarettes.

'It's only ten months, Abbu,' Ammi said.

'Even a day away from home is long.'

'She has to learn to be independent.'

'Didn't you and your sisters learn that,' Nana Ji replied. 'Look at you, you teach, you drive, you travel. You didn't have to leave the country to do that.'

'I had to leave this house to do that,' Ammi shot back.

Ammi prided herself on how unfrazzled she remained in her social interactions, boasting of the hushed nickname she knew her students used for her – 'Ice, Ice, Baby' – but there were moments like this when it was impossible not to feel the territorial insistence of her independence. It pained me each time, because we are taught that independent women are heartless women, and who ever wanted that in a mother? It also thrilled the part of me that would take after her.

'But you left when you got married, Seemi,' Nana Ji countered. 'Why send her away so young? This is her time to be near her own family, while her elders are still sitting.'

'Nana Ji, you're not an elder,' I said. 'You're still young to me.'

He shook his head.

'Not to myself. One day I'll stop dyeing my hair and you'll see how old your Nana Ji really is.'

I laughed and got up to take plates laden with mango peels to the kitchen. Meera, the maid from a nearby village, was washing dishes by the sink. The sleeves of her kameez were wet from tap water and hung loose on her thin arms. Her forehead was dripping with sweat; it was nearing 50°C. She couldn't have been a day past twelve years old. I felt anger at Nana Ji, at his desire for constancy and stagnation. He had spent his entire life in this house, inherited from his parents, in a part of the city where many streets had open sewage and not a single woman with her face showing. He had a girl Faisal's age washing his dishes. What would he know about independence, self-reliance, the thrill of a new place? I shook the plates over the trash can, unsticking mango peels. After putting them next to Meera, I went outside.

The house had a courtyard with light blue walls, the paint chipped in places. When we were younger, Faisal and I visited

34

every summer. Ammi and Abbu sent us here on Nana Ji's persistent request, staying behind in Pindi themselves. Multan burned each summer, hot dry winds stirring up so much dust in the afternoon that my grandmother sent us running to close every window. After the storm had passed, we would go around the house, drawing hearts on wooden tables covered with the gray sheen of the desert.

Now, I walked on the brick floor of the courtyard, trying to align my steps with every third brick. A large tree provided some shade, but it was still so hot the air felt like steam. Whenever Faisal and I came to Multan, we desperately willed time to stop, dreading the day we would have to take the bus back to Pindi. Despite the heat, Multan offered a respite from the restrictions of home. Here, we went to bed late and slept till noon, swaddled in the foreign cool of an air-conditioner; Abbu said ACs were wasteful. We flew kites on the roof all evening, without Ammi around to account for hours. When it came time to leave, Nana Ji would get on the phone with an exasperated Abbu and ask for an extra day. He would wait till the last minute to book the return tickets and once, when we got to the bus station and found out there were no more seats, we rushed back with joy, happy to get an extra day in the house with the blue walls.

I leaned against the tree, wondering why Nana Ji was worried. America was a shining dream, but it was just that – a dream, an interlude. Mr Shahid had stressed this a lot. We had been told not to do anything irreversible, like getting a piercing or tattoo, because in less than a year we would return to Pakistan, to our real lives. 'Your home country,' Mr Shahid kept calling it.

In the distance, I heard the shuffle of a loudspeaker, and the azan began. The cleric had a deep voice that perforated every inch of afternoon air. The door opened and Nana Ji came out, putting on his white prayer hat. He slowly knelt to put on his sandals that sat by the door. He worked on one shoe, patiently, then the other. As he stood up, his chest rose and fell; he often had trouble breathing due to asthma. 'Allah-u-Akbar,' he said to himself, in the manner of old people when they are weary.

The azan continued, and my eyes filled up. He didn't see me underneath the tree. I stayed still as he got up and walked out, alone, onto the street.

IV

What else did I do in those arid weeks leading to departure, when everything — friends, habits, the curves of the mattress — threatened to soon become memory? For months and years after, I would try to grasp at that — what it looked like, the thing that was lost. I would chase after the texture of that time and place, zeroing in on that summer, when I knew only one home, had parents who had seen everything that had ever happened to me, had a sibling with whom I shared every night and day, besides the murky years before he was born, which didn't matter much because my first real memory was Ammi leaving for the maternity hospital. All these prelapsarian significances came later, though, because life is lived in one direction and understood in the other. In those days of summer dew, of Faisal returning from street cricket smelling of child sweat, of Ammi tugging at dusty curtains to keep the afternoon sun out, it was just life happening the way it always had. It was the furniture of days.

We had moved into that house when I was eight, Faisal barely four. The first time I walked in the empty living room, the terrazzo floor was scarcely visible under the dust. I wore new shoes that Nana Ji had bought me for my birthday — white, with cherries on them — and I worried they would get dirty from the floor. Ammi held Faisal's hand as she moved from one room to another, inspecting the walls and windows. 'Don't think they ever cleaned this place, harami log,' she said under her breath, and I must have laughed, because she turned to look at me, half smiling, half guilty.

After we moved in, there had been months of repairs. All three bathrooms were in bad shape, the floors cracked and dirty. Ammi insisted on buying tiles and got handymen to come in and fit them. She cribbed all day about the decrepitude of the house. She worried about costs and measurements and timelines. Abbu made flimsy promises of accompanying her on weekend trips to wholesale markets, but Ammi knew by then that 'phekta hai sala.' Those were the years when Abbu began leaving more and more things to God, taking all problems to the prayer mat and leaving them there, an attitude poised firmly between wisdom and indolence.

Faisal and I, on the other hand, were unequivocally happy to be in the new house. The windows with cracks that let in precious wind on summer nights, the garden where we tried to plant lemons and mint, the backyard with tall walls that prevented shuttlecocks from escaping. The most significant upgrade for me was my own room, a place where I could hide away with my books or the cassette player. A place where I could jumpstart the process, as much as Faisal hated it, of becoming a person separate from my brother, who was still my closest friend at the time and yet, only four, still sleeping with toys, unbearably stupid.

That same year, Faisal joined kindergarten and Ammi got her job at the university. She came home from the interview and told me how she had charmed the principal by telling him that *Anna Karenina* was her favorite book. 'I haven't actually read it, but I remembered the first line,' she said. When I was twelve and we finally got dial-up internet, I looked up the opening sentence.

'All happy families are alike, each unhappy family is unhappy in its own way.'

I turned it over in my head. I was, and remain, skeptical of Tolstoy, the insinuation that happiness comes without variance. Our family was happy in its own way.

*

Ammi and I were in my room, stacking clothes inside a suitcase we had bought from a wholesale shop in the inner city. It was made in China, like everything else in that market, but the shopkeeper had loudly chucked it to the floor several times to prove it was heavy-duty stuff. It was neatly organized with things Ammi had accumulated for me ever since she found out I was going to America: my first pair of jeans, a red fleece sweatshirt, and walking shoes.

'Your father asked me to put this in here too,' she said, carefully placing my copy of the Quran inside. I nodded, embarrassed. I should have remembered that myself.

'Make sure you read it,' Ammi added. 'And offer your prayers.'

'Of course,' I said. I tried to pray once a day, and sometimes even set an alarm for the dawn prayer. When I did manage to get up, I would wake Faisal too, because Abbu had told us there was spiritual reward for anyone who woke up another believer for prayer. Faisal hated me doing that; once, he woke up, slapped me on the cheek, and promptly fell asleep again, leaving me so stunned that I, too, had wordlessly crawled back into bed. Ammi hardly prayed though, so it was odd when she told us to. When I first learned of the word 'atheist' as a kid, I spent many weeks worrying that Ammi was one.

'I don't need this many shalwar kameez,' I said, picking a stray thread off a shalwar Ammi had just folded in.

'Your father says you should keep a few.'

'Yes, so I can be a nice Pakistani girl,' I said, suddenly feeling churlish. Ammi stared at me, her face so sparse I couldn't tell whether she was angry. Ammi was good at that. Whenever I lost my temper, she would look at me with remorse and shake her head. 'You didn't learn anything from me,' she would say.

'Good thing he's not making me take a burqa along,' I said, pulling the shalwar out and flinging it onto the bed. I wasn't going continents away to keep dressing how my father thought appropriate. Just that April, I had fought with him to wear a sari to the O Level farewell party. It was a school tradition, I told him. But it's not a Pakistani tradition, he said, it's an Indian one. What about the pant shirt you wear to work every day like some goddamn Mountbatten, I had wanted to ask, but didn't, because it had been years since I had gotten a beating and it would be a shame to change that, but also because I knew the game. Culture and tradition looked best on a woman's body.

'Why don't you go talk to him yourself?' Ammi asked curtly.

As always, Abbu was using her as his khalifa to dictate what I wore, just the way he had told her, the year I turned ten, that I should start wearing a dupatta over my chest. And as always, I would forgive him much sooner than I forgave her. Did she still not know how it worked? He was a father. She was a mother. His errors and cruelties I would forget, or at least learn not to hold against him. His acts of love – the jasmine buds he collected in a porcelain plate on spring mornings, the omelet he made one lazy Sunday, the times he took us to the doctor in a dusty '96 Corolla – were vividly imprinted on my mind as the events that they were. Hers – the lonely vigil over the cot, kettles of heated water for our baths, corrected homework assignments, matching socks – were the constant offices of love, invisible and uncounted.

Ammi shrugged and turned away without a word. She refolded the shalwar and put it back in the bag, then began neatly stacking in a pack of cotton underwear, a bottle of Head & Shoulders, and cardamom biscuits.

There was a ding from the new laptop my parents had gotten me. Yahoo Mail showed a new email titled 'Greetings from Oregon!'

'Finally!' I said.

'Is it the host family?' Ammi asked.

I nodded, clicking on the email.

'*Dear Hira,*' I read out loud. '*We are so excited to meet you soon. I knew I would pick you as soon as I saw your profile. The photographs of you and your family are adorable. You have beautiful hair. I also loved the one of you by the bookshelf – it seems like you're quite the reader!*'

'Your hair is very nice,' Ammi interrupted, looking at my hair as if for the first time.

'*I know you will be leaving Pakistan soon, but I thought I would send a quick email to introduce myself and my family. I am Kelly, and I live in Lakeview, Oregon, with my daughter, Amy, and our dog, Winston (named after a British Prime Minister!) . . .*'

'Allah, they have a dog,' my mother said, frowning.

'Ammi, can you let me read?'

'*I moved here from California in my twenties, and now work as manager at the Eugene Trader Joe's. Amy has spent all her life in Lakeview. She is the same grade as you, so you two will get along great. We love our beautiful little town and I think you will too. It's a great place for hiking and we are half an hour from the Pacific. I looked up Rawalpindi on the map and it seems like you're very far from the sea. We'll take you to the beach when you get here. I'm attaching a photo of the three of us with this email, although I warn you that none of us looks great, except Winston, of course. Can't wait! Hugs, Kelly (or you can call me Mom).*'

'You can call me Mom,' Ammi repeated in a high voice, lengthening the word with a mock flourish. *Mawwwm.* I glared at her and she laughed.

41

'Don't come back sounding like that. Show me the photo.'

I clicked to load the attachment.

'I wonder what happened to her husband.'

'Maybe she never had one,' I said.

'Hmm.'

I looked up with a serious face and saw Ammi struggling not to say the wrong thing.

'Well, maybe that's good,' she concluded with a shrug. 'No strange man for me to worry about.'

I laughed and looked down at the photo. It showed Kelly and Amy sitting on their patio in the sun, a cluster of fir trees behind them. They both had golden hair, Kelly's tied up in a bun and Amy's arranged around her shoulders, framing her face. They wore pajama shorts that bared pale legs, and smiled widely into the camera, their eyes crinkled. Kelly hung her arm around the dog. Amy had a coffee mug in her hand. Was she really the same age as me? She looked older, more stylish.

'They look like a nice family,' Ammi said.

I nodded. As Ammi left to go downstairs, I kept looking at the photo. I pictured myself sitting with Kelly and Amy on that patio, having breakfast together under a limitless sky.

The newness of America beckoned. Kelly and Amy appeared crisp, like newly tailored clothes, the fact of them being strangers suddenly inviting. Abbu's tyranny, Ammi's coldness, Faisal's petty concerns – I would leave them all behind. Because I was sixteen, and I thought one did that, could do that – leave anything behind.

*

It rained on my last day. The first downpour of the season, it pelted thick and swift and eager. Afterwards, I went to the kitchen, where Aliya was making pakoray. I stood by her as she chopped onions and mixed potato slivers into the besan.

'So, why do you suddenly care about cooking?' she asked, sprinkling in chili powder and coriander. The past few weeks, I had taken to interrogating her about every dish she made – how long she fried onions before adding tomatoes to the masala, how much time it took to boil rice, what was the quickest dish she could make. She sometimes retorted with a frown, 'Have you ever seen a watch on my wrist?'

'I have to learn how to do things myself, Aliya,' I said now. She shrugged.

'Your mother's forty and still doesn't know how to cook.'

I let out a laugh, looking through the window into the unruly backyard, where Ammi and Abbu had unfolded metal chairs, dragging them out of the shadow of the jamun tree. The fruit was ripe and prone to falling off the branches onto the concrete, where it lay in its purple blood, turning moldy unless Aliya picked it in time. Ammi did cook, but only when Aliya wasn't around. 'Otherwise they get lazy,' she explained. Aliya's own daughter, the same age as me, cooked every day after returning from school. I wondered what Aliya thought of Ammi, or of me. She probably considered me spoilt rotten.

I took the tray out to the yard, where Abbu was on the phone with the family doctor.

'Finally,' Ammi said to me. 'Were you growing leaves for the tea?'

I set the tray on a weathered plastic table.

'What did he say?' Ammi asked, after Abbu hung up.

'He says she could take the medicine, but it's not necessary because she's young and healthy. I told him she'll be fine.'

A few weeks before, one of the medical tests required for the US visa had turned up a hard, fiery bump on my forearm, which remained itchy for several days. The scar was still fresh and red on my arm.

'Are you sure?' Ammi asked Abbu. 'She could just take the medicine with her.'

Abbu frowned the way he did when forced to revisit a decision he had already shelved.

'Who knows what these medicines do to your body,' he said. 'The doctor says she'll be okay.'

Cool air moved on us with long fingers. A murder of crows flew above. In the distance, a drainpipe gushed water down a neighbor's roof. I held my cup with both hands, watching the thin wrinkle of cream appear on top. Faisal, who was normally never allowed chai, had been permitted a cup in honor of the weather and my departure. He reached for it hungrily, stirring in two teaspoons of sugar.

'Bus karo,' I told him, and he glared.

'No bossy sister from tomorrow,' he said, looking up at the sky in gratitude.

'What about the backrubs? And all the times I correct your English spellings, jahil?'

'And who's going to watch *Madagascar* with you and laugh at the same jokes for the twentieth time?' He made a face that belonged only to him, pursing his lips and knitting his eyebrows together. 'Your new sister Amy?'

'Enough,' said Abbu, but he was smiling. He wore a white shalwar kameez from last Eid, the sleeves rolled up to the elbows. Ammi was leaning her head back against the chair, looking at the sky. Her hair danced around her face in the breeze. Her eyes – light green – were glassy, and I realized she was on the verge of tears.

For all their insistence on stoicism, my parents were a weepy lot. Abbu cried every time the Qaseeda Burdah played on TV and after every Maghrib prayer. I told him once I couldn't understand how he mustered tears every evening, and he stared at me with the silence of broken petals, before saying, 'That's because you don't have a living child or a dead parent yet.' Ammi wasn't half as profuse, but a few times when we frustrated her enough to push her to the brink and she couldn't hit us the way Abbu did because she, our mother, wasn't built for violence, did not consider the apples of our cheeks and the lobes of our ears hers to thrash, she crumpled and started crying instead. I wish I could say that felt worse than Abbu's beating, but it didn't. Nothing did.

Under the jamun tree, my heart sank in the reflection of Ammi's sadness. She was the one who had vacillated on whether I should be sent away or not, who saw some meaning in my departure that the rest of us could not.

It would be months before I fully understood what ached her, but my throat felt heavy. I was missing a moment that had not yet passed, and knew, as one sometimes does, that I would cling forever to that scene beneath the tree. There we are, sitting with teacups so old they are no longer white, in a yard that smells of sated earth and fried coriander. What of tomorrow? Perhaps if you imagine a moment long enough, it begins to exist outside of time. The chai is always pouring. The tree never dies. It is raining forever.

January

'Tuberculosis? Are they sure?'
        'Yes, Ammi. They're sure.'
    'Maybe it's a bad cold.'
    Something threatens to explode in me. I grip the handset tighter.
    'The doctor in Eugene ran sputum tests. I'm coughing up blood. I have a fever.'
    'Allah, what has America done to my child?'
    'America? Ammi, this was diagnosed back home.'
    Silence. Does she really not remember?
    'The day before I left. Remember, the doctor said I could take preventative medicine to be extra-safe.'
    'Oh, yes,' she recalls lightly. 'He said you were young and healthy. Who knew you'd be going to such a godforsaken place, where no one would take care of you?'
    'That's not the point. You two should have been more responsible.'
    'Hira, how could we have read the future? Many people test positive, it doesn't mean anything. You were there, remember, we all agreed it was okay.'
    'But I was a child,' I snap. 'Why did you let me do that?'
    She sighs.
    'We let you do many things we shouldn't have.'
    'Like?'
    'We let you go.'

Whenever I misbehaved as a child, Ammi would wait for Abbu to come home. She wasn't built for violence, but she had it in her to corroborate with it. She would watch as he shook my shoulders, tugged at my earlobes, whacked my head. Now, I want nothing more than for both my parents to be in front of me, so I can claw at them, grab them by the shoulders and shake them like the ugly dolls of childhood, ask them, over and over and over, *Why didn't you do what you should have done?*

Why did you let me go?
Why am I here?
Why are you not?

V

From the backseat, the half-moons of Ammi's shoulders appeared raised, drawn inwards as if in anticipation of accident. She hadn't said a word to me all morning, except to snap at me for not calling Nana Ji before I left.

The road, dried up from mere hours of July sunlight, showed no sign of the previous day's downpour. The air, on the other hand, told stories. A faint breeze blew in through Abbu's open window. In the distance, I could see the Margalla hills, turned sharply visible after the rain. The trees lining the road to the airport had shed their dust and turned that sharp shade of green that our eyes forgot each year.

We parked and Faisal wheeled my suitcases to International Departures, where other exchange students were congregating with their families. When it was time to leave, Ammi hugged me with more force than she ever had, then turned towards the parking lot as I said goodbye to Abbu and Faisal.

'Call us as soon as you get there,' Abbu instructed.

'Don't sleep through your layover,' advised Faisal, who had learned an hour ago what a layover was.

Baldwin says the world is divided between madmen who remember and madmen who forget, and my twist on that is that the world is divided between those who turn back for a last wave at airports and those who don't. At the gate, I looked back for a final wave, and saw that Ammi was still not looking.

*

Abbu had arranged for a customs officer to take me through security and immigration. 'The queue starts here,' an aunty called out in a British accent, glaring as the officer silently walked me to the front of the check-in line. I looked back with an apologetic smile but wondered if it was her first time at the airport, or in the motherland in general, so aggrieved did she seem at this rather commonplace injustice.

Within minutes I was standing at the Immigration counter, the officer flipping through my new passport.

'Kahan ja rahi hein?'

'Oregon.'

'Kahan?' He repeated the question, brows furrowed.

'New York,' I tried, and he nodded.

'My brother lives there,' he said. 'Jackson Heights.'

I stood silently. He had a neatly trimmed beard and hair that showed the slightest hint of product. His fingers, holding my green passport, were slender. I wanted to say something in response, something clever and charming, but what could a young girl say to a young man in this country? He stamped a page and handed the passport back to me.

'Fi aman Allah.'

Go in the custody of Allah. It was what Nana Ji had said to me on the phone, the last words Abbu had called out. On hearing it from the officer, I felt the threat of tears in my eyes. I walked away, blinking, to the last security check. Then I took the escalator to the lounge and sat down on the first seat I saw, lungs suddenly shallow, legs about to buckle.

*

Once we were on the plane, Zahra asked to switch with the uncle sitting next to me, pointing out that her assigned seat was between two men. The uncle got up and moved without a word.

'Always works,' she whispered, handing me her purse and squeezing in next to me. As we got steaming towels to wipe our hands, she nudged my arm, pointing out attractive members of the Emirates crew, red-lipped air hostesses with meticulous buns and skirts that fit like gloves. We had both only flown the national carrier before.

'PIA is nothing compared to this,' she said, rubbing the towel all over her arms, which were a shade lighter than mine. I stayed quiet as the plane began to move past single-story offices and warehouses. We throttled through air into the sky, and my heartbeat rose with the speed of the plane. I strained my eyes to look out at the city, trying to identify roads and landmarks from above, laying one final claim to the only place I had ever known. All I could think of was Ammi's shoulders, turned away from me at the airport.

*

In Dubai, Zahra and I walked around the airport duty-free, gasping at the price of perfumes and practicing our dollar to rupee conversions.

'What's $70 in rupees? 70 multiplied by 86.'

'Do 90 to make it simple . . . That's Rs 6,300.'

Zahra shook her head in disbelief.

'How much money did your parents give you? I got $1000.'

She was a person who could ask that question. I was a person who could never.

'$500,' I replied, thinking back to the five separate notes Ammi had stuffed in different parts of my hand carry. 'For safety,' she told me. When I took one out to pay for an egg sandwich at a café, the Emirati cashier stared at me.

'We don't accept $100 bills,' she said, her eyes almost pitiful. Zahra giggled behind me. I decided to wait until the next flight to eat.

At JFK Immigration, I waited nervously, shuffling through my passport, the acceptance letter from the program, and a handwritten note with Kelly's address. I had gathered a variety of testimonials on how the officer might treat me, from family friends eager to share their experiences. Being Pakistani didn't help. Being a Pakistani girl did. Flying Emirates wasn't ideal. British Airways would have been better.

I was called to the booth, where I handed the officer my documents.

'Hello! How are we doing today?'

'Fine, thank you,' I said, remembering what I had read online about American greetings. Americans asked how 'we' were doing, but they meant just you.

'Exchange program, huh,' he said, looking at the letter of invitation. 'You must be a smart girl.'

Smart meant well-dressed back home.

'I hope so,' I said, smiling slightly to show I was also a pleasant girl. He thumped down the stamp on my passport and handed it back to me with a smile much bigger than mine.

'Welcome to America.'

*

In the departure lounge I said goodbye to Zahra, whose host family was waiting outside to drive her to New Jersey. Her journey was almost over while I had another continent to cross. We had both peered down as the plane descended into New York, the skyscrapers and bridges suddenly real below us. I had expected her to gloat about how she was going to be close by, able to visit whenever, but she seemed subdued. Now, she hugged me and held on for a while, long enough that I knew we shared the same fear. In that goodbye, we were letting go of the last familiar, the yar who had touched that ground hours ago and called it home. As she walked away, dragging her suitcases, my head pounded from lack of sleep. I went to sit by my gate, too tired to wander.

*

There were fewer than ten people waiting outside Arrivals at Eugene Airport. I quickly spotted Kelly, standing with a yellow sign that said my name. I waved at her and she ran over, across the spotless green carpeting.

'Welcome to Oregon!'

I stuck my hand out, but she hugged me – a bear hug, the kind Ammi had given me at the airport today. Or was that yesterday? I put my arms around Kelly's back, unsure how tightly to squeeze. She was about the same height as me. Her hair smelled like a chemist's idea of peaches.

'I'm so happy to finally meet you, Heer-a!'

Despite the late hour, she was full of energy, smiling as she took one of my suitcases in her hand. She wore a blue sweatshirt with 'Heceta Beach, Oregon' printed on it.

'I'm parked this way,' she said, leading me out the sliding doors towards a large, empty parking lot. We put my luggage into the trunk of her car.

'Mind putting your seatbelt on?' she asked as we exited the lot. I apologized and hastily clamped the buckle. My parents never wore seatbelts – Abbu had gotten the warning beeper shut off a day after we got the car.

'How was your flight?'

'Good,' I said.

I wanted to speak more, tell her about the movie I had watched and the nice man who had let me take the window seat, but I couldn't. Her thick, easy English, those orotund vowels, left my tongue weighed down. English, to me, was the language of the academic and the formal; conversing casually in it felt like learning to swim in the deep end. There is the one

52

about the Punjabi, screwed on all fronts – her mother talks to her in Punjabi, her friends at school speak Urdu, the textbooks are in English, and on the Day of Judgment, the accounting's going to be in Arabic.

'How far is the house from Eugene?' I asked.

'It's about an hour, a little past Horton,' she said, and I nodded, as if I knew exactly where Horton was. Was Kelly a reckless driver or did everyone in America drive this fast? We raced down an empty country road, nothing but darkness on all sides. There was no sound, and I suddenly realized she could go this fast because the road was perfectly smooth. The smoothest, quietest road I had ever traveled on.

'You must be so tired,' Kelly said. 'I'll take you to the store tomorrow so you can get anything you need.'

'Can we go now, please? I need a phone card to call my parents.'

She told me it was late and all the shops were closed, looking so apologetic that I felt bad for asking.

*

By the time we got to the Wilkins' home, it was past midnight. The car went up a long gravelly driveway to the cottage above. Yellow light shone from a bay window. There was a patio in the front, constructed of wood, and a slanting roof. The house looked like the illustrations of Western countryside homes I had seen in children's books, always more charming to me than the distempered, flat-roofed houses of Pindi.

Kelly showed me my room, on the first floor near the kitchen. I had my own bathroom, in which two pink towels hung. Amy and Kelly's rooms were upstairs.

'Amy's asleep, but you'll see her tomorrow.'

I went to the kitchen to get water. In one corner sat slender wooden chairs and a round dining table. The fridge was covered with photos of Kelly and Amy, a wedding invite, a grocery list. *Kale. Yogurt. Salmon. Ask Hira what she likes to eat.*

'Are you hungry?' Kelly asked. 'I didn't know if you'd want food at this hour, but I'm sure there is something in the fridge you could eat.'

I was starving. The domestic flight had no food except ham sandwiches for sale. 'I'm fine, thanks,' I said, making a note to myself: people here didn't present food as soon as you entered their house. I walked around, admiring the red mitts, A and K embroidered on them in white, that hung above the oven. Looking out the glass door leading to the patio, I coughed up the water I was drinking. A pair of yellow eyes looked at me from the dark.

'What is that?' I said, trying to keep my panic from show-ing. Kelly let out a laugh.

'Oh, that's Winston. He's such a sweet boy. Would you like to meet him?' she asked, moving towards the door.

'No, no, it's fine,' I said. My heart was an abnormally large object, knocking against my insides.

'I hope you like dogs.'

I nodded with force. Rabia had told me that Americans treated their pets like children and got offended if you didn't like them.

'Alright, Hira. It's way past my bedtime. Is there anything else you need?'

I shook my head. Where was my tongue?

'I'm so happy you're here,' she said, smiling. 'We're going to have a great time together.'

She came to give me another hug, then locked the doors and went upstairs. After she left, I went to the bathroom. Sitting on the toilet, I suddenly remembered what Abbu had said about keeping a water bottle in the bathroom. I looked around, panicking. There was, as he had predicted, nothing

I could wash myself with. On the sink sat a painted ceramic cup, a half-used tube of Colgate inside. I stared at it for a second, then took out the toothpaste and filled the cup with water. After using it, I turned it upside down to dry. The toilet paper caught my eye as I got up. How was that enough?

My new room was sparse, clearly unused. There was a small sofa and an empty chest of drawers. On the far corner, near the window, was a single bed with wheels underneath. Outside of hospitals, I had never seen a bed with wheels. I walked gingerly towards it and sat down, my legs dangling from the turquoise sheets. With gasping sounds, I began to cry.

The curtains were pulled back to a coaly sky. I tried to put into some measurable unit how far away from my family I was. All around me was water. The house sat on a hill by a lake, and the Pacific was twenty miles west. On the flight to New York, I had seen the white cartoon plane on the screen move over swathes of blue labeled the Atlantic. If oceans were measured in leagues, how many leagues from home was I?

As children, Faisal and I had spent weeks away from home, visiting family in Multan and Talagang. But never before had I known the gaping wideness of such distance, the impossibility of returning home on a whim.

I thought of Ammi and Abbu, sitting at the dining table on what must be their Sunday afternoon, wondering if I had gotten here safely. Ammi might be complaining, 'Don't you think that Kelly woman should have made her call us?' Where would Faisal be? Perhaps alone upstairs; the thought brought with it the nausea of winter mornings. Maybe for my first night away Ammi and Abbu had let him sleep on a mattress in their room, the way we used to do sometimes as kids.

I put my head on a pillow that was too soft. The only sound I heard was my own breathing, coming out stalled and violent. The road near our Pindi house never emptied; on summer nights, when Faisal and I stayed up reading till dawn, we would hear the cargo trucks that traveled after hours, the distant hiss of the night train. Every now and then, the local guard whistled to confirm that he was around.

My mind went to the Pindi airport, where I had last seen everyone I loved. Right as I left, I had let out a soft cry and Abbu had shaken his head at me. 'My daughter is a brave girl,' he had said, his own voice cracking, because that was and will always be the central myth of our family. It is brave to leave.

I got up from the bed, wiping at my face. Unzipping a corner of my suitcase, I pried out two thin scarves. With one I covered my hair. The other I laid down on the floor as a mat, tilting it towards the lake that I knew sat eastwards. There I prayed, rocking back and forth, putting my forehead to the ground until sleep came.

VI

I looked around in a rush to recognize where I was. Through the door, I heard Kelly's voice. The sky outside was bright, fir trees set against the blue. I readied myself to go outside, practicing my name under my breath, remembering the intonations Kelly had piled on to it last night.

'Hira. Heer-a. Hirr-aw.'

I got dressed and went to the kitchen, where Kelly and Amy sat at the dining table. Amy was wearing a pair of tight shorts and a gray sweatshirt with the hood pulled over her head. Kelly was in pajamas.

'There you are! Hira, this is Amy.'

Amy gave me a smile and offered her hand.

'So nice to meet you, Heer-a.'

'Me too,' I said, taking a seat next to them. Amy's eyes scanned my clothes. *Me too*? Why did I say that?

'Did you sleep well? Any jet lag?' Kelly asked.

'Yes, thank you. I slept through the night,' I told her, making a note to look up jet lag online.

'What would you like for breakfast?'

'Anything is fine,' I said. I hadn't eaten in so many hours I was no longer hungry. 'Maybe some cereal?'

'Hmm,' Kelly said, tilting her head. 'Amy, do you remember if we have any cereal?'

Amy was typing away furiously at her phone. She looked up and quickly shook her head.

'No problem,' I said, eyeing the bits of abandoned egg on Amy's plate. I immensely disliked cereal; I had merely thought it was a staple in American houses, like tea leaves or flour back home. 'I can make an egg for myself.'

I moved slowly towards the kitchen, the tile foreign under my feet. In just a few weeks, I would start going days on food that I cobbled together myself, and it would seem laughable to me how stressed I was, that first morning, about an egg. I half hoped Kelly would offer to make it, and after she didn't, I took one out from the fridge door and cautiously carried it to the stove. I cracked it open over lukewarm oil. Kelly toasted some bread for me while making plans with Amy.

'We should go to the lighthouse,' she was saying. 'I think she'll like that.'

'Sure. Can we also go into town? I need to buy new shorts for volleyball.'

'That reminds me,' Kelly said, turning to me. 'Would you like to join the volleyball team?'

I looked up from the egg, wondering what might happen to the universe if I flipped it.

'I don't know how to play.'

'That's no big deal, the coach is always looking for fresh faces. And Amy will love the company.'

Amy didn't look like she cared much about the matter at all. I agreed to attend practice the next day.

After getting dressed, I used Kelly's desktop computer to send Ammi a quick email, telling her I had reached Oregon and would call soon. Kelly's room was softly carpeted, the bed half made, jewelry in shades of blue and green displayed on the dresser. The closet door was fully covered with ugly drawings and tattered birthday cards, likely products of Amy's childhood art classes. I tried to imagine my own mother saving such mementos. Ammi, who had no nostalgia for the soft, blurry days of our childhood, who said she liked us better as we grew up and became more independent. 'My happiest moments with you two began when you no longer needed me,' she told us.

*

The three of us drove to Heceta Head Lighthouse. We took the highway out to the coast, the lake winding itself down on our left, glinting every now and then through towering trees. Twenty minutes into the drive, Kelly asked me to look out the window. As the car drove up a slight hill, land fell away on one side. A vast blue emerged, stretching incomprehensibly. I held my breath, knowing I should squint against the glare but feeling unable to.

Kelly parked the car at a viewpoint, and we got out.

'Welcome to the Pacific,' Amy said, putting her sunglasses on. The water appeared like a solid object, a sheet of azure marble. I couldn't look away. Once, Ammi and Abbu had gone for a weekend trip together, leaving Faisal and me with Aliya. They had come back with tales of a rest-house built by the mighty Indus, with windows that opened startlingly close to the water. They had trouble sleeping their first night, overwhelmed by their proximity to so much water.

In the coming days, it would strike me as an oddity, even a lack of imagination, how often my points of reference flitted to that other continent. I would tell myself to be more present, that not everything was a slanted version of that thing I remembered from home. I took it to be a frustrating sign of my newness in America, and not for what it was – the forever condition of anyone living away from the city, town, street she had known to be the world.

'Stand together,' Kelly told me and Amy, holding up her camera. Amy walked over and placed an arm around my shoulders, seamlessly orchestrating intimacy on demand. I stood next to her, trying to keep the shoulder where her hand touched me very still.

The lighthouse stood spotless and majestic. While Kelly went to pay for parking, Amy and I walked towards the cliff. I let her walk slightly ahead of me, sneaking glimpses of her bare shoulders that seemed to burn golden in the sun.

'What's Pakistan like?' Amy asked.

Has there ever been a more stupid question?

'Very different from here,' I said.

She was pronouncing it the way American pundits did while discussing the Taliban. *Pah-kiss-tahn.*

'How is it different?' she asked.

'Not as green,' I said. 'And much hotter.'

Nothing I had experienced in Oregon – neither the smell of the pillow nor the sound Kelly's car made on asphalt – could be likened to life back home, but I didn't know how to formulate a more complex answer.

Next to the metal railing by the cliff stood a child with a mop of thick brown hair. He was looking intently at the blinding ocean with the same wonderment I felt. As we walked past, I leaned forward and touched his cheek, so pale it looked like the cream that collected on top of milk.

'Hello,' I said. 'How are you today?'

His beautiful eyes looked deep into mine as he opened his mouth and screamed, 'Don't touch me, stranger!'

His mother turned to us.

'What's the matter, honey?'

I stepped back, apologizing profusely. She ignored me, calling out instead to her husband to proudly recount how their son had just protected himself against a stranger. I felt heat on my face and saw Amy staring at me with pity and confusion. I opened my mouth to explain to her how innocuous my gesture would have been back home, how I

60

had spent an entire childhood getting my cheeks pulled by enamored aunties in markets. Straightjacketed by English, I knew there was no way I could explain myself. Just then, Kelly joined us.

'When was this lighthouse built?' I asked her, willing the moment to fade away.

Next, we drove to Eugene. Farmland stretched far into the horizon, dotted with houses every now and then. Hills greener than I had ever seen rose ahead of us.

'This is beautiful,' I said, looking out the window.

'Mhmm,' Kelly and Amy said in unison. I waited for them to say more, before realizing that the sound stood by itself, conferring the meaning of language.

'Would you like me to look into a phone plan for you?' Kelly asked as we looked for international calling cards at Walmart. 'It'll be around $40 a month.'

I shook my head, thinking about my monthly stipend of $150. I didn't have anyone to call except my parents, and I'd need calling cards for that anyway. Next, we went to the grocery section, where there were aisles upon aisles of cereal, sauces, pasta boxes. An entire aisle read, simply, 'Candy.' Kelly saw me looking around and laughed, no doubt delighted by what she thought was my wonderment at the bounties and excesses of America. But Lord, it was 2010, and everyone knew about America, the place that would upsell you on the thread count for your deathbed.

'They don't have a Walmart in Rawalpindi, huh?'

I shook my head, trying to look adequately bereft.

'I don't care too much for their labor policies,' Kelly continued. 'But it's so much cheaper to shop here. For spices and produce, I go to Trader Joe's.'

She picked up a few packs of frozen chicken.

'Do you know if they have halal meat?' I asked.

'What is that?'

'It's . . .' I struggled, realizing I didn't exactly know what made halal meat halal. 'It's the way Muslims eat meat.'

'Oh, I remember that from my California days. It's the same as kosher, right?'

'No, it's halal meat,' I said dumbly, not knowing what kosher was and deeply regretting bringing up the matter. Later, I would think back to this with incredulity. I had been given list after list of things to keep in mind in America, what to say, what not to do, while Kelly hadn't been made aware of something as basic as this – the chief dietary restriction of the entire Ummah.

She walked up to a store representative. He gave her a confused look when she asked him and shook his head.

'It's not a big deal,' I said, catching up to her. 'I can just eat vegetables.'

I did not yet know what travesties Americans wrought on their vegetables – the boiling and steaming, that naughty sprinkle of salt. She looked upset.

'You'd think they would try harder to accommodate all kinds of people. Don't worry, we'll find it somewhere else.'

I nodded, suddenly aware of the pink dress shirt I was wearing, a new one Ammi and I had bought in Saddar. All the other shoppers were in shorts, tank tops, T-shirts. A cashier stared as I walked by, and I wondered if it was the shirt.

'Can we go to the clothes section?' I asked Kelly.

Half an hour later, I had decided on an Oregon sweatshirt and three T-shirts, their fabric tight against my skin, the sleeves short and flimsy.

'Is this too revealing?' I asked Amy, who frowned and asked what I meant by revealing. Abbu never let me wear shirts with sleeves shorter than the elbow. Once, he made me change out of a black T-shirt I had paired with a shalwar, accusing me of trying to look like a heroine, and I had been livid, but also puzzled, because there wasn't a single film actress I had ever wanted to be like. Heroines were kittenish. The clever, intrepid assholes in movies were always men – men who lounged and smirked, men who rumbled, tumbled on the earth like they owned it.

When I was young, I spent hours burrowed under the blanket on weekends, imagining scenarios, furbishing boy-meets-girl stories filled with romance and flirtation, scene by scene, dialogue by dialogue. The perspective I inhabited, the person I associated with, the character I entered and left imaginary rooms with, was always the man.

I didn't want to be a heroine, Father. I wanted to be Shah Rukh Khan.

*

I stood by as Kelly exchanged pleasantries with the Walmart cashier – about the weather, how it was so wonderful that day, but how last week had been hot, so very hot, it felt as if they were melting. It was better now, they agreed, but who knew what next week would bring. I stared at the magazines and mints placed near the counter, trying to remember a time Ammi had talked to a cashier other than to request small change.

Then Kelly asked the woman if she knew where we might find halal meat.

'Are you Muslim?' the lady asked back, her face brightening.

'No, but my host daughter, Hira, is,' Kelly said, gesturing at me. The woman turned to me.

'Assalamu alaikum!'

I stared, taken aback. She was black, with an American accent. Did she know the greeting as a party trick, a requirement for good customer service?

'Hello,' I said. Then, quickly, 'Walaikum salam.'

'Mashallah. Where are you from?'

Perhaps I was imagining the hint of discomfort on Amy's face. Abbu would be delighted to hear I had met a Muslim on my first day in America. He would call it a sign of auspicious beginnings. But the exchange was making me self-conscious. I wondered if any of the other shoppers could overhear.

'Pakistan. And you?' I blurted.

The woman threw her head back and laughed.

'Portland, Oregon, my dear,' she said, extending her hand. 'Nice to meet you. I'm Amina.'

Then she turned to Kelly and gave her directions to the closest halal shop, a Bangladeshi store ten minutes away. Walking out of Walmart, I remembered what I had read in the newspaper about twentieth-century Islamic movements in America, Malcolm X, Elijah Muhammad, Muhammad Ali. I should have been warmer with Amina. Kelly was beaming.

'What a fun coincidence!'

*

It was 6 p.m. when I started unpacking my suitcases, but the sun still hung high, forming patterns on the bed. I opened a window to let in air that smelled of sunshine and grass, and placed my new laptop on the bedside table, checking its smooth cover for scratches.

The new clothes I had bought in Pindi already appeared frumpy to me: patterned shirts with sleeves that reached my wrists, pants that would circle loosely at the ankles. I hung them one by one in the closet, their tags swinging from the movement. I had also packed some scarves – woven in chiffon and wool, dyed in hues of pink, orange, seafoam green. I had imagined wearing them around my neck at school, my new friends complimenting them and asking to touch the fabric. Scarves did not seem to be in vogue in Lakeview.

I took Kelly and Amy's gifts to the living room, where they were watching TV.

'I got these for you,' I said, offering one wrapped kurta to each of them.

'Thank you!' Kelly exclaimed even before opening it. Amy unfolded her red one, holding it at arm's length.

'What size is this?' she asked dubiously.

'They're Pakistani shirts. They're meant to be big and loose.'

'Ah,' Amy replied. 'It's beautiful. Thank you!'

'Gorgeous,' Kelly added, getting up and taking off the shirt she was wearing. Amy followed suit. I stood, petrified into stillness, as the two of them stripped down to their bras to try the clothes on. This was normal, I told myself. This was normal in America.

'No, no, the pants stay on,' I said hurriedly, as Kelly reached for the button on her jeans.

'So bohemian,' she said, twirling around. 'I love it.'

I made them stand under the soft yellow light so I could take a picture for Ammi and Abbu. I could see it already, them circulating the photo among family, everyone commenting on how nice white women looked in desi clothes. They were already so beautiful; add to that the modesty of Eastern attire. Wah, wah.

'These prints were all the rage when I was in California,' Kelly said, changing back into her shirt. 'Maybe I can wear this to church next week.'

Amy was folding her kurta into a neat square. I could tell she had no plans of wearing it in public any time soon.

*

At eight, I scratched off the calling card and dialed home.

'Assalamu alaikum?'

65

Ammi answered.

'Amjad!' she called out loudly, after greeting me. 'Your daughter has finally remembered she has a family.'

'So dramatic,' I said, smiling. She would still be in bed, her back against the headboard, eyes puffy the way they always were in the mornings. Their bedroom would be flooded with light by now. It was 8 a.m. in Pindi, half a day ahead.

'We've been worried. You should have called.'

'I emailed you in the morning! Kelly said it was too late to get a calling card yesterday.'

'Allah,' she said. I heard the clink of her teaspoon stirring sugar in a cup. 'It's as if we've married off our daughter and the evil mother-in-law wouldn't let her call us.'

I laughed, checking to make sure Kelly wasn't around before remembering that she didn't understand Urdu. Ammi would betray a simmering jealousy towards Kelly the entire time I was in America – it is both touching and naïve of our parents, to think they must compete for influence in our lives. Kelly, too, would once tell me that while the program had instructed her to limit calls back home to once a week, she was happy that my parents called more often.

'I don't want them to feel like I'm replacing them.'

I had nodded, dumbfounded. Who has ever replaced anyone?

'Wait,' Ammi said. 'Let me put you on speaker.'

I told her and Abbu about Kelly and Amy, about Amina from Walmart, about the Taco Bell we had for lunch.

'Sounds good,' Abbu said doubtfully, after I described my bean burrito.

'How is Amy like?' Ammi asked.

'Theek hai,' I said. 'Not very friendly. American teenager.'

'Uff,' said Ammi, and I imagined her nose wrinkling in disapproval. 'Don't turn into one of those.'

I pictured myself in Amy's clothes, bra straps visible underneath a white tank top, arms and shoulders bare to the sun and wind. The thought thrilled me, even as I told myself I would look terrible, my darker arms obscene against the white.

Before I hung up, Ammi told me she had given away some of my clothes to Aliya's daughter.

'I asked Farah to choose whatever she wanted. I don't feel like going into your room right now.'

I had put several of my old clothes in a corner before I left. 'They might not even fit you when you return,' Ammi had joked. 'America fattens everyone up.' The room would be empty now, the bedsheet taut against the mattress, the window to the backyard tightly shut. Again, the feeling from the previous night – a stone against my ribs, pushing them inwards, constricting my lungs.

'I miss everyone,' I said, keeping my voice low so it didn't waver. 'If you talk to Nana Ji, tell him I send salam.'

VII

'We'll start with jumping jacks.'

The coach was a woman in her early forties, hair pulled back in a severe ponytail. Her voice ricocheted off the walls of the school gym. All twelve girls around me began to jump, flapping their arms in and out like birds flying low over water.

I looked at Amy and tried to match my movements with hers. Next, we did squats, lunges, and something called burpees. Amy wore her new Spandex shorts, as did the other girls – when their legs bent, flecks of golden hair shone on their thighs. Kelly had come along to the first practice to introduce me to Coach Lindsay and tell her, rather baldly, 'Hira will practice in leggings because she is Muslim.'

Within fifteen minutes of practice, I was gasping for breath. It had been years since I played sports, and I didn't yet realize that the cornerstone of American high school athletics was unadulterated pain.

'When will we actually play volleyball?' I whispered to Amy, as we leaned against the gym walls, our legs jutting out at right angles. 'Engage your core!' Lindsay was shouting from the other side.

'Next week,' Amy replied. 'First week back is just cardio and strength.'

Next, Lindsay made us jog in a row around the gym, while the person at the helm ran laps, trying to catch up to the snaking tail of the line. Several of the girls sprinted down the gym, catching up to us before we had completed a full lap. Everyone else clapped and cheered. I kept my eyes on the dwindling line ahead of me, dread and fatigue weighing me down. When it was my turn, I dragged like Sisyphus, hurtling down the gym as the line continued to move forward. It took me three laps.

'Let's go, Heer-a!'

'Yeah, Heer-a, you can do it!'

Lindsay and the girls cheered me on, but at some point, I could tell the line had slowed down, everyone realizing I would need help beyond verbal encouragement.

'Sorry . . . I'm not a runner,' I panted to the girl in front of me after finally catching up.

'No, you did great!' She lied with a smile and kept jogging.

*

On the way back, Amy turned to me from the front seat.

'Why do you run to the bathroom every time we switch our jerseys inside out?'

I opened my mouth to explain, but Kelly interrupted.

'Amy, that's rude. Not everyone's comfortable being in a sports bra in front of a dozen people.'

'I'm just curious. We're all girls there. Is it religious?'

I shook my head.

'It's something I never did growing up. I realize it must have looked odd.'

'No, just asking.'

We were driving past the post office, the only shop in town.

'I'm sure everyone understands, Hira,' Kelly said. 'Amy, this should teach you to be grateful. Not everyone grows up with the freedoms you take for granted.'

There were freedoms I had wanted to jealously claw at my entire life – walking alone on empty streets, whistling in public, holding the ember tip of a cigarette between my fingers – but I had never considered stripping to my bra as freedom before.

'Sure, Mom,' said Amy, and looked back to roll her eyes at me. 'Don't worry, it'll get easier in a few days, once your body gets used to it.'

At the gym, my teammates would look over with concern every now and then, as I heaved away like Winston did lying on the sun-lit patio. Twice, Lindsay had told me to step aside and hold my arms up so I could widen my chest and take in more air. I had stood like that, imagining my hands upturned in clamant prayer, beseeching Allah to take the wheel.

*

'I learned this recipe in my vegan days,' Kelly told me, crumbling a slab of tofu into a bowl. She was making tofu enchiladas.

'Back when Mom was a hippie in San Francisco,' Amy added, opening the glass door for Winston to slip in. 'Before she got knocked up with me.'

I tenderly moved out of his way as he padded into the kitchen, looking like all bulldogs do – slightly unwell.

'Amy, language, please,' said Kelly, clearly enjoying Amy's characterization of her past. 'Yes, I was young and silly. Didn't have a hundred bucks to my name when I moved here. An uncle of mine got me a job at the Lowe's in Eugene, and here we are.'

'Why did you stop being a hippie?'

She laughed.

'Why did I stop? Let's see. I guess there's a time and place for everything. I made some questionable decisions in those years.'

Behind her back, Amy pointed at herself.

'And then I bought this house. Settled down here, joined the church. Things just felt more in place.'

She was sautéing onions on the stove, their fragrance taking me back to Aliya's cooking. I realized the smell I had grown up associating with home food since childhood was not that of cumin or turmeric or the spice blends TV chefs measured out in fancy little bowls, but simply this – onions shivering in oil.

As Kelly stuck the enchiladas in the oven, she asked me and Amy to chop vegetables for a salad. I stood next to Amy, discreetly copying her. We cut tomatoes into small cubes and slit green onions to form lush ringlets. I held up an avocado and stared at it.

'Have you never cut an avocado before?' Amy asked.

'We don't have these back home.'

Kelly was delighted by this deficiency, and explained in detail that avocado was a fruit, yes, not a vegetable, wasn't that crazy, and that the best ones came from Mexico, and that you could tell how ripe one was by how easily the stub popped off. Then she sprinkled a homemade dressing on the vegetables, listing the ingredients that went into it – balsamic vinegar, raw garlic, rosemary sprigs. As I set the table, her voice remained a constant hum in the background. They had told us at orientation that Americans were verbose, and of course, I would go on to meet quiet Americans, but I listened to Kelly with the delight a confirmed stereotype brings. It seemed marvelous to me that someone could talk so much, and with such little reciprocation required.

Dinner was flavorful, with ingredients I had never had before – corn tortillas, enchilada sauce, jalapenos. I savored each bite, not telling Kelly or Amy that this was the first dinner I had ever participated in making. Both my parents had grown up in households where cooking was the wretched task of the least respected – the wife or the eldest daughter – and the kitchen itself a grimy architectural afterthought. They had replicated the same conditions in our house, adjusted for urban professional sensibilities. Abbu prided himself on never having to enter the kitchen. Sometimes over dinner, he told Faisal and me to be grateful to God for the food that appeared, fully prepared and steaming hot, on our dining table, which was an odd way of referring to Aliya's labor. Ammi had gotten her first job a month after getting married, mostly as a way out of the kitchen.

*

I hobbled around the house, my knees threatening to buckle whenever I went up and down stairs. I Googled 'why do my legs hurt after volleyball practice' and read up on lactic acid and muscle metabolism. Ammi, whose idea of exercise was a twenty-minute leisurely walk after dinner, told me to stop going to practice.

'It's okay, Ammi, it's a good way to make friends.'

It wasn't. Everyone was nice enough, but I spent most downtime standing on one side as they talked among themselves, drinking water out of shiny squeezy bottles and planning trips 'into town,' as they called Eugene. These were effortless friendships, unhindered by the mess of disconnected biographies. I didn't want to interject and force them to communicate at a level I myself found superficial.

'I talked to Kelly,' I told Ammi. 'She said sports are an essential part of the American high school experience.'

'But you're not used to this.'

'She said Americans don't quit.'

'You're not American!'

Ammi's voice was shrill, an oddity for her. Abbu spoke up in the background.

'Let it go, Seema. Hira, have you been going to the lake?'

The lake sat at the foot of the hill. Amy and I walked down in the afternoons, crossing the highway to reach a dock that the Wilkins shared with another family. Some days, her friend Crista joined us. She and Amy lay in their bikinis, turning every now and then from their backs to their stomachs. 'Like chickens in the bazar,' I described to my parents, explaining how they loved to roast in the sun and turn several shades darker. I sat next to them in a full-sleeve shirt, carefully tucking my hands under my crossed legs so they did not change color.

*

The Saturday before school started, Kelly came downstairs wearing a silky blue dress.

'I'm sleeping over at a friend's house tonight,' she said. Her eyes were dark with mascara. 'There are some Trader Joe's meals in the freezer. Amy, can you heat those up for yourself and Hira?'

Amy was sitting on the couch, petting Winston. She said nothing.

'Amy? I'm talking to you.'

'I heard you.'

Kelly looked at her for a second, then shook her head. She often did that – respond to her daughter's rudeness with a fatalism that I could not imagine in my parents. Even when Kelly and Amy did fight, it was quick and torrid and finite. A singularly unsettling revelation of adulthood has been that

73

not all families let their disagreements hang in the air, making everything unbearable for hours. Whenever Faisal and I were disciplined as kids, it was never Abbu's slap or ear tug that lingered like henna stains. It was the silence that followed, silence like the cold of December that burrowed into every nook. It was the self-annihilation, because how could one exist without the approval of the father? It was the tear-soaked pillow at night, into which I whispered, 'I'm never going to love him,' because I was young and thought love was the opposite of fear.

After Kelly left, Amy and I heated up two frozen meals – meatballs and pasta for her, lentil soup for me.

'Do you want to watch a movie?' she asked.

'Sure. Pick whatever you want.'

She began to type on her laptop.

'We can watch *Slumdog Millionaire*,' she said.

'It's not Pakistani,' I blurted, knowing she was choosing it for cultural fit.

She looked up crossly.

'I know. It's Indian.'

'Let's watch *Bend It Like Beckham*. Have you seen that one? It's older.'

I had seen very few movies in my life, and *Bend It* was one of my favorites. I had watched it with the door locked, so Faisal stayed away, and so I could rewind again and again when Jess almost kissed her Irish coach outside the club.

Amy and I watched the movie mostly in silence, her laptop propped on the floor, both of us lying with our stomachs pressed against the rug. Winston settled next to her, breathing out in harsh, asthmatic grunts. After some initial enthusiastic overtures on his part, we had both fallen into a cordial acquaintance. I was surprised to find out that I did not mind sharing a house with a dog, and in fact enjoyed observing him go about his day, stretching on the rug, chomping at the Purina kibble Amy put out for him every morning. I felt about him the way most people feel about polyamory – fascinating, but simply not for them.

At some point during the movie, Amy hit Pause and asked, 'Do you want a glass of wine?'

Kelly sometimes poured herself a glass at dinner but had never offered us any.

'I'm not allowed to drink.'

'Me neither,' said Amy. 'No one's home, in case you haven't noticed.'

'No, I mean, because I'm a Muslim.'

Amy nodded, then went to the pantry where Kelly kept her box of Franzia. I had walked past it the first day, thrilling at the image of a tilted glass flowing with red wine. Amy came back with a cup filled to the brim.

'Your mother's going to notice that,' I said.

'No, she's not. She'll be too busy being all nice to me when she gets back.'

I kept quiet, waiting for her to say more, but she turned the movie back on. After it ended, Jess having been allowed to go off to America, Amy asked, 'Did you also have to fight your family to come here?'

'They wanted me to come.'

Amy's glass was half empty, eyes and limbs languid.

'Did you want to come?' she asked.

Of course, I'd wanted to come. Who was sixteen and intelligent and didn't want to leave home?

'It's a great opportunity to learn about a new country,' I said instead.

She laughed, the wine making her friendlier.

'Bet you weren't trying to end up in Lakeview, though.'

Suddenly, she put the wine glass on the carpet and sighed.

'Mom's with her boyfriend Ethan.'

My elbows were itchy, but I tried to remain still.

'He lives in Eugene,' she continued, scowling. 'They started dating a few months ago.'

'And you don't like him?'

'He's okay. Reminds me of boys from school. We went out for dinner once, the three of us. Mom paid. Can you imagine?'

'Maybe she really likes him though.'

'She's lonely,' Amy said dismissively, as if the idea of her mother liking anyone was quite out of the question. 'Everyone in Lakeview is too backward for my organic, Obama-loving mother.'

I will forever wonder why Kelly chose to settle in that town. Almost every house but the Wilkins' had an American flag waving from its porch. This was pick-up truck and RV country. Kelly was an ex-vegan with a German Catholic mother.

'Can I taste that?' I asked Amy, pointing to the cup. She raised her eyebrows, then wordlessly handed it to me. I took a small sip.

'It's not sweet!'

'Why would it be?' she said, laughing.

The Quran mentioned wine alongside milk and honey as delicacies the righteous would receive in Heaven. I had always imagined it would be a combination of the two – thick and sweet, like the fortified Complan Ammi gave us when we were small.

'I can't believe people like that. It tastes horrible.'

I grimaced, more for effect than anything else, but from that day on, I drank alcohol whenever it was offered to me in Lakeview, joining the long line of Muslims who abstain from pork but capitulate to alcohol. While the former has been posited as dirty and disease-bearing since the time of the ancient Egyptians, the latter is intricately woven into mythology. Wine flows in poetry, where the eyes of the lover are a pair of taverns. Persia and Mesopotamia were essential to viticulture. Even the Quran, while forbidding alcohol in this world, promises it in the next one. Perhaps many Muslims consider their noncompliance simply an advance on future earnings.

Amy was lying on her back now, facing the ceiling.

'I love how it makes you less afraid. I'd still be a virgin if it weren't for alcohol.'

She said it with a shudder that also seemed for effect. Then she turned to me.

'Have you ever had . . .?'

'No.'

'Let me guess. Because you're a Muslim, right?'

There was something in Amy — hard, impolite — that I respected more than Kelly's apologetic ways.

'Right,' I said. 'Can I ask you something?'

'Go for it.'

'What do you think of when you daydream about yourself?'

'What?'

'Imagine you're doing something cool, something you aspire to. What is it?'

She thought for a while, then closed her eyes.

'I'm Prom Queen, I guess.'

'Describe the scene.'

'Umm. I'm wearing a dark green dress with golden edging.'

'Okay.'

'Kyle's there. He's kissing me, and everyone's cheering.'

'Who's Kyle?'

'You'll meet him, he's in our class.'

'Have you kissed him in real life?'

She opened her eyes.

'Not yet. Isn't this supposed to be a dream?'

I nodded.

'What about you?' she asked, correctly inferring it to be the kind of question one asked to be asked back.

I wondered how to describe it.

'There's a highway that runs between my city and Islamabad. I'm driving on it alone. I'm smoking a cigarette and ashing it out the open window.'

Amy waited for a moment, then asked, 'And?'

'That's it.'

'What are you wearing?'

'I don't know,' I said. 'That's not part of the dream.'

'Is someone watching? What makes it so cool?'

I couldn't explain to Amy who would watch a girl smoking a cigarette back home.

'I'm on the road. The whole world's watching.'

VIII

My first class was English Lit, with Amy and the rest of the juniors. The two other exchange students, a boy from Oman and a girl from France, had opted for sophomore English, but Kelly had called ahead about my placement.

'She has to be in the same class as Amy,' she told the superintendent. 'Her English is so good, you'll be amazed.'

My first two weeks in Oregon, I struggled to express myself, telling Ammi over the phone that living in English felt like wearing shadi ke kapray to bed. Kelly, however, interrupted me often to marvel at my sentences, asking me what that word I had just used meant and how I had learned such good English. I detailed for her the length of British rule in the subcontinent, but felt irritated at the lowliness of her expectations. I was used to my parents with their painfully high standards, who, when they called to tell me my O Level grades had come back all As, sounded happy but unsurprised. I didn't want to be patted on the back for knowing what fecundity meant.

Since then, I have developed other theories for why certain foreigners get offended at being complimented on their English, objectively a pleasant appraisal, and a reasonable one given the many people in their home countries who don't speak the language at all. Raised in places standing in the long imperial shadow of English, we are taught to peg our worth to how well we know the language. I had grown up reading only in English, respecting teachers more when they instructed in English, envying Dawn TV anchors when they delivered

79

the news in clipped English. I claimed – claim – the language dearly, and it made me angry that someone could question my right to it, even in compliment.

In class, I rifled through the heavy textbook, worried. Poe. Thoreau. Arthur Miller. I had never heard these names. My literary world had consisted of Dickens and the Brontës, Blyton and Austen, books set in the English countryside, pubs, and boarding schools. That, by the way, is a clear sign of class. If you were reading Blyton in '90s Pakistan, you were undoubtedly the bourgeoisie. The only American I had read was Nathaniel Hawthorne, and that because *The Scarlet Letter* was part of a Gender Studies course Ammi half-heartedly took once. She stopped attending the evening classes after a week, citing exhaustion from her day job. I, on the other hand, remained enrolled, sneaking the readings upstairs at night, learning, at age twelve, about female genital mutilation in African countries and the misogynistic machinations of the burqah, becoming a gullible convert to Western feminism at a tender age.

My worry subsided soon after class began. The teacher, a lean man with a graying mustache, asked the students what they remembered of Emerson from sophomore year. Such silence ensued that I could hear the superintendent scold a student in the hallway. Mr Avery resumed talking after a brief pause; he seemed to have expected the silence. He gave a short summary of Emerson's life and then said, 'Samantha, why don't you read out the first paragraph of "Self-Reliance" for us.'

Samantha sighed and began to recite Emerson in the dull register of the condemned.

'A little louder,' said Mr Avery cheerfully, annoying me. Why wasn't he telling Samantha she was eating half her words and sounded like an idiot? After she finished her paragraph, Mr Avery looked around and asked, 'Who wants to read next?' I raised my hand out of habit – we clamored to get selected for recitations back home – before realizing I was the only one who had. Everyone stared, including Amy. Even the teacher looked with suspicion at my lone hand, suspended limply in the air.

Amy avoided my gaze in the next two classes. I had never been the most popular girl in school, but I was sufficiently liked; back home, there was considerable cachet to being a good student, and that I'd always been. Things seemed to work differently in Lakeview, where students spent much of their energy vying to appear disinterested in class, in a race for the most authentic brand of ennui.

*

For lunch, I had no choice but to join Amy in the cafeteria line, where she stood with Crista and Nicole, the French girl. Hamid, the Omani student, came over as well.

'How's the first day going, Hira?' he asked, becoming the first person in America to say my name the way I had heard it said all my life.

'Good, thanks.'

I was trying to listen in on the conversation between the girls.

'French accents are so hot,' Crista was saying. 'Do you have a cute brother I should know about?'

They laughed.

'Are you doing halal?' Hamid asked, looking at the menu scribbled above the counter. 'I gave it up the first week. Too hard.'

'Yes,' I said in a low voice, irritated that Hamid was using our collective Muslimhood as a prop for small talk.

'Doesn't look like there's anything you can eat here then.'

At the counter, I asked the cashier if I could skip the beef entrée and pay half the price for the sides of potatoes and

81

fruit. She stared at me wordlessly, too confused to demand clarification. I shook my head and walked over to where everyone was sitting.

'You can have my potatoes,' Hamid offered when I sat down, pushing his plate forward.

'It's fine. I'll eat when I get home.'

'Are you vegetarian?' Nicole asked.

'Not by choice,' Hamid answered. 'She has to do halal.'

I felt like kicking him as he began explaining what halal meat was. It was less than a decade from 9/11, and I had read newspapers my entire life, and I really wasn't going for Halal Girl at Lakeview High.

'Basically, you let the animal's blood flow out of the neck,' Hamid said, and Crista pinched her nose in disgust. 'And you say Allah-u-Akbar when you put the knife to . . .'

'How was your English class?' I asked Nicole, cutting him off.

'Fine. Hamid and I had to give lengthy introductions of our countries,' she said, rolling her eyes. 'It was embarrassing.'

Amy was observing Nicole closely, taking in her thin arms and cotton blouse that looked much nicer than the T-shirts the rest of us were wearing. Hamid and I were scholarship kids, brought over by the State Department to do damage control in the Middle East. Franco-American relationships didn't require such measures, so Nicole was in Oregon on her own dime.

'The introductions were fun, actually,' Hamid said. 'There was this kid, Kyle, who asked me if I knew where Osama bin Laden was hiding.'

Amy laughed into the void.

'Kyle's such a joker.'

'That's a terrible joke,' I said, ice in my voice.

I could tell she knew that too, but the first rule of funny is that someone you want to kiss is often funny.

'I'm sure he meant nothing by it,' she said.

'Yes, I'm sure he would have said that to anyone. You, Crista, Nicole.'

'Well, no,' she said, frowning at me for not grasping something simple. 'It's because Hamid's Muslim.'

'And?'

I had to make her say it.

'Look, Osama is the Muslim we read the most about.'

Crista's eyes were glazed, and I could tell she was trying to recollect who bin Laden was. Nicole was staring at her potatoes. My ears were ringing.

'You should probably read more then,' I snapped.

'It's really not a big deal,' Hamid jumped in. 'We all just laughed in class and moved on.'

His poise was maddening. The three girls left soon after, Amy coldly informing me that she would drive back at 3 p.m. sharp. Hamid looked at me after they left.

'They told me to expect this,' he said gently, wary of setting me off again. 'My coordinator said not to speak in Arabic too much. It scares them.'

I stared at a space above his shoulder.

'You should complain if that happens again.'

'You're lucky,' he said teasingly. 'You're a girl.'

'Why is that?'

'Americans think our women are so oppressed, they can't do any wrong.'

One of Abbu's friends had traveled to New York the previous year and spent three hours in secondary screening while his wife sat at a Starbucks in the arrivals lounge. 'She downed two cappuccinos while they searched my undies,' he had complained.

'I've heard that before,' I said to Hamid.

He shrugged.

'If only they knew the biggest terrorist in Oman is my mother.'

I stared at him, struck by how familiar he felt. Then I started laughing, so loudly I could hear my cackle echoing off the cafeteria walls. A moment later, Hamid joined in. I banged the table. He stomped his feet. We both threw our heads back in mirth. It went on for minutes that felt like hours, until we were both wiping our eyes, safe inside the joke, next to a friend in America.

IX

Soon, we were eating lunch together every day. We learned to rush to the cafeteria as soon as the bell rang, before the line got so long it snaked into the adjacent gym. There were unspoken rules to the queue, like the one where you could cut someone in line only if you were in a higher grade. Teachers could cut anyone. We learned that certain tables were bagged by certain people, and no one else sat there. We often sat near the door, and no one bothered us. Lakeview High was a small, rural school of about 150 kids, all of whom had known each other their entire lives. With some relief, we realized that no one was trying to be our friend.

At the time I thought it unusual, a quirky coincidence, that my closest friend at an American high school happened to be an Omani boy who loved Jay-Z and video games and disdained books and newspapers – in short, the kind of person I would never have befriended back home. I've since learned to recognize the specific closeness that comes from being outsiders together. Yes, there is no shared history, but when you are new somewhere, you have no history to begin with.

Hamid did seem to take America much more in his stride than I did. He was only mystified by the country, while I had also decided to be offended by it at every possible turn. It helped that he could eat everything except pork at the cafeteria, while I sat around, gnawing at his fruit or starch. One day, Nicole slammed her tray next to us and sat down, saying she was 'sick of the Americans.' We expanded our circle

85

of outsiders and spent the lunch period listing our respective ticks with Lakeview. The food was bad. The streets were lonely, the air smelled of nothing. The cheese sucked, the pillows were too soft, the bread too hard. From then on, a protocol was established. Whenever the three of us got together, we talked incessantly about the gap between here and there. With each articulated difference, we flattened ourselves and let America define us. We were only ever what it was not.

*

Dark morning water edged the church grounds. Blades of grass leaned in, pregnant with dew. A swing hanging in the yard swayed gently. The air carried a hint of cold, making me shiver in my dress shirt. Back in Pindi, the days would still be swollen with heat, the nights starting to bring relief.

Church was a mystifying sequence of standing and kneeling. I sat next to Amy, whom I hadn't spoken much to since the cafeteria incident, setting the tone for our relationship in the coming months. Kelly had come of age in San Francisco, and was hungrier for the world, more cosmopolitan than her daughter. Amy had spent her entire life in that small town full of people she knew, and she had little need for me. To her, I was only an object of casual interest, an add-on to her daily life. And I didn't help matters. Some people walk into friendships with open arms, and it'll come as no surprise that I'm not one of those people. With Amy, too, I withheld. I kept a scale in my hands, always careful to be fair with her, but rarely kind.

Kelly was in the church choir and stood by the piano, from where she and two other women smiled and sang lovingly about God and Jesus. She had asked me the previous night if I wanted to come to Sunday service. 'It'll be a new experience for you,' she said, in a tone that indicated it would be tactless to refuse.

I could count on one hand how many times I had been inside a mosque. Most mosques back home were all-male affairs, offering at best dingy little compartments for females in the back. Women were placed at the end of the congregation, Abbu told me once, so that men weren't sidetracked while praying. Ammi had rolled her eyes and asked, 'And what if we get distracted by the men's behinds?'

I had visited the Badshahi Masjid as a tourist, craning my neck to look at the domes above, walking gingerly on red bricks so hot they could have been freshly kilned. Once, Aliya took the two of us and her daughter to Faisal Mosque, which sat near the Margalla hills in the shape of a Bedouin tent. We walked on the cool marble and took pictures. Aliya told Faisal, then five, that the mosque had been named after him. While she did wuzu in the women's bathroom, I furiously whispered to a smug Faisal that there was nothing special about him, that the mosque was in fact named after a Saudi king. Sitting in church, I thought of this and my heart grew smaller. Why hadn't I let him associate himself with beauty and grandeur? The problem with throwaway cruelties is you don't know which one will come back to haunt you.

After the service ended, Kelly took me around to meet people.

'Have you met our Pakistani girl, Hira?' she asked Mrs Sinclair, one of the women who sang with her. Mrs Sinclair beamed at me.

'Welcome! I hope America's been treating you well.'

'Very much so,' I said.

'On the news, they were talking about a terrorist attack in Pakistan,' she said, shaking her head at Kelly. 'I'm glad you're here, in a safer place.'

I had offered a banal answer to a banal question, but Americans love any indication that theirs is a country people flee to.

87

'I didn't hear of any attack,' I said, though I hadn't checked the news in days, and had no doubt she was right. Those were some of the worst years – school was closed for days the previous December, after a mosque was attacked during Friday prayer.

'Yes, it was in Peshawar,' Mrs Sinclair pressed on, like a patient teacher explaining an elementary concept. She even pronounced Peshawar correctly. I hated her.

'That's not where I'm from.'

Kelly jumped in, her voice smooth and mediatory.

'Hira, Mrs Sinclair's husband was stationed in Afghanistan for quite some years, so she knows a lot about the Middle East.'

Kelly pointed to a tall, broad man talking to the pastor, his haircut sharp and perfectly edged. In 2003, the newspaper back home began dedicating a daily page to photographs of the Iraq war: the toppled Saddam statue, clouds of smoke and dust, marines giving thumbs up to cameras. They all looked like Mr Sinclair.

'How did you like our service?' Mrs Sinclair asked.

'The music was beautiful,' I said, forcing a smile. 'You guys did a great job.'

'It must be very different from a mosque,' she said. 'Sometimes, when Henry called from Kabul, I could hear the azan in the background. Such an imposing sound.'

'Yes, especially when it's accompanied by the bass of American bullets,' I snapped back.

In the following silence, I excused myself to get water, and then lingered in the church kitchen for as long as I could. I thought back with envy about Hamid's poise at school. A couple of boys had taken to calling him Ahmed the Terrorist, and he either didn't mind or did a great job pretending.

What grated on me was Mrs Sinclair's insistent knowledge – nothing more dangerous than an American who thinks she knows the world. Kelly sometimes asked naïve questions about Pakistan, but they were curious and sincere, conscious of the place of unknowing they came from. This hag, on the other hand, was chewing up random facts gleaned over a telephone and throwing them at me as expertise.

*

Ammi and Abbu called me on the eve of Ramzan and insisted that I not fast the next day.

'The traveler is excused from fasting,' Abbu said.

'We're all travelers through life, Abbu. I should never fast then.'

'Clever. You also shouldn't bother Kelly to wake up and prepare food for you.'

'She's barely feeding you as is,' Ammi chimed in.

I didn't tell them how preposterous was the assumption that Kelly would wake up at dawn to cook for me. In my first week, she had shown me how to do laundry and clean my bathroom, while Amy watched on amusedly, cackling at any sign of my ineptitude. These were tasks made seamless by hi-efficiency machines and Scrubbing Bubbles, and I didn't mind them. Or perhaps I minded them a little bit, in the way of someone who's never had to clean the place where they shit, but it was hard to begrudge her the expectation that I start. She also told me that dinner was the only meal I could expect from her.

'I'm a single, working mother,' she said, with force, and what could one say to that, except to remind her that she was also a single, working mother when she agreed to host me for a year. I didn't say that. Instead, I silently kept score, resenting her each time I popped a frozen meal into the microwave or boiled water for ramen. Amy was resourceful in this matter and could put together meals out of stray objects in the pantry – hot dog rolls, frozen pancakes, slices of Muenster.

89

Sometimes, we shared Trader Joe's frozen meals; they had Indian varieties like chana masala and saag paneer, almost-black spinach speckled with cubes of cardboard tofu. It was, and remains, one of America's biggest mysteries to me – how can a country with such richness be so deficient in food? Perhaps the scarcity they had so proudly banished took taste with it too; maybe food needed to be exiguous for people to be generous with it.

The next morning, I woke up at five, hastily shutting off the alarm before it woke up anyone else. In the kitchen, I mixed flour with water and spent ten minutes trying to knead and roll the ball of dough into a round shape. As I put it onto a large, heated pan, one side slipped under my fingers, fissuring the already tenuous identity of the paratha. I shook a spoonful of butter on top, flipping the paratha until it glistened all over. The heat was on high, and the butter burnt. Suddenly, the fire alarm began to wail.

Kelly came running down.

'I'm so sorry!' I said, paralyzed by the sound. I didn't know where it was coming from, having only ever heard such a siren emitting from ambulances or police vans. She grabbed a hand towel and flapped it underneath the alarm until it stopped. I apologized again and again.

'No worries,' she said, her eyelids heavy as she surveyed the kitchen, blonde strands coming out of a loose ponytail. Walking back to her room, she stopped by the stairs and turned. I cracked two eggs in the pan.

'How can they expect such a young kid to fast by herself?' she said, her voice full of pain for me. I stared down at my eggs.

'No one's making me fast.'

Maybe she had hoped I would corroborate her indignation, spill into complaints against 'them,' because she sounded almost offended.

'Well, maybe you can make something else tomorrow. Fried bread at this hour is probably not good for you anyway.'

I turned off the kitchen light and took my plate to the dining table. I set it down and took a photo for Ammi and Abbu. Then I ate, enjoying the taste of fried bread so much that I forgot I was alone, that no nearby mosque would announce the start of the fast, that there was no one else in the entire town up at this hour, readying themselves to fast for God.

The next day, Abbu responded to the picture.

'Mashallah. Happy to see my daughter appeasing both cultures. You're fasting, but that paratha looks like a map of the USA.'

*

Hamid gaped when I told him I was fasting.

'Are you crazy?'

Then he looked down at his own food and his face fell.

'I shouldn't be eating in front of you.'

'Don't worry,' I said, 'I'm not hungry yet.'

'Maybe we can all fast together one day,' Nicole offered. 'In solidarity.'

Hamid looked like he'd rather die.

'I didn't come to America to fast,' he said, with a clarity I could only admire.

'But isn't it required by your religion?' Nicole countered.

'Yeah, so? Life is long. God forgives.'

How did some people live life without anything to prove to themselves, no central myth to protect? Mine was that I cared enough about my heritage to abstain from food and water for thirty days in America, even though I had never particularly enjoyed fasting back home. Perhaps Hamid had other myths that he held dear. He had taken to flirting with Nicole at any given opportunity. Maybe he wanted a Catholic conquest, another storied Islamic tradition.

'Come on, it'll be fun!' Nicole said. 'Wait, so you can't drink water either? Isn't that unhealthy?'

'Probably,' Hamid and I said in unison.

'How long is the fast?' she asked. 'Maybe we can do it this Friday, there's no volleyball practice.'

I felt some alarm. This was the kind of thing people back home would lap up – that I was making white people fast, showing them the ways of the Ummah. An uncle had told me that if I could return home with a couple of conversions under my belt, I would book a special place in Heaven for myself. People frequently talked about Heaven like that, as if it were a boutique hotel during high season. But I had no desire to save anyone. In his last book, Ibne Insha tells the one about the sea traveler who jumps overboard to save a drowning man. After they have both been brought back to the ship, and while everyone is applauding the hero, he asks them all to shut up. 'Tell me,' he thunders. 'Which bastard pushed me into the water?' All this to say that making your own peace with God takes a lifetime or more. I didn't have the bandwidth to explain to farangis what iftari was.

By the time volleyball practice came around, my stomach was shrinking into itself. I kept up with everyone for warm up, then went over to Lindsay and told her I would have to sit out because I was fasting. She looked at me blankly.

'What?'

'It's an Islamic tradition,' I started, preparing myself for the spiel I had repeated several times that day. She nodded with impatience.

'Just go slower than the others. Games start next week,' she said, before turning to yell at Crista for missing a serve.

In the car, I slumped against the seat with my eyes closed. Amy drove.

'I don't think you should do this anymore,' she said.

'But I want to fast,' I replied weakly.

'I meant volleyball.'

'Your mom said I shouldn't quit.'

'Mom's a bitch.'

I let out a laugh. She was, kind of, but in the way any older woman with authority is.

'Also, honestly, you suck at it,' Amy continued. 'I don't think Coach will ever let you play.'

I hated every single practice – the burning in my furious lungs, the shared shower I refused to use where everyone stood tits out, the collective masochism of it all. But I couldn't quit. What else would I fill my after-school hours with, besides homework that was so simple it was boring? Already, I had started feeling listless in the evenings, while Amy typed away at her cell phone and Kelly entertained Ethan, who had started coming over for dinner regularly.

That day, too, his car was parked in the driveway as we drove up the hill. Amy grimaced.

'He's not that bad,' I said.

Ethan was average height, with very thick hair and pleasant manners. Kelly seemed to laugh more, and genuinely, when he was around.

'They seem to be getting serious,' Amy said. She was frequently curt with Ethan, staying silent while Kelly and I laughed politely at his jokes about Obama. Ethan disliked Obama, and this made both Kelly and Amy uncomfortable. I didn't much love Obama either, but for rather different reasons – a half-black American in power is still an American in power. Back home, many of us associated him with drone strikes in the western borderlands, where a generation of children was growing up scared of clear blue skies, because that's when the drones came. But in Lakeview, Obama was a litmus test – a liking for him belied communist leanings, while

93

disliking him, according to Kelly, made you a racist. It seemed inconvenient to mention the drones to her, so I didn't.

That day, as we waited for sunset so I could break my fast with everyone, Ethan turned to Kelly.

'I heard a new one today. Babe, what's the difference between Obama and Osama?'

Amy glared at him, but he seemed not to notice.

'What's the difference, sweetie?' Kelly said, entertaining him like she would a child.

'The BS,' Ethan said, and slapped his hands together, bending over with laughter. Amy closed her eyes, as if willing herself to disappear.

'Wow, that's bad,' Kelly said, shaking her head. 'You're losing your touch with these.'

I hadn't eaten in thirteen hours and had spent the past two of them missing easy serves.

'I don't know who that's more insulting for,' I said. 'Obama, Osama, or the three of us for having to hear it.'

Ethan looked at me for a second, surprised. Then his smile returned.

'You know me, Hira. I'm just trying to have some fun here,' he said, going over to Kelly and hugging her from behind as she set the table.

'You can be so dumb,' she said, almost in a whisper, and I knew she was worried he had offended me.

'Well, there is something to it,' Ethan said. 'Did you hear, his people are allowing a mosque on the 9/11 site?'

I really had to start reading the news again. Back home, my mornings didn't begin without the paper, awash with updates on domestic terror attacks and global markets, but since coming to the US, the larger world had receded from my awareness. In America there existed only America.

'Well,' Kelly said, measuring each word. 'I suppose that's a little insensitive.'

'It's very insensitive,' I chimed in. 'Couldn't they find another place in the entire city to build a mosque?'

'Exactly,' said Ethan. 'Look, I respect all places of worship. But right there? That's just looking for trouble.'

Later, I would bring this up with Abbu, and he would tell me it wasn't a mosque but a planned community center with a prayer area, and it was two blocks away from the site, and the one thing I shouldn't ever do was take an American's word on America.

For dinner, Kelly had baked salmon, the fatty pink flesh melting in my mouth with each bite. I wolfed it down, trying to throttle the now sharp pangs in my gut. There were Brussels sprouts on the side, and hazelnut ice cream for dessert.

After clearing the dishes, I sat down in the living room, so full I had to lean back into the armchair. Ethan left for trivia night in Eugene, and Kelly came over with a glass of wine in her hand. Amy was upstairs.

'I'm sorry about Ethan,' she said, sitting down on the couch.

I couldn't bring myself to dislike Ethan. He was loud and exuberant, with mannerisms that were addictive; I sometimes copied them to myself alone, the way he clicked his fingers when excited or smacked his lips when he liked Kelly's food. He was also the only person who routinely forgot that I was from elsewhere, using slang with me that I had no way of knowing and offering me sips of beer every time he cracked open a can, which in turn allowed me to momentarily eschew the exhausting posture of the foreigner. So unlike Kelly, who delicately referred to the bottle in my bathroom as 'your water bottle,' despite my disclosure in the first week that I used it to wash my ass.

'Not at all. I like him, he's a good person,' I said, smiling.

'He is,' Kelly said, with sudden force. 'I wish Amy could see that.'

She studied my face for a second.

95

'I can't tell what she really thinks of him, you know?'

I checked the staircase for shadows. There's something faintly embarrassing in seeing a parent's obsession with their child.

'I sense she doesn't think he's good enough for you.'

Kelly's eyes lit up for a moment, then she shook her head and said, 'If only she'd try more with him.'

'If you don't mind me asking, where is Amy's father?'

'Oh, I can't believe I haven't told you,' Kelly said, shaking her head, as if I had asked for the Wi-Fi password. It wasn't the kind of thing one forgot to mention.

'I got pregnant right after college. Some guy I was briefly seeing, who upped and left as soon as he found out. I was silly and perhaps brave, so I kept her. Thank God.'

Last week, Nicole, Hamid, and I had been talking about the tyranny of fathers over lunch, sharing horror stories of well-placed slaps that turned cheeks stingy red, brutal cur-fews, confiscated pocket money. Nicole had asked Amy about her father, and Amy, eyes flashing, had only said, 'He's not like that at all.'

I blinked, a tear scratching the back of my eye.

'How did your parents meet?' Kelly asked, sipping her wine.

'It was arranged,' I said. 'Family friends.'

'Right, of course,' she said. 'Maybe that's not a bad idea after all.'

'It's a terrible idea.'

Kelly looked at me with surprise.

'You think so?'

'My parents spent the first year of their marriage as total strangers to one another.'

'But I'm sure they grew to love one another.'

They did, although their love little resembled what books and movies had told me to understand of it. Ammi and Abbu were excellent partners – they shared a frustrating number of inside jokes and never disagreed about money. I had never seen them run out of conversation.

People complained of how there was no way to say 'I love you' in Urdu. More than anything, this showed a lack of imagination. You couldn't say 'I love you' in Urdu because you weren't speaking English in Urdu. There were so many words, so many proofs – just no quotidian three-word ellipsis that could be proclaimed as seamlessly to a drunk girl in the bathroom queue as it could to a spouse of twenty years.

X

There's a strain of story this could fall into. The foreigner trying to fit in, hindered by accent and Fahrenheit and the Imperial system. The intelligent immigrant turned hapless by America. The outsider on the periphery of America. The entranced documenter of America.

The truth – I was bloody bored. It is hard to overstate how much of an abstraction a new country remains to the foreigner, and for how long. America was a concept, and I was there to testify to it. It was metaphor, and not the thing itself. Nothing I did there had any material weight; nothing sated, nothing seeped.

The counter-intuitive thing about newness is that it's not interesting. Within weeks, I went from homesick, to curious about America, to realizing how elementary my curiosities were, such clichés within themselves that I lost any desire to entertain them. It was a lift, not an elevator. Toilet paper, shoes inside the house, bananas with stickers on them. The month came first, then the day. Everyone loved it when you brought these things up. But I could grasp at America only from the outside, surmise only what was obvious, and that didn't excite me. It was an artificial entanglement, one that made me feel like I had been sent back a few grades. Abbu had moved to Pindi from the village in his twenties, and sometimes talked of the richness he had abandoned, swapping a place he understood in all its complexities and contradictions for the bland offices of the twin cities.

'Life loses color on the two-hour drive to Pindi,' he said.

In moving westward to that enormous country where great, shiny things supposedly happened, I, too, had lost color. And so, again, that old itch, for something beyond.

That's where Ali came in.

*

Twenty days into Ramzan, the telephone screeched me awake in the dark. I fumbled for the bedside light, heart pounding against my ribs. The clock in my room read 5 a.m. Who was calling at this hour? Had something happened? My mind went to Nana Ji.

I walked towards the phone cradle in the kitchen, hardly able to pick the receiver up. 011-92. It was the home landline.

'Hello?' I whispered into the mouthpiece.

'How are you, Hira?'

'What happened?'

'Were you sleeping?'

'What happened, Ammi?'

'Nothing,' she replied, sheepish. 'We thought you'd be up for the fast.'

Reflexively, I slid down the wall I had been leaning against, muscles melting with relief.

'Allah. It's your father's fault, I told him we shouldn't call, but he said you'd be up. And you had said the phone's near your room . . .'

She was rambling, perhaps to calm my nerves. I couldn't keep my voice from breaking when I spoke.

'Never do this again.'

'Never, never,' she promised.

'You can't imagine what I was thinking.'

There was silence, then:

'I have a daughter oceans away, so I probably can.'

In the background, I heard the Maghrib azan. Has there ever been a sadder sound? Abbu cleared his throat.

'Also, the bell can wake them up,' I added.

'Haan, haan, relax,' Ammi said. 'God forbid, if something happens, we're not going to call you in the middle of the night.'

Now, another fear.

'No! You have to tell me as soon as anything happens.'

'Acha, Ms Know-it-All. Go back to bed.'

'Now I'm up,' I said grumpily, irritated at the entire conversation that was meandering around my worst fears without addressing them. 'I gave up fasting a few days ago. Too tough to balance with the volleyball.'

It had first felt like defeat, and then a lot like relief.

'That's a good idea. You've got your entire life to fast.'

I talked to them for a few more minutes, until I calmed down enough to fall back asleep. They mentioned that Nana Ji's asthma had flared up again, that he had visited Pindi to see a doctor. Ammi told me about a family friend at NYU, in case I wanted to reach out. After putting the phone back, I stumbled back to bed with my arms outstretched in the dark, thinking how the curves of this place were still not familiar, not like my own room where I knew exactly how many steps I could take before stubbing my toe against the bed.

*

An unease lingered on the yellow bus to school, in Lit and History, even as I ate my favorite cafeteria meal of powdery mac and cheese with Hamid. I told him about the late-night call.

'I thought something had happened to my grandfather,' I said.

'Why?'

'He's sick every now and then . . .' I trailed off, then rushed into the words before my voice wavered. 'I didn't know I was living with this fear until now.'

He nodded.

'It sucks.'

'What would we do? If something happens? We wouldn't even make it back in time for the funeral.'

'Don't go down this rabbit hole,' Hamid said. 'I tried to talk to my father about it before leaving. Begged him that if something were to happen, they should wait for me to return, but he said the rules are what the rules are.'

I imagined Hamid – jovial, nonchalant Hamid – discussing death and Islamic burial with his father before leaving Muscat.

In the clan of the far-flung, of those away from home, there is a worry so common it is banal – The Call, The Call, The Call. Everywhere, there are people steeling themselves daily, convinced that if they imagine disaster over and over again, if they walk themselves through the horror of the worst thing that can be relayed on that long-distance line, they will manage to inoculate themselves against grief. To this day, I sleep with my phone on silent only when I am home. Home is the place where late-night phone calls don't seize the ground beneath you.

*

That evening, we were playing a nearby school at volleyball. While waiting for the bus, I went to the library. I logged onto Facebook and typed in the full name of the NYU student Ammi had mentioned. Ali Zaidi. I could tell his profile because his picture showed him with his mother, whom I had once met at a wedding. Ammi had whispered to me when the aunty got up to get food, 'Incredible woman, divorcee. Raised her only son so well he's studying in New York.'

101

I scanned his profile details. He was born on 13th November 1991, three days after Ammi and Abbu's wedding. Wavy hair, a beautiful jawline, space between the two front teeth. I sent a friend request, along with a message so he knew who I was. Seeing Zahra online, I sent her a link to his profile.

'Cute?'

'Yep. Who is it?'

'Family friend. NYU mein parhta hai.'

'Ooh, go for it,' she wrote. 'You're not going to find anyone in that white-ass town.'

It prickled me, Zahra's presumption that I couldn't get someone white, but she was right. In theory, I liked the idea of being the kind of girl who could date some Lakeview boy and then leave him in tatters when I flew back home, but the boys at school were indecipherable to me, a mystery that I didn't feel compelled to solve.

On the bus, I sat with Sam and Alicia, teammates that I had become friends with. Sam was tall and strong, with tan legs that peeked from underneath the array of polka-dot dresses that she wore. She loved Nicholas Sparks, the outdoors, and Jesus. Alicia wore pigtails and patterned tights to school every day and also loved Jesus. She told me daily that she would quit volleyball if I did; she was the only one nearly as bad at it.

Right now, she was listing for Sam the foods that made her burps smell bad.

'Milk? No way!'

'Yes. Especially low-fat.'

I listened wordlessly, wondering who had taught them to talk like this. Then Sam turned to me.

'I heard Amy and Kyle got really drunk this weekend.'

I nodded.

'She's such a . . .' Sam shook her head, as if words failed her. 'I hope it's not hard for you to live with her.'

I shrugged.

102

'She's nice to me. We do our own thing.'

My relationship with Amy was now comfortable, though not at all intimate. She always waited for me after school and cut up fruit for both of us in the mornings, but there were no late-night conversations under fleece blankets, no movie marathons, no confessions – all things I had imagined in the months leading up to America. I had the habit of envisioning every new girl in my life as the best friend I would ever have, thinking we'd sleep on beds pushed together, paint each other's nails, know each other inside out. The disconnect persists to this day – the female friendships I have is a sad fraction of the number I have imagined.

'I don't think she's very nice,' said Alicia softly. Amy was sitting at the very back with Crista.

'She's gone around with half the junior boys,' Alicia added. 'And now she'll destroy Kyle too.'

'Destroy Kyle?' I asked.

Sam's voice was a whisper.

'She loves going after virgin boys. And then girls like us can't date them.'

I leaned back, offended at the distinction she was making. Sure, I had as little social status at Lakeview as Sam and Alicia did, probably less, but I certainly wasn't in the business of virginity valuations. I was a virgin because most unmarried people back home were. In American high schools, I was coming to find out, being one was a personality trait.

Before the game started, we all stood as a girl from the other team sang the anthem. Men removed their baseball caps. Everyone held a hand to their chest. The first time I had heard the American anthem, sung by a Lakeview sophomore whose high-pitched voice filled the gym, the hair on my arms rustled at the invocation of dawn's early light. Then she began to sing about rockets and bombs, and Hamid and I looked at each other, eyes wide with disbelief.

103

We won the game, and thankfully I didn't have to play – Lindsay usually played me and Alicia only when we were clearly losing. On our way back, we stopped at McDonald's, where I ordered a Filet-o-Fish and fries, wolfing them down, reacquainting myself with the now rare joy of a full stomach. Muslims and the McDonald's fish filet in Western countries – that's an essay for another time. After getting home, I dug out one of the ice-cream tubs Kelly kept in the garage freezer. Whether I was allowed to eat it was unclear, since she had said she kept that freezer stocked for emergencies, but she was with Ethan for the night and I couldn't fathom an emergency that would require Ben & Jerry's.

Ali had accepted my friend request but hadn't responded to the message. I clicked again on his profile. Sophomore. Born in Lahore. There were photos of him sleeping in a library, holding a coffee cup on the Brooklyn Bridge, laughing with friends whose names hinted at many places in the world: Tina Chen, Ayesha Pervez, Tsega Berhane. In the list of friends currently online, his name showed up. I hurriedly clicked back to Home, as if he had caught me swimming two years deep into his photos.

'Hey!' he wrote. 'How're you doing? Happy you reached out.'

I hesitated. Typing back would initiate an entire conversation, instead of the offline messages I usually swapped with Zahra and Rabia. Then I wrote back.

'I'm good, how're you?'

'Good. The semester's ramping up.'

'How's Aunty?' I wrote, not sure what else to say.

'She's great. Listen, give me a phone number and I'll call you sometime this weekend.'

I stared at the screen. Why did he want to call me? Maybe his mother had told him to check in. I typed the number, annoyed at my quickening heartbeat.

'Looking forward to talking.'

I sent back a thumbs up and immediately logged off.

*

On Saturday, I kept my door open while studying. There was no reason he would remember to call. Maybe he had also been trying to find a way out of the conversation. At noon, however, the phone rang and Kelly picked up.

'The Wilkins' residence. Yes, she's here. Who should I say it is? Ah, one second.'

Kelly brought over the phone to my room, her eyebrows arched.

'It's a young man called Ali.'

I nodded wordlessly, then waited for her to leave the room. She stopped in the doorway, and I stared at her. She laughed and walked away.

'Hello.'

'Junab. Kaisi hein?'

Was he flirting, or was it Urdu?

'I'm good,' I said. 'Doing homework.'

Nice.

'Me too. So naturally I looked for the first distraction I could get. Tell me, what brings you to America, and Oregon of all places?'

I gave him the details of the program. He told me he was in his second year, majoring in History. He was at a coffee shop; in the background, I heard the clatter of saucers and the whir of a coffee grinder.

'How long have you been here?' he asked.

'Two months.'

'Miss home?'

'A lot, sometimes.'

'And a little bit, all the time?'

'Yes.'

Mostly, it was like a sore gum, subtle and constant. On occasion, it was nausea, crashing in like a wave, leaving me unable to carry on simple conversation.

'That's how it is in the beginning,' Ali told me.

'So it gets better?'

'It does,' he said, his voice softer. 'But the fact that you're from elsewhere never leaves you.'

We talked for twenty more minutes, during which I had to go get water from the kitchen, my mouth parched. He told me NYU had a big celebration for Eid-ul-Fitr, that I should try looking up something similar in Eugene.

'I don't know about that,' I said. 'The other day, I saw an Indian family on the coast. I went to say hi, and they just stared at me.'

He laughed loudly.

'Why would you do that?'

'What do you mean? It was my first time seeing desis here.'

Kelly and I had gone walking on the sand dunes south of Florence. I had excitedly walked ahead of her to approach the family. 'Yes,' they said, when I asked them if they were Indian, and swiftly walked on.

'Hira meri baat suno, there are millions of South Asians in America. Can you imagine if everyone started greeting one another? Also, people don't like being asked where they're from.'

'Why not?'

He sighed.

'So young.'

'Only two years younger than you,' I said, making sure he knew.

Too soon, he had to go, but told me we should keep in touch. I hung up and went to put the phone back in the cradle. Kelly looked up from her book.

'Long call,' she remarked.

'Family friend,' I said, turning away before she could see my face, worried it was painted too well with the hues of my heart – the golden of budding hope, the dark restlessness of a summer night, a shimmering belief that life would have more color after that phone call.

XI

Autumn arrived in flames. My walks were paved with leaves that burned scarlet, sometimes yellow, like a bride's dress. Unlike Pindi, where autumn was a brief, forgettable interlude between summer and December, Lakeview turned golden and splendid. The school posted a list of fall activities on the board – one could go apple picking, visit a corn maze, carve pumpkins. Amy painted her nails a 'fall color'. One weekend, Kelly baked an apple cobbler, checking the consistency of the crust with obsessive precision.

'Eid mubarak,' I wrote to Ali, glad to have an excuse to reach out. He was offline, perhaps at the celebration he had mentioned. I waited a few minutes, then logged off to get dressed. I put on the ajrak kurta Ammi had bought me for Eid and stepped in front of the mirror. The kurta was looser than when I had tried it on in Pindi, but I appeared far more significant to myself. Why had I swapped out the clothes my body had always known for shirts that dug into my armpits and a sweatshirt that made me look lumpy like everyone else at Lakeview? Kelly had noticed the unworn Pakistani clothes in my closet and told me I should wear them more often.

By the time the car rolled into the school parking lot, I desperately wished I was wearing anything else. Amy had looked sideways twice while driving but hadn't said a word. No doubt everyone would stare. I tried to shake off the feeling, telling myself that if I had decided to wear it, I should also be confident enough to walk in it without my spine curved inwards.

As luck would have it, it was September 10th, and the next day being Saturday, the History professor spent the first fifteen minutes of class talking about 9/11. As he spoke, I closed my eyes so they didn't catch anyone else's. In the moment, my clothes felt like some sort of confession. That's the magic of America – it'll make you feel at least partially responsible for a bunch of Saudi bombers hurtling to their airborne deaths nine years ago.

'Beautiful,' Hamid said at lunch. 'Eid mubarak!'

'Khair mubarak,' I said, sitting down with a Tupperware of tuna sandwiches. We had sat in two classes together but were only acknowledging Eid then. That entire year, Hamid and I treated parts of our ourselves like my tuna sandwiches – packed in little boxes, to be retrieved only during these lunches.

'You didn't wear anything traditional,' I pointed out.

'Nah,' he said, shaking his head. 'It's you South Asians, and your obsession with traditional clothes. We wear T-shirts and jeans and shorts, like normal people.'

I had never seen Abbu in informal Western attire. Any time he saw an uncle in the neighborhood walking around in shorts, he shook his head. 'Farangiyon ki aulad,' he'd complain.

'Where's your food?' I asked Hamid.

'They're serving pork today,' he said, making a face. 'Can you believe it?'

I laughed and pushed my lunch his way.

'Have these, it's too much for me.'

Out of the corner of my eye, I saw Kyle walk past our table and nod at Hamid.

'Hey, what's up, Ahmed?'

I stopped swallowing the bit of bread in my mouth. Hamid nodded back and Kyle kept walking.

109

'Don't fucking call him that,' I shouted, standing up. Kyle stopped and turned, his eyes moving up and down my frame. I put my hands on the table to stop them from shaking.

'Wasn't talking to you, Miss Pakistan.'

'Well, I am. That's not his name, stop calling him that.'

Kyle stared for another moment, then shook his head.

'Crazy bitch,' he said, not too loudly, before walking away as if in a rush. I considered yelling after him, but I had made my point, so I sat down, more than a little proud of myself. Hamid's jaw was glued to itself.

'Why did you do that?'

'Excuse me? Because he was calling you . . .'

'Yeah, so? He's a friend. Friends joke around.'

'What's funny about calling you Ahmed the Terrorist?'

'I don't need you defending me, Hira.'

Spite prickled in my throat.

'Clearly, you do.'

'No, I just know how to pick my battles,' he said. 'I know who I am, and no one can change that.'

'But why would you let him walk all over you?'

He took a deep breath, as if to calm himself down.

'Because I don't care. I'm not like you, always angry at the world.'

Hamid had known me for two months; was I that transparent? Over the years, his assessment is something I've thought often about. Angry at the world. I have never known another way to be.

'But did you see him?' he continued, now distracted. 'He didn't say a word to you.'

'He did call me a bitch,' I pointed out, trying to keep the murmur of pleasure low in my voice. Unknown to myself, I had waited for this moment all my life – for some American villager to tell me I was a crazy bitch.

Hamid seemed deep in thought, his forehead curled in a frown.

'It's as if he didn't know what to do with you.'

'At least you get to be his friend, as you call it.'

He sighed, picking up one of my sandwiches and biting into it.

'Not if you can help it.'

I knew what he was talking about. In class, I often took on the role of the overly judicious cricket umpire, shutting Kyle and his friends up when they made fun of the teachers or the girls. In return, they looked at me as if I were an insect – not frightening, but odd enough to be kept at a distance. A week ago, Kyle had turned in his chair to face me.

'Hey, Amjad,' he said. 'They say Pakistan's hiding bin Laden. What do you make of that?'

'Hmm, I should tell my family to hide Uncle Osama better.'

He snickered but then kept looking at me, as if trying to confirm that was a joke.

*

After getting home, I checked my empty Facebook inbox and slumped down on the bed. Last Eid, we had visited Abbu's family in Talagang. I had worn maroon, my arms painted in henna and ribbed with silvery bangles. We had gone to so many houses that I stayed up for hours that night, too wired from the cups of chai. Now, it was so quiet I could hear Winston scratching the living room rug.

I woke up from my nap as it was getting dark. Disoriented, I walked to the kitchen to get water, wondering why my body ached. Kelly was not home yet, but I could hear music from Amy's room. I opened my laptop, checked Facebook again, then searched for pulao recipes. As I was chopping onions, the phone rang. I wiped my hands and ran to the cradle, but it wasn't a New York number.

'Eid mubarak!'

'Khair mubarak, Ammi,' I said, trying to hide my disappointment. I heard Faisal in the background and told her to put him on.

'Hello, Amreeki sundi. How're "Mawm" and your new sister?'

'I like my old sibling more,' I said, wondering if he was wearing blue, his favorite color, for Eid.

'Duh,' he said, a word he had picked up the first time we watched *Friends* on a DVD we rented for Rs 10 a day from Lalkurti. A lump rose inside me. Here was the only person I knew inside out, because I had been there for every moment that the world shaped him.

'Do you miss me?' I asked.

'I did, but now I've moved into your room and replaced all your stuff with mine.'

'Like the land mafia in Defence.'

'Exactly.'

'Well, I miss you,' I said, 'I can't yell at anyone here.'

Then I remembered Kyle.

'Although, I did shout at this American kid in the cafeteria today. He was being mean to Hamid.'

'Ahan,' said Faisal, sounding unimpressed. 'You and your anger management issues.'

'No, he was calling Hamid a terrorist.'

'And you just had to step in and save the day.'

I didn't tell Ammi or Abbu the Kyle story, even though I knew it would make Abbu's eyes light up like fireflies. Ammi would be disappointed in my lack of self-control. My parents are both terribly proud people, but their arrogance manifests very differently. For Ammi, it means never showing your hand – no one is worthy of her anger. But Abbu, Abbu respects anger, thinks it deserves every expression, bows down to it the same way he kneels for God.

When he came on the line, I told him instead about the pulao I was making and the Eid presentation I was giving at church on Sunday. There was a pause, in which I heard him walk to another, quieter room.

'Hira, I thought you were going to church once to make Kelly happy. Why are you doing this presentation?'

His voice was wrapped in worry. I imagined his forehead creased with the same lines I would wear one day. *Because there isn't anything else to do in this town*, I wanted to snap back. *Because I'm in the middle of nowhere, chopping onions so I don't eat vacuum-sealed chana masala on Eid.*

'It'll be a nice opportunity to represent Pakistan, Abbu,' I said instead, feebly. I told him how the pastor had come up to the house and asked me if I wanted to do something for Eid at church. I had been taken aback, knowing I was the only Muslim he knew of. Hamid's family never went to church. Kelly had told me to invite him, and I had nodded without following up. Church had grown exceedingly boring, making me grateful that women were excused from congregational prayer back home. I had little choice but to keep going – Kelly loved taking me along and using my latest observations about America as a conversation topic among her church friends – but I had no intention of taking Hamid down with me.

I told the pastor I didn't want to do anything that might be considered inappropriate in a church, partly because I remembered Hamid's counselor, who had told him not to speak too much Arabic, and partly because the whole thing felt sweet but useless, like visiting an orphanage. But he kept waiting for ideas, his face expectant, until I offered to dress myself and my schoolfriends up in Pakistani attire and do a show-and-tell.

'You can represent Pakistan at school and home,' Abbu said, in that strict voice of his that used to send shivers down my spine. Across the phone line, it sounded smaller, as if he himself had shrunk. I said a non-committal 'Yes, Abbu,' knowing I would do it anyway, surprised and somehow sad that I didn't feel the old fear.

Later, I took my plate of chicken pulao to the bedroom. Kelly didn't like me eating anywhere except the dining table, saying the smell got into the upholstery. The Wilkins were always smelling things. Amy never took fruit with her to school so that her bag didn't smell like apples. Any half-cut vegetable had to be wrapped in pinchy plastic wrap for storage, so it didn't 'make the fridge smell like food.'

I took a deep breath and dialed the number I had noted down from the CID machine.

'Eid mubarak, junab,' he said, his voice already familiar.

'Khair mubarak. How was your day?'

'Great. Had the most amazing halwa puri. If you ever visit New York, I'll take you there.'

I skipped a breath. Did he want me to visit? I told myself to get a grip and relayed to him the details of my eventless Eid, leaving out the Kyle incident. It seemed too early to tell him I yelled at classmates in the cafeteria. Instead, I complained about my call with Abbu.

'If he doesn't want me interacting with people here, why did he send me to America?'

Ali clicked his tongue in impatience.

'That's second-gen nonsense, yar. There's more than one way to experience America. Maybe he thought your way wouldn't include a church.'

'Yeah, but isn't it nice that the pastor offered? No mosque back home would ever invite a Christian to speak about their faith.'

Faisal was once told off by the local maulvi for reading an English book while he waited for Abbu to finish his prayer. 'Arabic only,' the maulvi had insisted. Abbu had come home bristling. 'That duffer couldn't tell the Quran from a Darwish poem if he wanted,' he had said.

Ali asked if I liked going to church, and I told him I didn't mind it, although it sometimes felt like Kelly had loftier ambitions in taking me along. I had made the mistake of complaining to her once about the strict strain of religion I had been brought up on. Unlike Kelly and Amy, who went to meet God once a week, Faisal and I had spent our childhoods being asked to acknowledge Him in every single moment, in the clothes we wore, in the way we yawned, the direction our feet faced while sleeping. Kelly had nodded enthusiastically, telling me Christianity was much simpler, and she could give me the name of a great website if I wanted to learn.

Children are prone to exaggerating the cruelty of others, but there are times when one realizes the magnitude of someone's unfairness only in adulthood. Looking back, it shocks me that Kelly did something like that. Then again, perhaps she saw a young girl showing the first signs of a spiritual crisis and offered her whatever she could by way of guidance. Or perhaps, in her own flawed way, she genuinely worried for me; Islam was having quite the PR crisis in America.

*

The tiny church bathroom was a flurry of pale limbs fluttering around in silk and cotton. We were getting ready for the 'fashion show,' as the pastor was calling it by then. Kelly and Amy wore the kurtas I got them. Sam, Crista, and Alicia were changing into clothes I had brought from my closet.

'I feel like Jasmine,' Alicia said, twirling in a blue kameez that reached her knees. *Jasmine walks around her father's palace in a push-up bra*, I thought.

'There is no way this will fit me,' said Sam, holding a purple kurta at arm's length.

'Of course it will. I'm quite chubby,' I said, laughing.

Crista and Amy turned to me.

'You're joking, right?' Crista said, tugging cloth down her chest, her face without a hint of amusement. 'I bet you're underweight.'

I had been mostly joking. Back home, I was averagely sized, always worried that I weighed a kilo or two more than the most attractive girls in class. In the church bathroom, I realized that everyone around me was taller and thicker, with strong, full arms and postures that elongated their spines. This is what I mean when I say my mother didn't teach me to think about the body; it took me more than a month to realize I was smaller than every American girl I knew.

'Sam, you can switch with me if you want,' I said.

'Yes, please.'

I turned towards the wall to change.

'You can see her ribs,' I heard Crista whisper.

The 'show' lasted less than five minutes, all of us in a fit of awkward giggles as we paraded around the stage, holding one hip and jutting an elbow out. Then, I took the mic. Standing by the pulpit, I spoke haltingly about Eid, the importance of fasting, the lunar calendar. I sounded like an Islamiyat textbook or the Wikipedia page on Ramzan.

'We . . .' I began, then restarted like a car engine in wintertime. 'Muslims fast for thirty days, which means no food or water from dawn to dusk.'

Many in the congregation shook their head in disbelief. Perhaps the pastor had organized this so his flock could know how good they had it, showing up once a week in Lakeview Football jerseys.

'It's not too bad,' I added hurriedly. 'Back home, the government bans public eating and reduces working hours so everyone can rest during their fast.'

No one looked particularly impressed. Now I was making it sound as if everyone lazed around for an entire month a year, millions of able-bodied adults whiling their days away, waiting for dusk so life could restart.

'But at the end of the thirty days comes Eid,' I said, cringing as I heard myself list foods like seviyan and chana chat with performative American notes. Abbu used to tell the story of an old Christian man in his village, who, when asked if he had ever considered converting to Islam, hadn't wasted a beat before retorting, 'Do I look like a mad dog bit me?' Had a mad dog bitten me, that I was standing at an altar in rural Oregon, telling pews of stone-faced Americans what chand raat was?

After the presentation, Mrs Sinclair came up to me and said she'd love to get some of those delicious recipes.

'And this beautiful scarf, is it for modesty?' she asked, fingering the gauze of my dupatta.

'No, it's an embellishment,' I replied.

Of course it was for modesty. Of course its purpose was to hide my breasts and my hair and my neckline, but I wasn't going to give her the satisfaction. 'If there is trouble at home, you don't go around telling the neighbors, do you?' Abbu had pointed out while advising me to be a loyal ambassador in America. For years after, this was the tightrope that mattered – either confirm a stereotype to smug Americans like Mrs Sinclair or defend norms that had troubled me all my life. Then I realized two things. One, that my parents had raised me a snob, and universal legibility was not necessary, or even desirable, to me. Two, that I found no pleasure in translating culture, in working towards a greater understanding between one pack of duffers and another. There are people paid to do that – consular officers, foreign correspondents, and such. Not me.

The six models congregated near the altar and Hamid, who was there for the occasion, took photos. I tried not to be alone

117

with him, worried he might ask me what was more embarrassing – being called a terrorist every now and then, or the corny show I had just put on.

'Never again,' I wrote to Ali later. 'Culture is a farce.'

Alongside, I slipped in the photo I looked best in, worried his eyes might glaze over me and find the other girls, on whom the clothes looked like strange, wonderful adornments.

'Purple's a good look on you,' he wrote back.

January

After I am diagnosed, a nurse from the county health department comes to the house, her car sputtering up the gravelly hill. I sit on the porch and wait. She slams the car door and walks over, holding a small container in her hand.

'What are you doing outside?' she asks by way of greeting.

'Just sitting.'

'Let's go inside.'

Standing by the dining table, she carefully opens her container and takes out a Ziplock bag with four shiny pills. She lists the names of the first-line drugs involved in treating tuberculosis, while I take fastidious notes on an orange notepad.

Isoniazid, Rifampicin, Pyrazinamide, Ethambutol.

She emphasizes that all four of them must be taken daily, without any gap, otherwise the bacteria can become resistant to all medication. That opens the door to MDR-TB, multidrug-resistant tuberculosis, which I should be grateful I don't have. I nod to indicate gratitude.

'Where are the rest of the pills?'

'I'll bring them with me every day.'

'Oh, no need for that,' I say, horrified at the thought of her driving two hours daily. 'I can just keep them here.'

'That's not how it works,' she snaps. 'It's called DOTS. Directly Observed Treatment, Short Course. I have to observe you swallow each pill.'

Erratic dosage can lead to drug resistance and relapse. She tells me this, and I nod along, but all I can think of is how much I already dread seeing her tomorrow. I ask about any side effects of the medicine. She mentions nausea and tells me Rifampicin will turn my urine orange, the color of clementines. On rare occasions, a patient's liver can entirely reject one of the drugs, and they have to use a process of elimination to figure out which one it is.

Before leaving, she says, 'Also, you absolutely cannot be outside the house.'

'Why?'

'Because you're in quarantine. You have a contagious disease.'

'The house is on a hill.'

Her eyebrows shoot up.

'Ms Amjad, you would be in a quarantine facility right now if it weren't for your host family. You likely brought this disease from a foreign country, and now it's a public health issue for an American community.'

The woman's Mexican, with an accent as foreign as my country.

'You are forbidden from stepping outside or meeting anyone but your host family.'

*

In my dream, I meet Nana Ji under the jamun tree. He is carrying around a sample of my urine in an uncapped test tube. I keep asking him to put it down, worried that the orange liquid will flow onto his fingers, staining them. He tells me he has to carry it to the doctor's house, so he can make sure he isn't the one who gave me TB.

'But you don't have TB,' I call after him, frustrated, but he is walking away, telling me he has to be sure, he has to know.

I wake up shivering under the blankets, my body damp with sweat. I clamp my legs into myself, thinking it's the dream, but a few minutes pass by and my chest remains unbearably cold, my forehead slick. I run to the bathroom and shove the door shut to contain the sound and fury of my body. I shudder in recognition of that dreaded sensation of childhood, of guts defying gravity and rejecting what they have been fed. I vomit into the bowl, retching again and again until nothing comes out except clear liquid.

For a while after, I sit on the fluffy mat, damp forehead against the vanity, hair in clumps around my temple. I stare at the contents of the bowl. Remains of the pasta Kelly made for dinner float in bile that is tinted a deep, dark orange.

XII

October 15th was my birthday, and Alicia invited me and Sam to a sleepover at her house. Used to Abbu's strictness – how many nights I had tossed in bed, frothing with rage, while Rabia and the others got together to order late-night burgers and dance to K3G songs – I expected resistance from Kelly. She seemed very happy though.

'Glad to see you're making friends,' she said, and called Alicia's mother from the town directory to arrange pick-up.

Alicia's house was the nicest in the area. We pulled into a long driveway leading to the homestead. The accompanying barn, tall and red, had been built in 1905. The main house had three floors, with a music room and a game room in the basement. In the backyard sat a hot tub.

Dinner was slow-cooked chili, with a small vegetarian pot for me. I was still doing halal, although it was starting to wear down on me, restricting what I could eat everywhere I went. Alicia had also baked a thick chocolate cake with white lettering, the kind I had only ever seen at Rahat and Bread 'n' Butter back home. They told me to close my eyes and make a wish, and I wished for a trip to New York. Everyone sang the birthday song and then asked me to sing it in Urdu for myself. I told them we just used the English one, so they laughed and sang it another time.

Afterwards, Sam, Alicia, and I watched *Pretty Woman*, because the two of them found my lack of exposure to Hollywood classics appalling. Like many unpopular kids in American high schools, both Sam and Alicia were huge movie buffs, with interests wide enough to traverse soft-core Christian ones like *A Walk to Remember* as well as *Grease* and *Silence of the Lambs*.

'That's Julia Roberts,' Sam told me.

I was intimately familiar with Julia Roberts's face. While I had never seen any of her movies, I had gone through a phase in early adolescence where I would cut up photographs from the celebrity section of the newspaper and tape them onto the walls of my room. Each night, I would sleep with the pale ambassadors of turn-of-the-century Hollywood – Roberts, Tom Cruise, Jennifer Aniston, DiCaprio – gazing down at me.

After the movie ended, we went out to the hot tub that Alicia's father had going for us. Sam and Alicia wore their bathing suits, but they were used to my shenanigans by then, and didn't bat an eyelid as I got in wearing my T-shirt and leggings. Steam rose from the water, and it felt like a bewildering luxury – to be submerged in hot water on a cool night, looking up at a sky studded with stars.

'How's Ali?' Alicia asked.

I had given them the basics – he was Pakistani, he was in college, I was in love with him.

'I have to figure out a way to visit him,' I said.

'Why don't you just go?'

'I can't just show up. We've never met.'

'Do it! What if he's your soulmate?'

'What if I go and we have nothing in common?'

'Time to be bold,' Alicia said. 'I just signed up for the Nicaragua mission trip.'

'How long is it?' I asked.

'A year. I'll do it between junior and senior year.'

'Aren't you scared?' Sam asked.

'I have Jesus on my side. I'll be fine.'

What could one say to that? We all sat in silence for a bit, the hum of the hot tub the only sound.

'What do you guys want to do after graduating?' I asked.

Alicia said she wanted to go to Oregon State for Environmental Sciences.

'I want to study worship arts at Eugene Bible College,' Sam told me.

Sam consistently performed the best among all the juniors, did both drama and choir, and was editor of the school magazine.

'You could get into a much bigger school with your grades,' I said.

She shrugged.

'I don't want to. My parents both went to EBC, and all my siblings.'

'Aren't you curious to see if you could do better?'

She frowned.

'EBC is a good school.'

'But it's not the best.'

'So what?'

All my life, I have observed a certain kind of person with baffled envy. The person who has never felt the desire to flee. I feel the least in common with this person, and yet I am endlessly fascinated by her. How can one be that content? Is she lucky, the draw of the universe birthing her in a place that fully aligns with her in temperament and ambition, or is she just complacent? Often, I have to remind myself that staying and leaving can both be matters of luck and class, but I can't help it; my vagrancy disdains such a person.

'This here is enough for me,' Sam said, waving her hand to indicate the lonely forest in the distance, the endless sky, this small town at the edge of the continent.

What I was realizing was that it wasn't enough for me.

*

'That smell, huh.'

In the ten minutes at the halal butcher's, Kelly walked around with her nose wrinkled. Now, as I put five pounds of chicken in the backseat, she asked, 'Have you considered relaxing this rule for yourself? I worry this meat isn't very hygienic.'

I got into the front seat and we started driving towards Trader Joe's.

'I was reading online,' she continued. 'Many of these religious rules were made hundreds of years ago, to keep people from getting sick.'

Her tone was intrepid, revelatory, as if telling me my religion was 1400 years old would shatter some dearly held conviction. The previous week, the church pastor had told us that Christians had a religious duty to stand beside Israel, as if the Bible had been referring to modern-day Tel Aviv all along.

'I'll talk to my parents about it,' I said, looking out the window.

'You should feel empowered to make these decisions yourself,' she said. 'You're not eating enough.'

'Well, that's because we barely cook at home.'

'You mean to say I barely cook?'

I stayed quiet. That is what I meant, yes. Most days, I got home from practice and walked straight to the fridge, opening the door and hoping its contents had magically transformed into food I could heat up and eat. Kelly had dinner at Ethan's some nights of the week – they were spending more and more time together. Even when we all ate together, Kelly preferred foods like spaghetti squash and chicken Caesar salads. I often went to bed with my stomach gnawing at itself.

'I've said this before,' Kelly said, frowning as she drove. 'I'm a single mother with a day job. This is what I tell my own daughter – if you want something done, get it done.'

Years later, it's still hard to parse out where the boundaries of fault – hers and mine – lie. Undoubtedly, I was not getting

125

fed. Looking back at photographs, I can see a waning of my body over those initial months – sunken cheeks, thinning wrists. Some of it was Kelly's Americanness – the brash individualism of thinking you owed cooked food only to yourself would be horrifying to anyone back home. And yet, she was juggling a relationship and work and two dependents. I was seventeen, not a toddler. Why didn't I have the sense to feed myself as required?

'Hira, we don't have servants in America,' Kelly said, sighing, as we pulled into the Trader Joe's parking lot. 'You have to take care of yourself.'

As we walked around the produce aisle, Kelly checking beets and avocados off her list, I wondered about her words. Class was hard to translate across the two countries. It was true that on winter mornings, Aliya brought Ammi and Abbu's breakfast to their bedroom. Afterwards, they sat in the backseat of the Cultus and read the newspaper while Uncle Shafiq drove them to work. Whenever we had to see the doctor, Abbu made a call and the next day we could zig-zag our way through the unventilated corridors of the military hospital, past the snaking line of people sicker than us.

The Wilkins' house was much nicer than ours, as was Alicia's, with wooden floors, hot water for baths that wasn't boiled on the stove beforehand, an extra freezer in the shed. Lakeview High had facilities we could not imagine back home – a wood workshop, a music room, a football field, a gym with bleachers and changing rooms. Amy had the latest iPhone, Kelly had been to London and Amsterdam. But Kelly had a steady job with insurance, making the Wilkins better off than many families in town. Crista's parents never went to the doctor, even though her father's sugar levels were rarely under control. Every first Saturday of the month, the school organized Food Box – handouts of Pop-Tarts, watery juices, baby cartons of milk, and candy – for families in the area, including Hamid's and Crista's. The first time I passed a parked RV, I remarked that it looked like the cute wandering caravans of Enid Blyton books, and Kelly stared at me. 'That's someone's house,' she said.

Americans appeared less likely to carry the stilted noblesse oblige that weighed down on Ammi and Abbu each time we were around someone poor, the hyper-awareness of difference that rendered any genuine interaction improbable. However, I was learning that this was in part because Americans didn't even acknowledge class, thought of it as a quaint concept from other parts of the world, like yoga or turmeric. When I asked Kelly why so much of Lakeview was poor, she took a second to think, then said, 'I would say it's bad decisions and a distance from God.'

The hippies, they were dying out.

*

I told Abbu I was considering breaking halal. He sighed and quoted a verse from Iqbal.

'Log asan samajhte hein musalman hona.'

'Abbu, no one thinks that.'

'It's the hardest things in life that test one's convictions.'

But everything was hard. Living oceans away was hard, making small talk with Mrs Sinclair was hard, the idiom of English was hard. Worrying about piously butchered fowl felt like a stupid kind of hard.

'Have you read Surah Baqarah in the Quran?' Ali asked, when I told him about my conversation with Abbu. 'The Children of Israel were asked to sacrifice a cow, and it could have been any cow, but they kept asking for clarifications about exactly how old it should be, and what color, and in doing so they made the rules stricter for themselves.'

'What does that have to do with anything, Ali?' I asked, feigning impatience. That mode of conversation, the act of palavering and circuitously reaching a conclusion through anecdote, was the most familiar he had felt to me yet.

'What I'm saying is, don't complicate things for yourself. Do what you need to do.'

He and I were writing to each other more, my days punctuated by frequent Facebook logins to see if he had left a note. During the week, he took days to respond, leaving me weaving through my past messages to see if I had said something boring. He seemed busy, his profile a menagerie of tagged photos and college events he RSVPed to. Each weekend, however, he called and we spoke, uninterrupted, for an hour. I put him on speaker and changed for church, hoping he could hear the rustle of fabric and know I was unclothed. Each night, the thought of him was its own heat.

We conversed mostly in English because he seemed to me like one of those people who had never grown up entirely comfortable in Urdu, so speaking it with him felt like a boast. Even when I pushed for it, he invariably tumbled into English. I pointed this out to him, calling him a burger, and he said we were both burgers, he was just gourmet, which stung because so much of my identity – what with Abbu being from the village and us not having cable TV – was centered around not being a burger. Those were the years when the easiest, perhaps only, way to define yourself was to decide what you weren't.

He often began sentences with yar, and I did the same with him. Yar, *you wouldn't believe what happened today*, yar, *suno*, yar, *I'm tired*. Years ago, Abbu had told me gently, after hearing me say it to Faisal, that yar was a very masculine word, that respectable women didn't use it. A thrill ran down my marrow when he said that, and I found my favorite word in the language, a word that would forever be chocolate syrup, heated honey, red wine – yar, yar, yar.

Ali told me about his father, who had moved to Karachi after his parents' divorce, and about his mother, who worked for a bank. He said what he missed about home, besides her, was walking to get halwa puri on Sundays from the same man his father used to go to. Sometimes, he talked about the classes he was taking on European nationalisms and the Cold War, mentioning a professor's quip or a passage from his readings. To me, Ali was like the blue Oxford Urdu-to-English dictionary Abbu kept at home. I gave him my observations about America that reeked of naivete and newness even to myself, and he translated them back to me, setting them in time and place. When I told him I continued to find it hard to form effortless friendships in America, seeking Hamid's comfort instead, he wrote back about large Pakistani communities in Queens that were universes within themselves, about foreigner enclaves in Islamabad that had shops with dollar prices.

I couldn't decide whether he made my life better. There was certainly more pleasure to my days. I now had a reason to wake up early, to see whether he had left a message while studying late. Mundane events at school – the Hollywood classics we saw in Film class, the Christmas choir Sam had convinced me to join – became valuable as fodder for our next phone call.

I asked him if he had dated anyone in college.

'Yes, this white girl from Virginia,' he said. 'It didn't work out because of the songs.'

He said he didn't want to spend his life taking turns playing songs in Urdu and Punjabi, which seemed like a sweet and bullshit reason. I crawled through his friend list until I found her. Great teeth, Obama fan. RSVPs to events hosted by the NYU Pakistan Students Association. Perhaps it didn't work out because she had been insufferable.

Some days, the idea of him deepened the patches of loneliness that had begun appearing on my days. I kept myself occupied as much as I could – volleyball practice, babysitting at church, sleepovers at Alicia's. Walking down to the school bus one day, I thought I heard Ammi say my name and stopped in my tracks, my breath shallow, until the bus came around the bend. Sometimes, while talking to Kelly, I stumbled around a sentence, unmoored by language. Even after the conversation had moved on, I remained unsteady, like I was riding a bike that had narrowly escaped a hedge.

There's a certain purgatorial period after you've moved to a new house, when your reflexes are still set to the old one. You expect the cabinets to open a certain way, the light switch to be right by the door. As time goes on, you start quizzing yourself on whether your body still remembers the old place. What type of lock was on the front door? Which way did the bathroom faucet turn? Did the window creak when opened? I was at that stage of missing home, where I was wondering what I remembered and worrying that I had forgotten too much. Of course, what I didn't know then is that one forgets things only to remember them again.

But it wasn't just home that I yearned for. Talking to Ali, hearing him describe a college protest about drone strikes or an Italian restaurant he had tried in the West Village, made me feel provincial, stuck in a part of the country that no one seemed to know or care about. Why had I been placed in the Chichawatni of America? Most other exchange students were spread out across the East Coast, often in the suburbs of large cities. On weekends, they uploaded photos in front of grand city halls and skyscrapers, holding halal cart food and tacos, their locations tagged as 'Philadelphia, PA' or 'Boston, MA.' Once, Zahra posted a photo in the shadow of the Statue of Liberty, her teeth showing in the wide smile she had picked up in America.

'New York, NY.'

I sent her a chat the next time she was online.

'Hey, how's it going?'

She told me she was eating leftover nihari and my stomach growled. What seemed like years ago, I had made fun of her for wanting biryani in America. We chatted about our classes and she listed to me all the states she had been to so far.

'You should visit,' she wrote.

'New Jersey, you mean?'

'Yes, and New York's close by.'

I stared at the screen, taken aback by how easily the invitation had been extracted. It could have been an off-handed suggestion, but I wanted this too badly to worry about Zahra's sincerity. I opened Google Maps and put in directions from Edison to NYU. An hour by train. I hadn't touched most of the money Ammi had sent me with. I flipped back to Facebook.

'Should I visit for December break?'

*

The night was cold, the tall pine trees moving in lazy whistles. Amy and I shivered on the bleachers, cheering Hamid on as he aided a decisive touchdown in the last minute of the game. Unlike me, Hamid had created value for himself through sports. He was smaller than the other boys but athletic, a fast runner.

After the game ended, Amy invited me and him to drive with her to Fifth Quarter. In the brown tiled kitchen of the church, some volunteering parents set up a weekly joint after football games. It served Costco pizza, Hot Pockets, and root beer floats; mostly, it was meant to provide celebrating high schoolers a release, keep them from driving out to Eugene late into weekend nights. I bought slices for myself and Hamid and went back to the table, where he was sitting with Amy, Kyle, and Crista.

131

'Here's to the champ,' Crista said, raising her float.

'We need something stronger than that,' Amy added, taking out an opaque water bottle from her bag. Ever since she started dating Kyle, she had graduated past drinking Franzia while her mother wasn't home. Now, she and Crista went to games armed with highly spiked juice, their eyelids growing heavier with each quarter.

'Here,' she said, offering it to Hamid.

His eyes immediately flickered towards me, and I sensed his calculation. Drinking in front of another Muslim is a high-beta move. At best, you can thrill in sharing the gifts of Heaven with each other, knowing that the two of you are on a different high from the rest – one part tequila and two parts forbidden pleasure. At worst, the other person abstains, and you look like the lone harami all night long. I nodded in encouragement, and he shrugged and took the bottle.

The tequila went around the table. The conversation turned to a college fair Amy was attending in Eugene next week.

'Are you coming with me?' she asked Kyle, in a manner that suggested this had been discussed before.

'Nope.'

'Fine, suit yourself,' she snapped.

Kyle turned to me and Hamid.

'Do you guys think you'll go to college?'

Again, we caught each other's eyes.

'As opposed to?' I asked.

'I don't know. Working at a farm. Or a Target or something.'

'Why would I do that?' Hamid asked, perplexed.

'Oh, yeah, too good for that?' Kyle said, but his tone wasn't unkind. In their own way, he and Hamid had formed a friendship that seemed to transcend the fact that he still called Hamid a terrorist every now and then. Cruelty and intimacy often sit together.

'My mother would kill me if I didn't go to college,' Hamid said.

'Come on, Kyle,' Amy interjected, a little red. 'Some people actually want to achieve things. And these two are fancy. They're going to be bigshots.'

'What's bigshot about going to college?' Hamid countered. 'It's what everyone does.'

It wasn't, but everyone Hamid and I knew did.

'It means you have the money to go,' Crista replied.

'Yeah, fancy pants. It means your terrorist father is rich,' Kyle said.

For many Lakeview kids, college was either an impossible dream or an unnecessary nuisance. Amy and Alicia were the only juniors registered for the PSAT. Hamid and I, on the other hand, plucked as emissaries by the discerning hands of the State Department, little go-betweens drained from that continent to this one, had never considered life without higher education. We were children of the professional class, training to become obedient, ascendant members ourselves. And only in retrospect can I see how much this biased me against my classmates at Lakeview, because at some level I knew that while they had gushing hot water and my family didn't, and they were American citizens and I would spend my life groveling at embassies, I had prospects in life that they did not.

By the time I walked home an hour later, my head was light from alcohol, the world twisting around me like the phoropter in an optician's office. I checked my laptop. No message. I wanted to tell Ali about the night, the warmth of alcohol and conversation, all the delicate ways in which I was learning to define myself against the world.

The phone rang. I walked over with the measured gait of the inebriated and squinted at the Caller ID. Multan.

'Assalamu alaikum, Hira.'

'Nana Ji, how are you? I miss you so much,' I said, suddenly horrified at myself for picking up the phone. I could barely stand.

'Beta, I miss you too. Do you have a cold?'

'Nahi, I was just outside.'

'Make sure you don't end up wheezing and coughing like your grandfather.'

'I'll be fine, Nana Ji. I don't have thirty years of smoking on my resume.'

He let out a loud laugh.

'That's true. Seemi sent us a picture. You've grown so thin. Are you eating enough?'

I told him about the challenges with halal meat, about how Kelly barely cooked.

'Haan,' he sighed. 'This is the independence your mother wanted for you. Life is not easy in pardes.'

Pardes – the country that is not yours.

'When do you come back?'

'June.'

'You have to come to me as soon as you get back. Tell the pilot to land the plane in Multan.'

I laughed and told him I would. Then I spoke to my grandmother, who asked if it was true, if America was as big as people said it was. I told her it was vast and endless, instead of admitting just how small I was finding it.

XIII

Some objects:

Abbu's nail cutter, with yellow edging, sitting on top of the TV stand. The telephone directory, its pink flowers faded from time and dirt, Ammi's slanted hand on every page. Ammi's lipsticks, assembled like a tiny army next to the mirror in the hallway. The inside of the microwave, speckled with dried bits of food. The one dining chair that always creaked. The garden hose, chalky with dust. The plastic table in the yard. An enamel teapot. Faisal's blue pajamas. Abbu's winter shawl.

My parents had no fetish for objects. Wedding cards and letters ended up in the pile of paper Aliya collected for the scrap-collector. Old toys were donated the moment we outgrew them. Abbu patronized libraries and never bought his own books. Ammi collected the tiniest things – hotel soaps, the sachets of conditioner that came with her hair dye – but their value was only in the promise of future utility. Faisal loved his Sims CDs, but little else. I have always been the most materialistic person in my family.

And being thus, I appreciated all the ways in which the Wilkins' house was more comfortable than ours, while remaining unpretentious. The lighting was superior, yellow and cozy. No paint peeled off the walls any time a door slammed shut. Lizards didn't incubate near the windows. The oven worked. I reveled in it all, because it was still years before I would learn to take irrational pride in the eccentricities of my childhood home. Defending dysfunctionality as character is a singularly adult trait.

*

Much to my relief, Lakeview High didn't make it to state playoffs for volleyball. Unlike what Amy had said, it never got easier for me. When I lifted my shirt up to the mirror, I thrilled to see shapes I had never seen before – a long trough cutting down the middle of my torso, an abdomen hard as bones. But the fire in my lungs never abated, always following me on the ride home from practice. After the season ended, I began taking walks in the afternoon, making my way down the hill and onto a side road where a spring ran. Walking around Lakeview was a joy, meditative and mindless, like moving the beads on a rosary. There was seldom anyone on the streets, the only thing to be wary of the occasional car rushing down the highway. I had never walked for leisure back home, where the streets were made for people like my family, who owned cars. In the market, Ammi often waited for someone else to pull out so she could park right in front of the store. Uncle Shafiq was instructed to drop me off as close to the school gate as possible. The brief moments I did spend on the streets were a cacophony to the senses – looking out for erratic motorcyclists and blindly reversing cars, turning this way and that to avoid the sprawling bodies of men, adjusting my dupatta so it didn't sweep the floor. Each foray out of the car was a ten-second odyssey.

Kelly sometimes joined me on my walks. I liked her best on such days, when she wore loose sweaters and walked around squinting in the sun, in possession of a quiet confidence. With Ethan, she was often nervous and watchful, letting him do much of the talking but making sure he didn't offend me or Amy. Around Amy, she curtailed herself into the role of the worrying mother.

'Why did you sign up to be a host parent?' I asked her, as we made our way past the lake, its surface ablaze in the late afternoon sun. She looked surprised.

'Why would I not? It's a wonderful opportunity. How else would I learn so much about Pakistan?'

She hadn't learned much about Pakistan. Our conversations were mostly about the day-to-day of school and work. She told me about growing up in northern California, about the early, lonely years of being a single parent in a highway town. I had drawn for her brief sketches of my parents and life back home.

'You could learn about Pakistan from the internet. Why did you really do it?'

It was the kind of thing Ammi and Abbu would never do. And while it was true that Kelly had an openness to the world that neither of my parents possessed, I still felt that anyone who would willfully sign up to host a stranger, voluntarily add to the list of people they had to put up with, had to have an itch to scratch.

We walked in silence for a few minutes.

'I always wished Amy had a sibling,' she said. 'She was a lonely child.'

An itch to scratch or a hole to fill. I fought the urge to reach over and squeeze Kelly's hand.

'Is my presence helping?'

'I think so,' she said, not sounding convinced. 'You two are very different. It seems like you had an easy relationship with your mother growing up, so it might be hard for you to relate to her.'

'Was it not easy between the two of you?'

'I was set up for failure. I suppose every single mother is. There's only ever one person to blame.'

'Well, there's also one person to credit,' I said. 'Amy is who she is only because of you.'

She stayed quiet.

'Also, if it helps, even when there is a father, the mother usually gets the blame,' I added.

A cloud of rage flitted over her face, then disappeared. She laughed a brittle laugh.

'I suppose you're right.'

Kelly was the anxious mother Ammi had tried her hardest never to be. 'Children will consume you if you let them,' I had overheard my mother advising a friend on the phone once. And yet, it was still she who laminated our school notebooks in brown paper at the start of each term, she who sewed every loose button and mended each hole. And when we cried, it was still her arms we sought. Perhaps it didn't matter whether you embraced motherhood like Kelly or treated it with suspicion, like Ammi. If you were a mother, a mother was the most you'd ever be.

Kelly pointed to a wooden bench, painted a bright yellow. We sat down. When she turned to me again, her eyes were shining.

'When she was a kid, she would lock herself in the bathroom at school and refuse to come out. They would call me at work, and I'd have to drive all the way back from Eugene.'

She blinked; a tear fell.

'As soon as she heard my voice outside the door, she would unlock it and just smile at me, and everything would be normal. It was always a test, and I had to pass it.'

Yes. For the child, a mother was all a mother could be.

*

By mid-November, everything was windy and wet. Kelly kept the house warm through a central wooden stove that crackled deep into the evenings, but by each morning, the cold had penetrated every corner of my room, threatening to crawl in through any nook in the comforter.

One Sunday, Kelly and I went to visit her church friend Megan and her husband. They played Lady Antebellum on a portable speaker as we sat outside and quartered apples for cider. Megan brought out an electric stockpot and put in the apples, along with oranges, cinnamon, and cloves. While the cider simmered, she served us warm pumpkin bread and milky coffee, insisting that I wear her spare coat on top of my red fleece sweatshirt. 'She'll need a real jacket soon,' she said to Kelly. My hands were numb from the juice and I had started shivering.

The next day, I woke up to a distinctive lump in my throat. I tried to discreetly clear it several times, until Hamid frowned at me in class. Even more than usual, I begged the clock above the classroom doorway to move along. By the time I got home, my head was heavy, legs weighed down by gravity as I made my way up the hill. The next morning was worse; the cold had traveled to my nose and chest. Kelly took one look at me from the doorway and said, 'You don't look too good,' which I knew by then was the American way of saying you looked like shit.

'Well, I better keep away. Stay home and rest, I'll bring back some cough medicine,' she said, her eyes moving to the couch, where my textbooks and clothes were carelessly strewn. 'Maybe you can tidy up your room since you're home.'

Whenever Faisal and I got sick back home, our parents roamed about us like moths drawn to the heat of our bodies. They forced us into bedrest, plied us with boiled eggs and doodh patti, massaged our aching limbs. Aunts and uncles visited, honey and broth in tow. Being sick in America appeared like a social misstep – you had to stay away from people, sparing them embarrassment, contagion, any unseemly reminder of physical vulnerability. I closed my eyes to hot tears gathering under the lids, plotting to spill over.

I knew I was being sensitive, the illness breeding spongy self-pity. I chided myself, thinking that I was now too old to get bent out of shape by an adult's careless words. Of course, that, right there, was how young I was, that I thought there would ever be a day when nonchalant words lost their power to sting.

Amy promised to hand in my homework and forced me to take a Dayquil before she left. I tossed in bed for an hour, then got up, fluffed the pillow and pulled the comforter over it. I stuck clothes in the laundry, put my books in a neat pile, and took the vacuum cleaner out of the hallway closet. Kelly told me I shed too much hair, and that I should take multivitamins, and it felt petty to point out that all other living beings in the house – she, Amy, and Winston – had much lighter hair, thin whiteish strands that became one with the wooden floor.

I boiled two eggs and peeled them the way Abbu did – yanking swiftly at the shell so that the chewy membrane came off as well. I ate the eggs with the chai I made with Kelly's Twinings teabags. Then I went up to Amy's room, my breathing shallow by the time I got to the landing. The room was spotless, decorated in yellow and gold, the curtains pulled back with ribbons. The comforter was tucked in tightly, without a single crease. On the dresser was a makeup organizer. I sat down on the dainty ottoman next to it.

The only makeup I owned was a stick of kajal and a tube of sticky gloss that glued my hair to my lips in the wind. I had gotten them as gifts from an aunt, whom Ammi had railed against the entire car ride home. 'Why does she think that's a proper gift for a young girl?' Ammi fumed. Abbu simply forbade it, telling me I should wait till marriage to wear makeup. I was twelve then, and marriage was an unreasonable while away, so instead I just waited for the car ride to school. Uncle Shafiq learned to turn the rear mirror as soon as I got into the backseat, so I could rub in the kajal without poking my eye.

I squeezed out some of Amy's foundation, then used my fingertips to spread it across my cheeks and nose. A ghost stared at me in the mirror. I was parchment, the color of starch. I picked up the foundation bottle and saw the shade code. Light Beige.

Then I flung open her closet, pulling out clothes like I was in a store. One by one, I tried them on, letting the cloth run down my body, then discarding it into a shimmering pile on the floor. Shorts and halter tops, tube dresses, sequined skirts – anything that showed ample skin. I twirled around, looking at my legs and chest from every angle, jutting my jaw out, tugging the fabric up and down. Part of me felt obscene – it's a particular shame, to see yourself scantily dressed for the first time. Part of me felt I had never seen anything sexier in my life.

After putting everything back in place, I went down and returned to bed with the cordless, feeling delirious from the fever and from all that skin – mine – that I had just seen. I called Ali to wish him a happy birthday, asking if he was doing anything to celebrate.

'Dinner with Sameen and a few others,' he said. Sameen was in his year, also from Pakistan. In her Facebook pictures, she had her nose pierced, hair dyed, and legs perpetually draped over this thing or that. Most recently, to my relief, they were draped over her new boyfriend, some boy from Connecticut.

'Has anything ever happened between you and Sameen?' I asked.

Ali sighed.

'You sound like my American friends. There are thousands of Pakistanis in New York. We aren't all hooking up with one another.'

'I'll see that for myself soon,' I said, and told him about the flight I had booked to New Jersey for December. I deliberated over each syllable, forcing myself to keep my tone even.

'Wait, what?! Why didn't you tell me? And why aren't you staying in New York?'

I told him about Zahra, whose Indian host family lived in Edison.

'Of course they do,' he said, amused. 'Well, good thing you told me. I was about to buy my ticket home for the break.'

I struggled to remain casual as we discussed what day I should visit New York.

'Also, wear that purple kurta when you come,' he added.

A memory from long ago surfaced in my mind. A newly married woman, Ammi's friend, had visited our house in a deep red shalwar kameez.

'He asks me to wear this all the time,' she told Ammi, referring to her husband. 'He says I look sexy.'

Her voice tapered into a whisper at the end. They both laughed like girls while I held my breath, stationary, so Ammi didn't remember I was there and send me off. The woman had stuck to my memory like Elfy. 'Sexy,' she had said. From then on, she became Ammi's most beautiful friend in my mind. I envied her the giddy surrender of her voice, the delight of having a man affirm what a woman hoped was true – that she wasn't merely beautiful, but sexy.

I told Ali about trying on Amy's clothes and he laughed.

'Did you feel different in them?'

'Giddy.'

'Why?'

'Just the freedom of bare skin. But also scared. What if America's changing me?'

'That's not how change works,' he said.

What did he know? He was raised a rich boy in Lahore, assured that the streets were his. He wasn't reminded to always cover up before heading out, instructed to hide the polythene wrappings of Always pads, told to hang drying underwear in a dark storeroom. Ammi had once asked me, as we drove in Saddar, who I would be, if I could be anyone in the world. 'A Pakistani man,' I had replied without a second thought.

She had inhaled sharply – whether out of shock or empathy, I would never know.

'Tell me how change works, wise Pakistani man,' I goaded Ali.

'Acha, I'm going to shut up.'

'Good, because you have no clue what you're talking about.'

'Yar, wear the skirts if you want,' he replied, sounding annoyed. 'In fact, send me a photo when you do. Just don't be surprised when you feel like the same Hira you always were.'

He was right and he was wrong. Of course, one was only what one could ever be. The place I was from would stick with pungency to the rest of my days, like the ghost of the beloved, like a too-late diagnosis of a terrible illness. So, then, yes. I contained within me the seed for everything that was possible, yet who but God knew what that was?

January

The morning after I puke orange into the toilet bowl, I call up the doctor's office. Ethan sits with his bowl of Cheerios at the table, listening in. The doctor says I have to continue the medicine for a few days to see if my body will start tolerating it.

The nurse comes at the same time as the day before and watches me put the four pills in my mouth. I throw up again that night, and the next one. It's Ramzan in reverse – I eat during the day, then my body cleanses itself at dawn. The fourth time it happens, I tell her none of the medicine is staying in me.

'You're driving back and forth for nothing.'

She doesn't bat an eye.

'I'm doing what they tell me to do. Call the doctor.'

Kelly drives me to the doctor again, where the assistant notes down my weight and tells me I have dropped three pounds in a week. 'You're officially underweight now,' she says cheerfully, checking a BMI chart. Then she draws blood and hands me a paper cup filled with orange juice for hydration. I take a sip and remember the nightly contents of the toilet bowl – the color of clementines, horizon at dusk, chili oil. Before leaving, I spill the rest of the juice into the sink.

XIV

'Are sore throats supposed to sound like that?' Amy asked, after hearing me wheeze three days into my sickness.

'My asthma flares up whenever I catch a cold.'

Every winter, the dry, dusty cold of Pindi got me sick, and every time, the cold turned to bronchitis, sneaking into my lungs and turning their passageways narrow and swollen. I would spend sleepless nights with Ammi and a Ventolin inhaler on my side, head propped up on three pillows.

'Mom, you should take her to the doctor,' Amy said.

'Do you have health insurance?' Kelly asked.

I was sick and tired of Kelly not knowing things she really ought to know.

'Yes, but we can wait. I brought my inhaler. Maybe it'll get better in a few days.'

'Well, let me know,' she said, appearing concerned but also somewhat relieved. The months leading up to Christmas were her busiest time of the year at work. That night, she made a hearty beef stew; my cold had finally broken me and I had decided to give up halal. She offered the serving bowl to me again and again. When I told this to Ammi later, she said, 'Yeah, she's guilty because she's never around for you.'

'Well, the food was delicious.'

My body was satiated, my mouth remembering a taste it had forgotten: dark, fatty, salty meat.

'Did the meat taste different from halal?' Ammi asked, her tone light as whipped cream.

'Yes, the cow tasted sad that it wasn't killed to Allah-u-Akbar,' I said, regretting it even as the words spilled out. Ammi had asked that intentionally because Ammi did little without intention. She wanted to indicate, without saying as much, that she respected my decision to switch. In turn, I had mocked her.

'Is that how Americans talk to their parents?' she asked coldly. I stayed quiet.

'Remember that I'm not American, and neither are you.'

*

For Thanksgiving, we were driving to California to visit Kelly's mother. I counted down the weeks, looking forward to spending a few days without the bulky blue jacket Amy had lent me, saying it might help with the cough.

It snowed the weekend before we left. Kelly laughed at my shriek as I walked into the living room in the morning. Flecks were falling onto the front stoop. Standing by the backdoor, I stuck out my hand and watched them melt in the heat of my palm. Everywhere was covered with untouched snow, ready to be embellished with weaving footprints on the way to the school bus.

Ethan had begun spending nights at the house, a development Amy had narrowed her eyes at and then slowly made peace with. She was growing less edgy around him, and once I even saw the two of them with their heads bent over a laptop together. 'Mom's Christmas gift,' Amy explained. After breakfast, he took photos of me outside, telling me to grab fistfuls of snow and throw them in the air. Amy showed me how to make a snow angel. Kelly brought down a well-worn box of Christmas ornaments.

'Your enthusiasm's infectious,' she said to me. 'Why wait till after Thanksgiving.'

She and Ethan had just cut the tree at a farm that week. We spent an hour hanging the ornaments – a red cube that said 'Happy Millennium,' a miniature Space Needle, a stuffed doll with hair that had gone from blonde to brown with time. I hummed along to 'Jingle Bells' when Kelly played it on her laptop, telling her about music classes in primary school, when we would stand in neat rows and sweat in Pindi heat and sing about the snow we had never seen. She was quiet as she adjusted the tree skirt.

'It's quite strange, if you think about it,' she said after a while. 'You know so much about here, when we don't know anything about there.'

Yes. It was quite strange.

※

We left early on a Tuesday, Kelly and Ethan splitting the drive through Redding and Sacramento. I was almost out of the cough syrup Kelly had gotten me.

'We can get more at the next rest stop,' Ethan said.

'They're going to have cough syrup at a rest stop?'

'Why wouldn't they?' he responded, frowning.

The place we stopped at sold more variety than most general stores in Pindi – medicine for all common ailments, as well as coffee, hot dogs lazily swiveling on metal rods, watches, reflective jackets, DVDs, truck supplies, paper plates, lemon cakes, fuzzy blankets. For $10, one could take a shower.

We reached San Francisco by evening, as the sun drowned in the bay. Kelly had booked two rooms in a dimly lit hostel. The lobby was flooded with flyers advertising tour groups and day trips – Alcatraz, Fisherman's Wharf, Chinatown. Next morning, we made pancakes in the communal kitchen while chatting with backpackers from Manila and Lisbon. On the street, I heard a dozen tongues I couldn't identify. Restaurant menus boasted of dosas and idli and crispy pork belly. The red, soaring bridge we drove on was clogged with people the color of all earths – clay, loam, silt. I was in the American metropole, brimming with its most valuable import – labor – summoned from all over the empire. But I only saw its garb of cosmopolitanism, and it gave me a heady rush.

Amy must have felt it too, because she turned to me on a packed street.

'I'm so jealous you get to visit New York.'

It's funny, in retrospect. Whenever I would return to America later, it would be to its glittering cities – gleaming high-rises, subway vents blowing mystery plumes, Chinatown and Deevan Avenue and Arabized Motown. But deep down, my nostalgia for America is marked by its first imprints – the vast canopy of Lakeview sky, the fetid smell of sea lions in Florence, country fairs, the sadness of a rural Dairy Queen. It's a lonesome landscape, full of solitude and longing for other places. It is so disparate from the rest of my life.

*

After another half day of driving, we finally reached the LA suburb where Kelly's mother lived. The neighborhood reminded me of neat developments back home, run by the military, rows upon rows of houses with neatly tended lawns in the front. But unlike those houses, built with the unavoidable uniformity of a military contractor, these were custom-built, each with differently colored stoops and sidings. The air was dry and warm, like Pindi in October.

Hannah had divorced Kelly's father many years ago, and now lived by herself in a three-bedroom. As she showed me around the house, I noted her accent, distinctly not American.

'When did you move here?' I asked, stressing my own into-nations. *I am like you, also not from here.*

148

'Around forty years ago,' she said, pointing to a photo on her dresser that showed a teenage girl with braids, standing by the water. 'Kelly's father visited Germany as a strapping American with jokes and dollars, and I couldn't resist.'

I picked up the photo. It was dated 'Hamburg, 1968.'

'Do you visit often?'

She squinted, counting in her head.

'Seven years ago.'

'Long time.'

The picture was black and white, but I could see that Amy had taken more after Hannah than Kelly had – she had the same nose and forehead as the slim woman in the photo.

That night, we stayed up late after dinner, playing board games. Every time Hannah lost, she claimed the rules didn't make sense. 'That's not how we play the game,' she said, reminding me of the times I told Kelly and Amy, 'We eat with our hands,' 'We don't wear shoes inside,' 'We like sitting on the floor.' It seemed that this invisible *we* persisted throughout one's life, conjuring the first community one knew, the only one most of us could own.

*

'Why don't you make something Pakistani?' Kelly asked on Thanksgiving Day.

I balked at the pressure of more representation.

'I don't think we have the spices for it,' I said.

'We can get them before the stores close,' she said, and handed me a pen and paper to make a list. I Skyped Ammi and asked her for step-by-step instructions for bhindi, after which Ethan and I drove to the store to get okra, turmeric, cumin, and coriander. An hour before the turkey would be done, I chopped up the okra, discarding the tops, and fried it. Ethan walked over now and then, rubbing his hands in anticipation.

149

He told me about Tandoor, the Indian lunch buffet place in Eugene he went to every other week. The sizzling okra smelled so distinct that I kept my face low over the pan, inhaling its sticky redolence. Bhindi with boiled rice was Abbu's favorite meal in the world, besides those nervy chicken broths he loved to eat. Next, I fried onions and added the spices. Kelly rushed to open the backdoor.

'Don't want everything smelling like food,' she said. Then, looking at me:

'Would you like me to bring you a T-shirt? That pretty kurta is going to smell.'

I kept stirring the onions.

'It's fine,' I said.

'The smell doesn't bother you?'

'No.'

'For me, it's just a tad strong . . .'

Hannah, bent over the oven, said, 'Stop bothering her, Kelly.'

I put the food in a big bowl and sprinkled fresh coriander on top. Hannah carved out servings of turkey and we all walked around the island, making our plates before sitting down at her small table. She had put on a new tablecloth for the occasion – red, with silver half-moons sewed on top.

I was suddenly joyless. I knew what Ammi or Ali would say, that I was letting someone else's stupidity come in the way of my own happiness. Ali would tell me there was no way to survive in America except by holding one's head high. But I didn't want making bhindi to feel like holding my head high. I wanted it to feel like making bhindi.

'Just like Tandoor,' Ethan said, upon his first bite.

'Very good,' Kelly agreed.

'This isn't how it's supposed to taste,' I said, surly. The sauce was thick and viscous, unlike the thin shimmer of oil that bordered Aliya's bhindi. There was too much tomato.

'The good thing is,' Hannah said, copying me and scooping the bhindi with a piece of bread, 'none of us knows how it's supposed to taste.'

Later, I sat in the backyard on a white plastic chair, looking out at the other houses. Among the gifts America gave me: tank tops, avocados, and a fetish for peeking through windows, lit in warm yellow light, frilly curtains half drawn. I stared out and waited for someone to come by, but saw no one, though I heard them all: their glasses clanging, spring doors opening, engines revving as guests left.

I still felt unmoored in America, but there were ways in which I was beginning to understand it that were more nuanced than my initial observations. One of these was how the private and public blurred into one another, unlike the clear boundaries of home. Evening windows invited the voyeur; often, there were vases or porcelain dolls standing on the sills, enticements for the onlooker. People checked their mailboxes in pajamas. The first time Hamid visited the Wilkins' house, Kelly had given him a tour. He followed her awkwardly to all three bedrooms. 'Very nice,' he had offered, puzzled, as we stood next to Kelly's closet, well-worn beige bras peeking from inside.

Hannah came out to the backyard.

'They might watch a movie,' she said, sitting down on the chair next to me.

I nodded, and there was silence for a while.

'Why don't you visit home more?' I asked.

If it seems odd that I was fixating, almost obsessively, on Hannah's foreignness, let me tell you one of my most dearly held orthodoxies – for anyone who leaves home, that becomes the most interesting story of their life.

Hannah stretched her legs out, unfazed.

'California's home.'

I didn't buy it.

'I moved here around the same age as you,' she said. 'This is where I got my first house, my first car. It's where my life is.'

'I haven't moved here,' I said firmly.

'I see.'

I could feel her eyes on me, so I looked down and rubbed my feet against the dry, neatly trimmed grass.

'You know,' she began after a pause. 'Home doesn't stay the same after you move. You change, it changes. Especially since my parents passed, it's different.'

A brick landed inside me, weighty and unmovable. It was the world in which Pakistan wasn't home.

Then she shook her head.

'Oh, but you're so young. You have the rest of your life for these questions.'

'Great.'

She laughed and got up to turn the porch light on. Her forehead, above light blue eyes, was creased as she looked at me again – not with worry, it seemed, but with a certain bemused empathy.

'I know this sounds odd,' she said, 'but leaving doesn't have to be a tragedy. It can be quite freeing, to never be at home anywhere.'

'That sounds awful.'

'It's not. Imagine a life unburdened by history.'

Just then, Kelly screamed inside the house. We rushed in to find Ethan on his knees, a ring box cupped in his hands. I glanced at Amy and saw that she knew already. She looked serene, almost happy. Then Kelly was jumping, yelling, 'Yes, yes,' and Ethan was pulling her in for a kiss, and Amy was shouting, 'Gross, stop it!' Hannah, who was just as clueless as I was, clapped her hands and went to dig for champagne in her basement.

Later, as we got into bed, I asked Amy, 'Are you happy?'

'Of course,' she said, without missing a beat, and I could tell she wasn't lying. 'This is the best thing that has ever happened to Mom.'

'She'd say you're the best thing that happened to her,' I said.

'Well, she'd be wrong,' Amy countered, then continued in a low voice. 'It does mean he'll come live with us. I wish we were moving to Eugene instead.'

'Why can't we?' I asked, my heart fluttering with hope. Compared to Lakeview, Eugene was a cosmopolitan dream.

'Mom wants me to finish high school at Lakeview,' she said. 'It'll be good to have him around though. I wouldn't have to worry about her being alone.'

How much of filial responsibility is merely worrying about your parents' loneliness?

'You knew about this, right?' I asked.

'Yep, he and I chose the ring together,' Amy whispered, turning the light off. 'I told him to do it elsewhere. Getting engaged in your mother-in-law's house, imagine.'

I shrugged in the dark. Everyone in Pakistan got engaged in their mother-in-law's house.

*

By the time we got back to Lakeview, the wedding had taken over as the topic of most conversation. The atmosphere in the house turned manic with excitement. The wedding was very soon, on January 16th – Ethan's mother wasn't doing too well, and they wanted a small event anyway. There was still a lot to do, though, so Kelly put both Amy and me to work getting quotes from florists and looking up possible wedding favors, while she booked the flights and hotel for their honeymoon in Hawaii.

'It'll be my first vacation in years,' she said, showing me photos of a Maui resort with an infinity pool. 'I'm splurging.'

No one in my family had ever done a honeymoon; my parents' first trip together was to Saudi Arabia, where they spent forty days sharing dingy tents with other worshippers. The idea that you could have a wedding with fifty guests and spend that money on a hedonistic vacation instead was new to me and seemed quite brilliant.

For the first time, the rather separate lives that Kelly, Amy, and I led all converged on the focal point of the wedding. Instead of spending evenings at Kyle's, Amy came back after school every day so we could all sit in the living room and plan. We looked up hideous bridesmaid dresses and made fun of them together. It reminded me of the thrill that would run throughout the extended family any time a cousin's wedding was announced, a siren call for the clothes-stitching and the shoe-buying and the dowry-making to commence. More than anything else, matrimony gives people something to do.

Amy and I were to be bridesmaids. I was touched.

'Isn't Amy the maid of honor?' I asked Kelly.

'No,' she replied firmly. 'You're both my daughters.'

I most definitely wasn't, but it was a kind gesture. The three of us went into Eugene to pick out the wedding gown and bridesmaid dresses, and Kelly paid for one of her daughters while the other one did mental calculations about how much a $100 dress would set back her bank account. Next, we stopped by a catering company to see how much they would charge for a pizza cart.

'It's going to be so much fun,' I told my mother on the phone, the night before I left for New Jersey. 'Finally, some excitement around here.'

'Didn't you say it will be fifty people? That's a dinner party.'

'Haan, not everyone invites the entire village to their wedding. Also, she's letting me help plan it. Treating me like an adult, unlike my own parents.'

'Sure. That must be why she makes you pay for everything. You're an adult.'

What is evident to me in retrospect is that Ammi had decided very early on to dislike Kelly – not in the dull, constant

154

way that my misanthropic parents disliked many people, but with purpose.

She softened when I told her Kelly was making me a bridesmaid.

'That's nice. Why don't you give her the phone? I'd like to congratulate her.'

I walked upstairs with the cordless, a little taken aback and almost self-conscious. Ammi had never talked to Kelly before.

'Mom, you *have* to take her to the doctor when she comes back,' Amy was saying behind Kelly's door, which was half ajar. I stopped at the landing, wondering if Ammi could also hear through the receiver.

'Her cough isn't getting better. Crista was asking me if she has pneumonia. Why did you sign up if you can't take care of her?'

Heat pricked at my jaw and crept up my cheeks. In Pindi, coughing and sneezing in the classroom were commonplace, as much a part of the winter landscape as early sunsets and foggy mornings. How odd I must have looked in the hallways of Lakeview High, sick for days among strong, healthy bodies. Before I could let myself hear Kelly's reply, I climbed down a few steps and then walked back up, calling loudly for her so they knew I was coming.

XV

A towering Christmas tree was set up in the Newark arrival terminal. I walked out to the pick-up area where Zahra had told me to wait. She was already there, although it took me a second to recognize her. She had gained weight, her cheeks firmer than before. Or maybe they looked rounder because of the white scarf that hung around her face, tied at the chin.

'Hira!' she called out, running over to hug me.

'You're so skinny!' she exclaimed, holding my wrists in her hands. 'How did you manage to lose weight in this country?'

From the pictures other exchange students had posted on Facebook, it seemed like many of them were putting on pounds. It was something they had warned us about at orientation, that the body cannot remain unaffected by the bounty of America, its readily available ice creams, burgers, and sodas. Glee ran through me each time I saw a plump cheek, a T-shirt tight over rolls of fat. I was proud of my own abdomen, hardened from volleyball practice, of legs that slid smoothly into skinny jeans and showed the thigh gap Amy envied.

'Volleyball,' I explained to Zahra, trying hard not to stare at the scarf. She appeared fully at ease, not even realizing this was my first time seeing it on her. Her host mother, Sumaira, was waiting in the car. Sumaira had high cheek-bones and also wore a scarf. As we drove towards Edison, she told me she had family in Rawalpindi, distant cousins who had migrated to Pakistan after Partition. She and her husband came to America in the '90s, she said, speaking with an accent that reminded me of Ammi's. But while Ammi hesitated in the curves of the English sentence, stalling to formulate her next thought in a language she used only at work, Sumaira's words unraveled smoothly. The first few times she asked me a question I responded in Urdu, savoring the fact that I was again with people who spoke it. Sumaira continued to talk only in English, except when she laced her words with Mashallahs and Inshallahs. I felt myself put off by both her insistent English and her religious invocations.

We, of '90s Pakistan, of the shadowy years after Zia, of the backyard to the War on Terror, of bomb blasts near the Pearl Continental, of bomb blasts at the Marriott, of bomb blasts that shook the front gate, of Hazaras refusing to bury their dead, of Ahmadis unsafe even in their mosques, of enlightened moderation, of the never-arrived renaissance, of goddamn Lal Masjid, of the scourge of the fundos. We grappled with the faith we were born into, in its most rotten, mutated form, and those of us who didn't buy it turned suspicious. While waiting for the Atatürk that never came, we scoffed at those who loudly proclaimed this faith. A belief in God, I thought to myself while hearing Sumaira talk, didn't make one interesting. It did. It could, but I had yet to learn that.

Zahra sat in the front seat, mostly in comfortable silence, sometimes speaking to finish Sumaira's sentences. There was an ease between the two of them that I didn't feel with Kelly. I was envious, and annoyed. Of course Zahra was more at ease – she had never left her comfort zone, swapping Islamabad for a woman who could easily be an Islamabadi Al-Huda aunty. This wasn't comfort, it was complacency. And what was up with that scarf?

*

We stopped at Patel Brothers. From the parking lot, I could see several families coming in and out, husbands and wives, children in thick coats, old women with greyed hair in braids that dwindled down their backs. They were all desi.

'This is where we do our shopping,' Sumaira said as we made our way through a door plastered with advertisements for beauty parlors and sari shops. 'Celebrating our food, our culture,' said the sign above the entrance. Inside were aisles upon aisles of Shan masala packets, dal of all kinds, frozen chapatis in packs of thirty.

'Doesn't it remind you of home?' Zahra asked, taking a deep breath as we walked through the produce section. Back home, Abbu sometimes took me along on his weekly trips to the vegetable market, where he asked every stall keeper to hand him a plastic bag that he whipped with air before filling it with tomatoes the size of small eggs, cucumbers that Aliya peeled for salads, wounded aubergines and turnips. He would insist on picking each tomato and checking for scars or rot before bagging it. The market was uncovered and smelled like the world around it: in the summer, like rain, in the winter, like dust. This store, with its perfect baseball tomatoes, smelled nothing like it.

Sumaira put two bags of basmati rice in the cart. They were made of jute and held ten kilos each, unlike the delicate pouches Kelly sometimes got at Trader Joe's. We got bhindi, gobhi, and cilantro. Sumaira picked up biryani masala and loose tea.

'We'll get meat from the halal store. Beta, has it been hard doing halal? Is there a butcher nearby?'

I was expected to say it was indeed very hard, but what could I do, Aunty, Allah had ordained it and who was I to question His will. Alhumdulillah.

'I don't do halal anymore.'

Zahra's eyes widened. Sumaira shrugged.

'Yes, a lot of people have started giving it up. But we're old-fashioned people, what can we do?'

Like a gust of wind, home arrived. Sumaira was speaking facetiously, the same brand of facetious that came naturally to people back home. *We are so steadfast, so stubbornly pious, we can't help ourselves.* I looked around and saw the women at the tills, ambling with the slow gait of my aunts. Their shalwar kameez were in shades of popping pink and blue, colors Ammi would shudder to look at. They were wearing gold the way women did at weddings back home, except we were in a grocery store that smelled like disinfectant. Everything about the spectacle was disconcertingly familiar – it was home put under garish UV light and flipped on its head.

*

Sumaira and Aslam lived in a cul-de-sac surrounded by tall trees. The large lawn leading up to the house was covered in snow, although I could imagine the gleaming grass in summertime. The garage doors swung open automatically as the car pulled in. Four bedrooms, a basement, an attic, and a kitchen with a spotless island of dark marble.

'Very nice, Aunty,' I said, sitting down on an almond-colored couch adorned with Rajasthani cushions. I felt strangely tired from the flight, almost feverish.

'Thank you,' Sumaira said, eyes lit up with pride. 'We bought it two years ago. We're still renovating the basement.'

Show me a wealthy American not renovating their perfect suburban house.

Zahra took me to her room, which we were sharing for the next week.

'You can take the guest bedroom if you want, but I figured . . .'

'No, this is nice,' I said, settling onto the plush bed. 'Take the scarf off, we're home now.'

She unbuckled the safety pin. Underneath, her hair sat as curly as before.

'I take it in front of Uncle, since technically he's not related to me,' she said, folding and putting it away on the bedside table. I must have raised my eyebrows.

'What?' She laughed. 'Are you judging me?'

'A little bit.' I leaned back against the headrest. 'What, you came to America to become a full-on Muslimah?'

'So judgy. It feels good, yar, it gives me peace. Plus, everyone here takes it.'

'Yes, New Jersey is renowned for its hijab fashion.'

'Aray. Everyone I know. You'll see, it's almost a statement piece.'

Not even in the Pindi I remembered – that of loudspeakers blaring conservative sermons on Fridays and headmistresses starting assemblies with Quran recitations – was the scarf a fashion statement. You did it to show yourself, or Allah, or others, how pious you were. The stuff wasn't sexy.

'Did Sumaira tell you to take it?' I asked, and Zahra frowned.

'No one's making me take it, yar.'

'Sorry, sorry. It just seems out of character.'

She sat down on the bed, thoughtful.

'Yeah, I suppose it is. But it feels intentional, a choice I've made myself. Not like back home, where we follow Islam like robots. You know what I mean?'

I did know what she meant. I had just chosen to stop following it at all.

'Chalo, I'm happy for you. Did I tell you my host mother's getting married?' I said, opening my laptop to show her the bridesmaid dresses Amy and I had picked.

*

That night, Sumaira made biryani and kababs. We sat around a large dining table that could fit ten; 'We have so many parties, that's why,' Zahra said. Upon the first bite of the biryani, I let out a moan, and Zahra cackled. I bet she remembered.

'Beta, eat more,' Sumaira said.

Her husband Aslam cleared his throat. He was a physician who worked from his own clinic a five-minute drive away. Within moments of meeting me, he had inquired what my father did for a living and then expounded for a long time on the impossibility of being an honest civil servant in the subcontinent and the inevitability of corruption in the Third World. He was the kind of man taken to platitudes, rubbing me the wrong way with his loud, brash confidence. I liked men the way most men liked their women – confident, but largely silent.

'So, tell me, Hira,' he said now. 'How did your parents let such a young girl live with an unknown family for a year?'

I stared at him, then at Zahra.

'Of course. But this is different.'

I knew what he meant but arranged my forehead in puzzlement, waiting for him to elaborate.

'Zahra's parents knew she was coming to a house where the Quran is displayed in every room. Ramzan, no problem. Halal meat, no problem,' he said, and I wondered if Sumaira had told him about our conversation at Patel Brothers. 'All our friends here are Pakistanis or Indian Muslims. How did your parents agree to send you to Oregon, to live with those people?'

I had said it countless times – to Ali, Ammi, Faisal. I had referred to Amy and Kelly as 'these people,' with their unwashed butts and bacon breakfasts. Now, Aslam's words rankled me.

'They're very understanding and respectful. And it's a good way to learn about American culture.'

161

'We're an American family too.'

It was Zahra who chimed in.

'Yes, of course,' I said, wishing mostly to return to my biryani. 'But there is value in living with people different from you.'

Zahra shrugged.

'As long as they're not the white kids at school, whose first question to me is always "Where are you from?"'

I stared at her. *But you are from elsewhere, yar.*

'We're just as American as anyone,' she said, picking up another kabab. 'That's the beauty of this country. It's so diverse that there's no such thing as one American culture.'

Had she been watching too many Obama speeches? I saw that I was coming up against a belief close to her heart. In any case, I had, and continue to have, little tolerance for debate. My mind is too hazy and imprecise for declamation – never in my life have I convinced a single person of anything. Instead, I turned to Sumaira and asked about her children, who were both studying at Princeton. I understood Aslam and Sumaira's claim to America. They had become adults in this country, acquired passports, raised children and sent them off to college here. But why was my friend, five months out of Islamabad, so adamant on calling America her own?

*

We were at Woodbridge Mall because Zahra said that was what people in Central Jersey did for fun. Sumaira dragged me to H&M and picked out a winter coat for me.

'That sweatshirt is so thin,' she said. 'No wonder you're coughing all the time.'

She had come into Zahra's bedroom at night with cough syrup.

'Nahi, Aunty, this is too much, please.'

162

I had been steeling myself to make the purchase soon – I couldn't keep borrowing Amy's jacket whenever it snowed – but the coat Sumaira had picked was almost $100. She waved me off and asked the shop assistant to ring it up.

'Thank you so much, that's very kind.'

'Are you sure you don't want anything else? Maybe new jeans?'

She was eyeing mine, which had a rip over one knee.

'No, thank you.'

'It's just . . .' She was speaking slowly. 'We're going to have a lot of guests over for Christmas and it might look . . .'

'I brought shalwar kameez,' I said brusquely. Did this woman think I had left my common sense on the other coast?

'She can also borrow one of mine,' Zahra interjected. 'They don't fit me anyway.'

'Perfect,' Sumaira said with relief, handing over her credit card.

Afterwards, we went to the mall theater. Sumaira paid for the movie and bought us buttery popcorn, frowning deeply when I took out my wallet. I put it away, recalibrating myself. I had gotten used to Kelly, who let me pay my share for lunches any time we went into Eugene together. For the hotel in San Francisco, I had paid one-fourth.

One of the things I miss least about adolescence is the stupefying entitlement it sanctions. Looking back, I can see how generous Sumaira and Aslam were to me. In a country where people Venmo-ed each other for coffee, they were taking me in, sight unseen, for two weeks, plying me with familiar foods and buying me warm clothes, even though we would never see each other again, and there was nothing I could do for them in return. Then why did I judge them for how they were getting by, trying to convince their adopted home that they belonged?

*

Saturday was Christmas and we woke up to the smell of frying onions. Sumaira was prepping lawazmat for the haleem she had made last night – onions blackened in oil, thin wedges of ginger, lemons, rings of green chili. Aslam heated up some frozen parathay, while Zahra and I made omelet the way we always had it back home – scrambled eggs with onions, tomatoes, and green chili. The kitchen was stocked with all the accoutrements of desi cooking: several strainers for chai, rolling pin and board, a pressure cooker, and curvy pots I had never seen in America. We ate the parathay and omelet sitting on bar chairs that bordered the island, sticking the last bits of bread in chai to soak before eating them, leaning over the plates so we didn't dribble on our clothes.

Guests started arriving after two. Faiza and Habib came with two adolescent daughters who wore matching head-scarves and spoke with the bland politeness of well-adjusted suburban youths. Another couple came bearing a pot of nihari. The last to arrive were Hina and Arieb, a newly married couple in their late twenties, who worked in Manhattan and lived in Jersey City.

Unknowingly, I was being introduced to a cross-section of the techno-managerial class that forms the most visible part of the South Asian diaspora in North America – doctors and bankers and engineers who had left home not out of any desperate need for money or refuge, but out of professional preference, a desire to become even more comfortable than they were back home.

As I stood in the kitchen, I found myself surrounded by vanity and pretense, an artifice in dialogue and presentation, that I had never encountered in Lakeview, but one that brought to mind my parents' work friends back home. People fussed over one another, postured at humility, greeted each other as if they were meeting after years. I looked closely at Hina. Her hair, curled around a small face, shone with highlights. She wore a well-fitting green kameez and her engagement ring glistened across the counter, four times the size of Kelly's. Unlike the aunties at the grocery store, Hina wasn't wearing clothes that looked ten years behind what was trending back home, but still had the accent and perfect teeth of someone who had grown up in wealthy America.

The politics of teeth is pernicious. I was born to a mother who, despite growing up one of six siblings and never seeing a dentist, has the most perfect teeth of anyone I know. As children, Faisal and I were admonished daily for sticking our tongue into the gaping holes left behind by the departure of milk teeth. 'If you take care of them, you can get teeth like this,' Ammi would say, grinning to show hers off. We didn't, and it took America for me to realize that Ammi was an exception to the rule. Having beautifully aligned teeth was less the proof of discipline than of orthodontic access.

As people moved around Sumaira's house, everyone seemed to know their role. The three older men grabbed the cups of fresh chai Sumaira had brewed and took them to the living room, where they put a news channel on. The rest of us stood in the kitchen, chatting and helping Sumaira sprinkle the dishes with cilantro and count out plates and cutlery. That is how it always is – the stodgy fellowship of men on one side, and the vibrancy of women and children on the other. Sumaira insisted Arieb go sit down with the men, but he shook his head and started setting the table, saying he was far too young to act like an uncle.

'Don't you ever,' Hina said.

Returning from the bathroom, I caught a glimpse of the two of them standing by the front door, stealing a kiss. It was a chaste one, not unlike the ones Ethan and Kelly shared all the time. Yet, I averted my eyes, feeling warmth rise up my neck. Mine was a generation that grew up seeing violence – on the streets and in the house – but never a man kiss his wife.

165

After the table was set, the men were called over. They came with eyes gleaming, mouths lavishly praising Sumaira's food. They were served before anyone else, all three aunties acting like a collective Lazy Susan, handing the men brimming bowls of haleem and nihari. I caught Hina's eyes and she grimaced. These men with their ironed button-downs that accentuated carefully cultivated pot bellies, men who did nothing but show up – it was a reminder of home I did not need.

'Arieb, when are you buying a house?' Habib asked over a mouthful of naan.

'Not any time soon, Uncle.'

'We're actually thinking of moving to Pakistan,' Hina added, emptying half the salad onto her plate. She was the only one who had reached for it.

'What?' a few people exclaimed in unison.

Everyone was looking at Hina with horror. She shrugged, and I could tell she enjoyed the provocation.

'It's been a long time coming.'

'Why?'

'Arieb got a job offer in Karachi, and I've always wanted to go back, at least for a few years.'

'But why?' Habib repeated.

'I want to be around people who look like me.'

'You live in Jersey City,' Sumaira said.

Habib turned to Arieb.

'Are you also part of this madness?'

Arieb shrugged in mock helplessness, as if his wife had unilaterally decided they were moving countries.

'Plus, I want to raise my children in Pakistan,' Hina added. 'I want them to be grounded in their culture.'

Faiza frowned.

'What does living in that kabaarkhana have to do with culture? Look at us. Aren't we raising kids here? They go to

166

Quran class every day, they celebrate Eid, they can probably speak better Urdu than those rich kids in Islamabad.'

Arieb raised and lowered his eyebrows, as if to say he very much doubted that.

'Beta, I know it's daunting to think of raising kids here,' Faiza continued. 'But there are ways to do it. And think of all the opportunities they'll miss out on. Trust me, they're better off here.'

Hina's eyes narrowed.

'Ask that of the kids who did grow up here,' she said bitterly, in Urdu. She reminded me of Benazir, who had returned from Oxford with big dreams and atrocious Urdu. PTV dramas used the same accent to make fun of the uppity rich, but I was warming towards Hina. I tried to imagine what might have marred her childhood. She seemed so put together, every hair in place, it seemed impossible that she could have ever been bullied.

'Okay, okay,' Aslam said, leaning back in his chair to lighten the mood. 'May it be the best for the two of you. This country's going downhill anyway.'

Faiza nodded.

'You know our street, Aslam bhai. It's always been decent families. In the past year alone, all these strange people are moving in. Ayesha says the new kids in her school are all from South America.'

Arieb looked sideways at Hina, who had set down her fork. His hand moved under the table, perhaps to grip her leg, quietly beg for containment. He let out a loud laugh and changed the subject, mentioning an upcoming cricket match between India and South Africa. For the rest of the dinner, Hina silently chewed on cucumbers and tomatoes, not reaching out for anything else, while Arieb entertained everyone with the latest memes on Indo-Pak politics.

Nothing the older people said was shocking to me – it was such routine fare I almost judged Hina her naïve anger. Arieb, who had moved here from Karachi a few years ago, was likely the reason the two of them were invited to these parties at all. He, steeped in Pakistan himself, could give these people a certain margin she couldn't. I imagined him as an older Ali, with friends from all over the world, an apartment in which he probably hosted parties with white wine and charcuterie. And yet, he could also show up to gatherings like this armed with banalities that became the few commonalities – cricket, chai, politics. He knew how to read past the hypocrisies of these people to value what they offered. Food, gup shup, a shadowy replica of the places they had all left.

*

After dinner, Hina sent Sumaira off to the living room. She, Zahra, and I scrubbed the greasy pots and loaded the dishwasher while everyone else sipped on green tea.

'So, are you visiting New York?' Hina asked.

'Yes, tomorrow,' I said. 'I'm seeing a friend who studies at NYU.'

I said it in Urdu to make the pronoun clear. Hina made me want to impress her, show her I was the kind of girl who befriended boys and went to meet them alone.

'Friend?'

She winked. I smiled, putting away a washed saucepan upside down to dry.

'We've been talking for a few months,' I said, using the dating language people at Lakeview High used. You saw people. You talked for a while. Then you saw where it went. 'We'll see where it goes.'

Hina laughed a deep-throated laugh.

'Oh, young love. Is he Pakistani?'

I nodded.

'Good, good,' she said. 'I dated a few white boys in college but ended up with Arieb. Maybe it's hardwired into us.'

With that, she had let me into a special club, of women who were relaxed and self-assured, independent but grounded, who moved with their heads bare but when the time came, bowed them to values that mattered. I looked over at Zahra who was drying plates with a stark white towel. She said nothing but I could tell from her jaw, and was pleased to find out, that I had hurt her.

*

'Why didn't you tell me you were going to meet him?' she asked, after everyone had left and we were upstairs. I stared at her, deciding if I should pretend not to know what she was talking about.

'I wasn't sure how you'd take it,' I said, my cruel eyes moving to the scarf. She frowned and unclasped the pin underneath her chin.

'So, because I wear a scarf now you can't talk to me about a boy? What the hell?'

She looked down for a moment, neatly folding the scarf into smaller and smaller triangles. Then she angrily flung it onto the bed.

'Tell me, Hira. Does it ever get exhausting, being this superior all the time?'

Her jaw was clenched even further into itself. She must have figured out I meant to hurt her, and I remembered that this was Zahra, with the tongue that could slice diamonds.

'You think you're different. Out there, living some bold adventure with a white family. But honestly, you're so close-minded and judgmental. Faiza Aunty's got nothing on you.'

Her eyes were fire.

'How dare you judge me, Hira? How dare you? Have you considered for a second that not all of us are trying to run away from who we were?'

169

'Are you kidding me?' I sputtered. 'I'm the one running away? Look at that scarf. You go to Jummah, for heaven's sake. And this whole America the Great bullshit. How diverse and gleaming and perfect, like this street and this house and that stupid mall.'

'It's not my fault your America sucks.'

I shook my head. America wasn't mine, or hers.

'Look, I don't judge you. I used to wear the scarf myself.'

I did judge her, of course I did. I just thought I had the right to. Wasn't that the first prerogative of a shared history?

'That's the thing,' she snapped. 'You used to wear it and now you don't, and you think you're so emancipated for it.'

Her chest was heaving. I had deeply wounded her, which had felt good an hour ago, when I saw her face in the kitchen. Now I felt tired and somewhat ashamed. I could faintly make out that this was my own bitterness congealing into condescension. I envied Zahra the fact that America had brought her closer to figuring out who she wanted to be.

I sat down on the bed, weary.

'Yar, baitho, I'll tell you everything.'

After a moment, she sat down on top of her green comforter and I rushed into my words. I told her more about Ali, how I forgot to breathe every time the landline displayed his number, how he seemed so perfect to me – intelligent but sincere, worldly and wise. A good listener. Zahra clapped her hands in excitement.

'But wait, you said he's a sophomore in college? What if he thinks you're too young for him?'

I shrugged.

'I'm smarter than most people he knows.'

Some of it was bravado – I was seventeen, and dumb as dirt – but there was truth to it. I was intelligent in a way boys like Ali valued. I was willing to entertain the oddest thread in conversation, skeptical about the world in a way that was common neither among his NYU friends nor in his wealthy circles back home. I have disappointed people in love and obedience and loyalty, but I have rarely let anyone down in conversation. Also, I will never be disciple to the cult of the shitty, irresistible man. My insecurities reveal themselves in anger and resentment, but never in making gods of disinterested men. I liked Ali because he liked me.

Then Zahra told me about Fahad from school, who had left a box of chocolates in her locker. They had held hands on the bus once. She told me he smelled sexy, like cologne and sweat, and not like white boys, who all smelled like—

'Baby powder,' we said in unison, and burst out laughing. We cackled with our hands clasped, rolling in bed. I opened Facebook and we went through all 247 of Ali's photos, and it was a testament to her generosity that she let out appreciative hmms at even the ugly ones. 'Hot,' I announced truthfully when she showed me a photo of Fahad. He had great hair and biceps that threatened to rip out of a short-sleeved shirt.

'Brother's doing some serious jihad on his body,' I said, and we cracked up again, laughing so hard that Sumaira called out from her room. We turned the lights off and talked for another hour, about the boys we wanted, the foods we craved, the people we missed. We didn't talk any more about the women we were trying to become.

I would never again feel as close to Zahra as I did that night. A lot of it, I told myself, was circumstance – we would enroll in different schools when we returned home, and her house was across the intimidating boundary of the Faizabad Exchange. But as we whispered with our faces turned to the ceiling, I was happy that the dark blanketed over everything – our eagerness to make up, our delicate fear that the other person might erupt again, but mostly, our desperation to convince ourselves that the rift that had just presented itself was a minor fleck and not the inevitable result of growing old in different ways.

XVI

I rubbed the blush off as soon as I got on the train. Zahra had insisted on layering me with makeup she had collected on her trips to Woodbridge – liquid eyeliner that slid across my eyes, mascara, matte lipstick that was almost red, and very pink blush. In the glass windows of the NJ Transit car, I looked at myself with regret. I stuck a finger to my mouth, then rubbed the wettened tip across my cheeks. My eyes I kept as they were; it was how Hina wore her eyes at the dinner party.

Ali had told me to meet him at Penn Station. I got off and followed the post-Christmas sales crowd up a narrow flight of stairs, then walked down a hallway to the Pret a Manger where we were supposed to meet. I caught a sight of him before I turned the corner and halted, immovably shy. This was so embarrassing. Perhaps it wasn't too late to turn back and email him some excuse. Packed trains. A bad cough. Something with Zahra's family. But I remembered the vast spaces of loneliness Ali had helped me through in Oregon, the days and nights that would have been indistinguishable but for the words he wrote to me. I stepped forward.

'Hey!'

The hug coursed through me, molten, on that cold, cold day. He was wearing a dark blue coat that reached his knees. His hair was newly cut, shorter than I would have liked. He smelled of coffee and cologne. I made a mental note to tell Zahra.

172

'Welcome! How're you liking the East Coast?'

His head tilted towards the exit and we started walking out of the building. He held open the door for me, then pointed out Madison Square Garden and the imposing building of the post office that stood across the street, its Corinthian columns rising to a frieze. He read out loud the inscription, lofty words about snow and rain and heat and gloom, and I wondered if he was also nervous, trying to outtalk his agitation.

'So, how much time do we have?' he asked, rubbing his hands in anticipation.

'I have to be back for dinner.'

'What did you tell Zahra's family?'

'The truth, except you're a girl,' I replied, and he grinned. 'Classic.'

We walked south, past groups of tourists bundled in scarves and hats. We crossed one intersection after another, nestled within a flood of humanity. At every corner, there were halal food carts, subway fumes rising like a Vicks vapor steam, yellow cabs pulling to the curb. Ali laughed as I looked around.

'I told you, you ended up in the wrong part of the country.'

I described to him the America I had seen in the past few days – clipped suburbia, three cars to a house, biryani and chai, mehndi parlors.

'Well, hopefully it was a taste of home.'

'Not really. It made me uncomfortable.'

'Is that so?'

That was something he did often, and it annoyed me. Instead of asking why I felt a certain way, he reached obtusely for clarification, making me feel as if each intimacy, each disclosure of mine, was self-proffered, given and not requested.

'Yes,' I said.

We continued to walk in silence, my cheeks and nose frozen. I looked down Eighth Avenue and saw the island stretch for miles. It was bitterly cold. Sumaira had told me about wind tunnels, how the rows of concrete in New York trapped air that slapped you in the face and turned your eyes watery.

After a few minutes, I realized that any time I was not the one offering conversation – details of the upcoming wedding, jokes about Sumaira and Aslam – we receded into long patches of silence.

'Why don't you ever talk about yourself?' I asked him.

He looked over, surprised.

'I do.'

'Not as much as I do.'

'Well, you're infinitely more interesting.'

I shook my head, too cold to answer back.

'Alright, let's talk about me,' he said, and told me about his Christmas weekend, which he had spent in upstate New York with his roommate's family. He detailed the gifts the family had sweetly put for him under the tree, to make him feel included. A minute in, I was losing focus, thinking instead about Zahra, wondering if she was still angry at me.

'And I told you about the courses I'm taking next semester, right?' Ali asked.

I nodded, realizing I had heard little of what he had said. This would never have happened with Zahra or Kelly. Why are men so much less interesting in conversation, even those that make your legs weak? I tried to remember if this was how it was over the phone. Ali kept talking, and with every detail he gave, every synchronized step we took down that strange city of glazed eyes and hostile shoulders, I became convinced that anticipation was the greatest happiness of all, the anguish of waiting far more exquisite than the joy of meeting.

We walked all the way down to the West Village, where townhouses stood covered in ivy stalks, next to storefronts displaying cashmere sweaters. In front of a deep green stoop, a couple posed for engagement photos, their cheeks pinkened with cold. Italian restaurants greeted us on every block, cucinas and osterias filled with slender people pecking at pasta. Ali walked us into his favorite coffee shop, with a menu far more sophisticated than the Eugene Starbucks Kelly sometimes stopped at. I told him to order for me and the tattooed barista rang up two cortados. She turned around to prepare them, not looking over once as I fought to pay and Ali pushed my wallet back into my bag. Her lack of interest was disconcerting. In the five months I had been in Oregon, I had grown used to the glances I got at cash registers, volleyball games, the post office – glances that were never malignant but just long enough to inform me that my body was marked as different.

It's important to note that the entire time I was in America, I peddled in one stereotype or another, taking succor in their confirmation. Americans were rural and ignorant, or they were urban and slightly less ignorant, unless they were New Yorkers, who were exempt from any allegation of ignorance. New York was different – home to the dream, away from the nightmare.

Stereotypes happen when you don't understand the thing itself, and so you interpret it. This is not an account of how America was. It's an account of who I was.

I pointed out the barista's indifference to Ali, who nodded with enthusiasm.

'That's why I love this city,' he said, opening the door so we could step back into December chill. 'I could disappear into its anonymity forever.'

I thought of Hina.

'Will you stay here after graduation?'

'Absolutely,' he said, his voice emphatic. 'If I can.'

His lack of ambivalence bothered me. I was disappointed, wondering if he was not like Arieb or Hina after all, but instead a young, slick successor to those suburban Jersey couples, who had decided that Pakistan was simply

175

not good enough for them. Kabaarkhana, Faiza had called it. Junkyard.

'I'll also try to get my mother out of there as soon as I can,' he continued. 'It's so unsafe for us.'

'That's old news though,' I said dismissively. Had America brainwashed everyone? He turned to me, his face harder than I had ever seen in photos.

'No, Hira, I meant, for *us*.'

It clicked.

'I'm so sorry,' I said, my words tumbling over one another. 'I forgot.'

'Of course you did.'

'I swear.'

He shook his head.

'You should hear my father's stories about being Shia in Karachi sometimes,' he said, bitterness dusting his words. 'We know so many who've been killed, who've changed their names, who've had to leave.'

I was ashamed. Ali has talked about this before. Once, in a tone of measured amusement, he had told me about being asked to take off his shirt in high school so the other boys could check for welts. And even that testimonial should not have been necessary. I had grown up on the daily paper. I knew about the buses to Iran, about Parachinar, about Quetta.

We resumed walking in silence for the next few blocks, his tread a beat quicker than mine, shoulders angled away. Months of talking to him over the phone and Facebook had felt like speaking into a mirror, an access to memories that were plucked out of the same album, a link to the collective home we had temporarily abandoned. But that arbitrary place we both appended to our introductions in this foreign country, the part of our identity that had taken on a sweeping significance, meant different things to us, carried different burdens. There is no collective home.

After a while, he stopped in his tracks and turned to me.

'I got carried away,' he said.

'No, you didn't.'

He was looking at me intently, as if for the first time.

'I'm stupid,' I told him.

'You can be, yes.'

A tear ran down my cheek and he wiped it away with a thumb. We stood frozen, freezing.

'You're ruining that mascara.'

'I'm sorry,' I whispered.

He grabbed my hand and we continued to walk.

*

For lunch, we went to Xi'an Famous near St Mark's. The place fit fewer than ten people and there was a line, but he insisted it was worth it. We stood outside in the cold, which felt decidedly less cold now that I was distracted by my hand, which rested in his. Heat radiated from my body, and I worried he would notice and ask if I had a fever. Half an hour later, we sat on narrow stools and ate spicy lamb burgers laced with cumin. Chili oil ran down my fingers and tickled my throat. I tried to be discreet when I coughed, not wanting to send my lungs heaving the way they did each night. We shared a napkin to clean our fingers, the white staining scarlet. Outside, he pulled the hood of my coat to cover my head, knuckles brushing against my ears, every touch a strike of lightning.

We continued to walk, saying little. He pointed out this and that as we walked west – the Punjabi deli where he and his friends joined New York's cab drivers in their quest for chai and samosay, the city's most extensive wine store, the red, stark building of the NYU library. I half heard everything, impatiently waiting for my heart to calm down, to realize that this state, of my hand in his, shoulder rubbing against his arm, was the new equilibrium.

After a while my breathing got ragged from exhaustion and I told him I'd like to sit down.

'Are you okay?'

'Yeah, still a little sick from before.'

We found a bench in Washington Square Park. Dread-locked boys crooned on guitars as we watched the magnificent arch turn shadowy in disappearing daylight. He pointed to the Islamic Center across the park, where he sometimes went for Jummah.

Further west, weaving past Greenwich Village, we reached a promenade that hugged the Hudson. The sun etched indigo streaks on the sky over Jersey City. Lights turned on in gleaming apartments across the water, the windows throwing out seductive light. We stood leaning against the railing. I faced the river and he faced me. A gracious evening, I thought, and verses rose like dust in my mind. I said them out loud to Ali, surprised I remembered them from an audio recording heard years ago.

Ai shaam meherban ho
Ai shaam-e-shehr-e-yaran

'Shaam-e-shehr-e-yaran,' he repeated. 'Evening in the city of the beloved.'

I nodded, not trusting myself to say a word more. Soon, I would have to take a cab to the train station. He touched the sleeves of my purple kurta, peeking from underneath the coat.

'Thanks for wearing this.'

If we were any closer, our faces would touch.

'Maybe I'll visit Pindi this summer,' he said, winking. 'See if you guys do anything except kill off Prime Ministers.'

I tried to laugh, but it required an abandon I did not possess. Our eyes met and held. A second? A minute? Then he leaned in and kissed me, and I, who had imagined this obsessively, wished for it devotedly, practiced diligently on the back of my hand, stood still and let him, thankful that one of us had done this before.

For how long we kissed, I still can't tell, except that after the rose of his lips had withdrawn and we had pulled apart, after I had hungrily brushed back his hair and he had hailed a cab and closed the door and tapped the side, after the driver had begun rushing up the West Side Highway and I had collapsed onto the seat and set my blazing forehead to leather, I knew that there was a part of me, a shadowy outline of a person with my curves and my hair, that remained behind forever, leaning against the railing, in the city of the beloved.

XVII

Fever the next day, settling in for good. It was my last day in Jersey, which I mostly spent under Zahra's comforter, my body convulsing with shivers every time I got up for the bathroom. I promised Sumaira I would go to the doctor as soon as I returned to Oregon.

'This sounds serious,' she said, brows furrowed as she put two Advils on the bedside table.

It did sound serious, and I will never fully understand why it took me till that day, lying in Zahra's bed, to treat it as such. A tale of parenting and adolescence, as this one is shaping up to be, will always ascribe some blame upwards, and so here it is – perhaps I also carried Abbu's recklessness when it came to health, his condescension towards medical vigilance as an atheistic act. I ate little during my months in Oregon and repeatedly told myself that the cough that sent my lungs chafing against my rib cage was a routine hazard of winter. Kelly kept no scales in the house, saying she did not want Amy growing up with body image issues. On my first day in Jersey, Zahra had made me climb on top of Sumaira's weighing machine, telling me I looked very thin to her. 105 pounds, 48 kilograms. I had shed 6 kilograms in America, I had told her, trying and failing to keep the pride from my voice.

Lying in Zahra's bed, I began to have a budding suspicion of why that might be. I looked up TB symptoms on my laptop, and it was a catalogue of all I had been going through for weeks – the coughing, the exhaustion, the weight loss. Could it really be that? There had been the positive test, but the doctor had given me the okay signal.

I wondered what to do. Kelly's wedding was three weeks away. I couldn't possibly burden her with this information, and who even knew if it was what I feared? Right there, burning from a fever in Edison, I made the one decision that year that was solely, unquestionably mine. I would return to Oregon and continue with the preparations for the wedding. I would not rock the boat unless things got worse. I would keep my fears to myself and God.

*

'You should have saved your veil, Mom,' Kelly said, tilting her face in the mirror. 'I could have just worn that.'

Hannah shrugged.

'Didn't save the marriage, didn't save the veil,' she replied, adjusting the thin gauze blusher over Kelly's head. 'This looks good.'

Kelly continued to look at her own reflection, face full of doubt.

'It's too casual,' she fretted. 'I thought it would be a good look for a small wedding, but I think I bit off more than I could chew.'

Biting off more than could be chewed was a key Kelly trait, but I didn't know how to tell her that she need not worry; she looked breathtaking. Amy had curled her hair that morning, twisting soft ringlets that trailed down her freckled back. She was wearing a pair of gold earrings Hannah had gifted her, and no other jewelry. Amy had also brought over her makeup kit and worked on Kelly's face for less than ten minutes but, as is often the case with women who wear little makeup, the result was stunning. I, who had never seen a bride in white before, felt at the edge of tears. Amy's eyes were shiny too, even as she said, 'Yeah, that veil is very courthouse wedding, Mom.'

I did cry an hour later, during the vows. Hannah had wanted a Catholic ceremony, but Kelly chose the Evangelical church we went to every Sunday.

'The Catholic church doesn't allow couples to write their own vows,' she told me, shaking her head. 'They're sadly immutable in many ways.'

It struck me as rather sensible not to subject dozens of people around you to sappy, ill-worded ululations of love, when the church had a highly vetted, abbreviated version with centuries' worth of first mover advantage. Sure enough, Ethan read out his vows from a crumpled piece of paper, promising Kelly to put her first 'even during football season,' but noting that when he said *I do* he didn't 'mean the dishes.' Then Kelly took out a folded page from a sealed envelope. Her words, wavering with emotion, were proof of how so many men spend their lives failing to deserve the women they luck into.

'Fantasies, perfection, infallibility – that's the stuff of young love,' she said towards the end, as Amy and I stood behind her in chartreuse bridesmaid dresses and Hannah looked on from the first aisle. 'All I know is that the world keeps spinning, and only at the end of each night, when my head is on your shoulder, does it stop long enough for me to comprehend it.'

*

The ceremony was followed by a reception of about fifty people, including Ethan's parents, best man, and Kelly's friends from church and work. Mr and Mrs Sinclair were there, and Hamid came as my plus one. The bridal party took a few photos in the churchyard – first Kelly and Ethan, then various combinations of the newlyweds, the best man, me, Amy, and Hannah. Kelly insisted on getting one of just her and me, and I wondered, standing with an arm around her shoulder, what the picture would stand witness to. Years later, she might happen upon it while going through the photographs with a grandchild, and struggle to remember my name. What an odd, forced intimacy we shared, with a discrete end date.

Afterwards, we all congregated in the small events hall for the first dance. A DJ had come in from Eugene, and the pastor's wife took care of the flowers. Hannah and Kelly danced together to 'Wonderful Tonight', and Amy joined them for the final notes. This was followed by Ethan's dance with his mother. Then the floor opened to everyone, and it seemed as if elderly Lakeview had been raring for such a moment, because suddenly the room was packed with old couples swinging around in long skirts and tweed jackets. I asked Hamid to take a photo of me – the dress was long enough for my parents, and glamorous enough to show Ali. Then he and I settled at a table in the corner, sharing notes on how the event differed from weddings back home. It was far less elaborate, certainly, but also came with an ease I had never seen before. Kelly throwing her head back and laughing at the pastor's jokes. Amy squealing as Ethan dipped her back at the end of a song. Hannah buying three G&Ts at the cash bar and winking as she handed two of them to Hamid and me. I tried to imagine Ammi and Abbu at this wedding, how they would scoff at the lack of pomp, which they would take to mean a lack of seriousness. Abbu had already said as much to me, after I told him about the reception, with its cash bar and pizza slices.

'That's not a wedding,' he said flatly. 'It's a forty-year-old throwing a party for herself.'

This wasn't a cultural difference – nothing ever is. There were weddings back home, even in the family, where people made fires out of stray kindle, then danced around in dizzy circles and ate out of cracked plastic plates before walking through dark farmland on their way back home. It's just that my parents had made their way past that, had ascended into urban, professional Pakistan with its joyless celebrations. Those older, looser ways of doing things were not for us anymore.

I imagined Kelly as Abbu probably saw her – a haphazard woman with a child out of wedlock, about to marry a man she'd been sleeping with for months. Abbu's male friends were often colorful characters – poets cheating on their wives, witty officers wisecracking about everything under the sun. The women he knew through university or work were more monolithic, or at least presented as such because they rightly understood that for them, professional success required a much tighter sense of decorum. One of his colleagues was a woman whose husband had passed away when she was thirty. She had spent the rest of her years at her mother's house, taking care of nieces and nephews, dressing like a frump, fostering friendships with chivalrous men like my father. Abbu thought she was one of the most honorable women he knew. I thought she had let the world pass her by.

'My parents always said they wanted a simple wedding for my sister,' Hamid told me, shaking red pepper flakes over a margherita slice. 'Then they invited three hundred people to it.'

I nodded.

'I can't wait to show these photos to my parents.'

We continued to jest with each other in low voices, pointing to the paper plates for the pizza and the homemade jam jars Hannah had prepared as favors, but I could tell, from the way Hamid looked at the dancers with a half-smile, how we both joined in the raucous laughter during the best man's toast, that he was just as entranced as I was by this wedding, so lacking in pretense that it was almost a spectacle in its own right.

Amy came and sat next to us, her face flushed.

'I asked Hannah to get the three of us another round,' she said, putting up her feet on a chair.

'Careful with the drinking,' Hamid told her. 'I saw you almost fall on your face while dancing.'

She swatted his arm, then turned to me.

'Isn't it crazy? From now, we're a household of four.'

'Are you going to call him Dad?' I asked her, and she scoffed.

'No, he's Ethan.'

She looked over at Kelly, who was taking a shot with the Sinclairs.

'Mom's my dad.'

Why couldn't she say those words to Kelly's face? I felt frustrated at Amy, but then I remembered all the things, tablets full of things, that I could never say to my parents. Conversation is what happens when you can't say the things you want to.

Hannah came over balancing three drinks in her hands.

'This is the last round. I'm going to be broke before you're sated,' she said. Amy kissed her on the cheek and grabbed her drink before going off to dance again. Hannah sat down in her spot.

'Are you having a good time?' she asked me, but her blue eyes were not set on me with intent, the way they had been in California. Tonight, she was the doting mother, looking again and again at Kelly in amazement.

'Yes,' I answered. 'Are you?'

She nodded.

'My feet hurt. I haven't danced like this in a while.'

After a few moments, she spoke again.

'This makes me so happy. Kelly's been alone for too long.'

'So have you, no?'

She looked over in surprise, as if I had been just a little too personal.

'Yes, and sometimes you worry you're passing it down,' she said.

'What's wrong with that?'

'Some people are good at being alone. Kelly never was.'

185

That came as a revelation. Of course it was true, and it explained so much, perhaps most of all the question I had been asking myself for five months – what in the world was I doing in rural Oregon?

'I think she was relieved when she had Amy,' Hannah continued. 'Even without the father around. It meant she would never be independent ever again.'

We both laughed.

'Instead, she values goodness. Like hosting you. No offense, but it's an odd thing to my mind, to invite a stranger over for a year.'

Mine too, I wanted to tell her, but I curtailed myself. The night was the first time I felt comfortably on the outside, observing them all in ways that finally felt sharp and accurate. There was Amy, tapping Kelly on the shoulder so they could pose for a selfie. There was Ethan, his gait betraying all the beer he had been guzzling. Here was Hannah, looking at her daughter with the tenderness of a held breath. All of this had nothing to do with me. I was there in the shadow, peripheral, a foreigner in the most wonderful sense. For the first time ever, I did not mind.

*

Around nine, the guests started filtering out. I went over to Kelly to congratulate her in person, because I had not yet done that – the odd, shy ways of the adolescent. When I got to her, I didn't know what words to use, so I hugged her instead. She tensed for a moment; we hadn't hugged since that very first night I arrived. Then she wrapped her arms around me and swayed me from side to side. She smelled of lavender and sweat and red wine.

'I'm so happy you're here for this,' she said.

'Me too,' I told her, meaning it – my stated happiness – after a long time. 'The vow was beautiful.'

186

'Whose?' she asked, smiling slyly.

'His was good too,' I added reluctantly, and she laughed.

'I knew you wouldn't be impressed.'

'I haven't seen you so happy ever,' I told her.

'I never thought this would happen.'

'Marriage?'

She nodded.

'It feels like such a fresh start.'

Kelly's move to Oregon, her decision to raise Amy alone, her desire to host an exchange student – they were all motivated by this desire for renewal, the belief that a single action could change who she was. The mirage of the blank slate fools us all.

'It was a great party,' I told her.

'It looks like everyone had fun. Maybe too much fun,' she said, shaking her head as Amy and Ethan careened around in a tipsy dance.

'They have a lot to celebrate,' I said, holding up my glass to her. 'They're lucky to have you.'

'Thanks, Hira.'

She beamed.

'You know, I would love to meet your mother one day. I have a feeling we'll get along really well.'

Of course, Kelly was feigning closeness when there was none; she didn't even know Ammi's name. Of course, there was no world in which she and Ammi would get along, even if they had the opportunity; when Ammi congratulated her on the phone, their call lasted less than five polite minutes. And yet, what she said warmed me, and I hugged her again. She was thinking of my mother, which meant that she was looking at me and realizing that I, too, was someone's daughter.

*

As everyone said goodbyes, I trudged up the hill to the house alone, partly so that no one could see how out of breath it left me. I called Ali, who had just returned after winter break.

'Kelly wanted me to invite you to the wedding,' I told him.

'Why didn't you?'

'You just came back from Pakistan.'

'You know I would have come.'

I knew he would have come. And I would have loved it all – playing his tour guide in rural America, introducing him to Kelly, slow dancing with him in the chartreuse dress. But by then, I was too distracted by my body. I knew for a fact that I was terribly sick, and the deepest part of me knew, even if I had not admitted it to myself, even if I had spent an entire night dancing and sharing drinks with people, that it was only a matter of time before the secret was out.

It was on that same night that I spewed blood.

January

It's an ancient disease. Traces of *Mycobacterium tuberculosis* were discovered in bison that lived in Wyoming 17,000 years ago. Scientists found it in spinal samples from mummies buried in Thebes. In Atlit Yam, a Neolithic village now submerged in the Mediterranean Sea, they found it in the remains of a mother and child, buried together. By the 1800s, the disease widely known as consumption had killed one in seven of all people who had ever lived. Chekhov died of it, as did Keats. Austen, Orwell, Chopin, Thoreau. In 1924, Thomas Mann published *The Magic Mountain*. The same year, Kafka died of it; he had written to his friend from a sanatorium some years back, calling tuberculosis the 'germ of death itself.' In 1948, Muhammad Ali Jinnah succumbed to it in Karachi, despite the vials of streptomycin, among the first to ever be circulated, that were sent in from America. Until the antibiotic cure became widely available in the fifties, the disease remained a specter over every inhabited continent. In Europe, it was considered almost romantic, a sophisticated sickness, an aesthetic death. It was thought to produce bouts of euphoria, clarifying fevers, improved appetite, increased desire. Wasn't Helen Burns beautiful and serene as she lay dying in Jane Eyre's arms?

The Eugene doctor doesn't go that far back. Instead, he tells me over the phone that while the disease has been eradicated in most of Europe and North America, it remains a major problem in the Third World, with South

Asia accounting for 40% of the total 'TB burden.' I have to stop myself from reflexively apologizing, since it's hubris to assume that I answer for the Subcontinent. The disease festers in poverty and bad hygiene, he says, and I understand why the nurse who comes with the medicine always looks at me as if I am vermin; she thinks I'm poor and dirty. What I had back home, the doctor speculates, was likely a latent form of the disease, in which the body is able to fight off the bacteria without any sign of infection. A quarter of the world population has latent tuberculosis – asymptomatic, and therefore not contagious. Very few, less than 15% of them, get the active disease, with symptoms developing slowly and assiduously over several months.

'What causes it to become active?'

'A compromised immune system. Usually weakness or malnutrition.'

That's what the internet tells me as well – the disease manifests itself in bodies that cannot fight it off any longer. Once active, it consumes, infiltrating the lungs and moving on to other vital organs if left unchecked. Even treated, it is like a previous marriage, leaving scars and requiring disclosure on immigration forms and health histories. It is airborne, the internet tells me, and I read, horrified; it can be contagious for those living with the patient. The paranoia of this contagion led to the glamorous sanatoria of nineteenth-century Europe. In twenty-first-century America, it is the disease of the congested poor – city poor, prison poor, homeless shelter poor. In the sprawling poverty of the rural Pacific Northwest, it is unheard of.

*

Not anymore, though. The day I am diagnosed is my last day at Lakeview High. Kelly goes in to explain the situation to the superintendent, entering the tiny office lined with yearbooks and asking Mrs Gibbs to close the door behind her. Amy hands in my homework and tells the teachers not to expect me in class anymore. 'It's a private matter,' she says, careful not to leak any information ahead of the assembly next week, where Mrs Gibbs will announce that the school is organizing mandatory testing for every student, teacher, custodian, janitor, coach, and bus driver. The reason for concern, she will say, is a student, whose identity will remain anonymous, who has become an active vector of a potentially contagious disease. The school of 150 students will take ten seconds, perhaps less, to figure out who has not been attending class for a week.

Everyone at the wedding is to get tested as well. Tuberculosis spreads primarily through extended exposure, but most people at the party were older and therefore more at risk. I call Hannah in LA and apologize profusely.

'Why didn't you say anything?' she asks.

'I didn't know.'

'Kelly says you tested positive back home.'

'Yes, but a lot of people do. Even the TB vaccine they give infants can make you test positive,' I tell her, regurgitating information I have read online.

I continue: 'I was playing volleyball and not eating well, the doctor says that's probably why the disease became active.'

'Right,' she says coldly. 'You were coughing the entire time you were here. You didn't put two and two together?'

No, I didn't. My body is something I forget about until it betrays me. My period often surprises me. It sometimes inconveniences me that I have breasts. So, no, until that last day in New Jersey, I had not spent any time wondering if what I had was more serious than a long-drawn-out cough. I don't tell this to Hannah, who, in any case, doesn't care for my side of the story.

'I know you're young,' she says, before hanging up. 'But one has to take responsibility for things.'

I don't blame her. I've made her daughter's life hell. Kelly and Ethan spend a full day calling up airlines and hotels, trying to see if they can get a refund on their honeymoon costs. I'm not kin, so it's not considered a family emergency.

'You should go, I'll be fine,' I tell Kelly, and she stares at me.

'We can't just fly off tomorrow. What if we're also infected?'

Kelly, Amy, and Ethan's test results are still pending, but since they have been in constant contact with me, it's mandatory for them to start a preventative three-month dose regardless of the results. Same goes for Hannah, Hamid, Crista, Nicole, Sam, and Alicia. I message Ali on Facebook, apologizing profusely for meeting him in New York. He writes a long message back, full of sympathetic words; at the end, he sends a winking face alongside a CDC article saying the disease does not spread through kissing.

The doctor hands Kelly a list of quarantine facilities in Oregon.

'Your household will have to take the preventative dose in any case, so it's up to you whether you send her there or not,' he tells Kelly, although I am sitting right there. Later, I overhear Kelly speaking with Ethan on the staircase landing, her voice low and angry.

'Ethan, for God's sake. She's a child.'

'Not yours,' he points out.

I imagine a windowless room, with a single slot for food and water.

*

I open my laptop and scroll through photos of me and Zahra from the trip to Jersey. I zoom in and out over my arms, the circumference of my waist, my neck. Had I looked deathly to everyone? Had Faiza and her children noticed? Had Hina mentioned to Arieb after the party, 'That girl looked sickly, no?'

192

I had noticed myself thinning over these past months, and had felt no alarm. Leanness meant fewer of the vulgarities of the body, less of it to think about. It meant more refinement, because you became less and less body, and more and more mind.

Faisal is online. I open our chat box, but he is already typing.

'Ammi told me u have TB. That sux.'

'It does,' I respond. 'Why are you up? How are you online?'

'Computers in my room now. Need it 4 school homework.' He keeps typing.

'Ammi told me u yelled at her. This isnt just her folt.'

I picture him typing on the keyboard under fluorescent light.

'Fault*. And yes. It's both their fault.'

'They dint know ud get sick. And anyway, u shunt have gone.'

'What are you talking about?' I write. I add the angry emoji, then remove it. 'Ammi Abbu sent me here.'

'If u said u dint want 2 go, they wud have said ok. But u wanted 2 leave.'

The desire to leave. I remember it vaguely, its taste far from my tongue.

'Dont worry,' Faisal writes back, after I don't respond for a while. 'U'll recover and come bak soon.'

'Inshallah,' I say. The doctor tells me the disease is fully treatable, and no one really dies of it in advanced Western nations anymore, but he has given no date for recovery. The full treatment course runs for nine months, but I can travel as soon as I am no longer contagious. When that will be all depends on this body of mine.

'And dont yell at Ammi on the fone again,' he writes, before logging off. 'Nana Ji isnt doing too well.'

*

193

The doctor calls the next day, before Kelly leaves for work. I put him on speaker, and he tells us the bloodwork just came back. The reason I have been throwing up every night is because my liver is rejecting some of the medicine. My blood shows evidence of hepatoxicity, a word that Kelly writes down while shaking her head in disbelief. One of the drugs is damaging my liver function, but the question is, which one? There is silence, and then Kelly says sharply, 'Are you asking us, Dr Lane?'

These things are murky, Dr Lane replies, but he will start by removing Rifampicin, the most likely suspect, from the regimen and seeing what changes. If that doesn't help, we will reinstate it and remove another one. We must be patient, as it will certainly set back the treatment timeline.

'Fantastic,' Kelly says, her eyes on the calendar hanging above the phone set. She has managed to postpone the honeymoon flights to March. After the call ends, I apologize for my health getting in the way of her life.

'No, don't say that. Tell me, how are you feeling?'

I shrug.

'Besides the vomiting, I'm fine. It's all a haze.'

She nods, her brows knitted with worry. I'm angry at her, because it seems like this could have been avoided had she actually looked after me as she had signed up to do. But I'm also full of guilt for running a train though her newlywed bliss. Thankfully, no one else tested positive, but all we have talked about in the past few days is my diagnosis, the bloodwork, and the visits from the nurse. The wedding gifts sit unopened under the stairs.

Upon hearing of the liver tests, Abbu turns insistent that I get on the next plane to Pindi.

'The treatment is a simple course of drugs. You can complete that here.'

I panic. If Abbu insists on calling Mr Shahid, demanding my return, the program will have to acquiesce. I can't return midway through the year. What will I do, sit at home for seven months until school starts in the fall? Have the entire program find out I left early? Mr Shahid told us at orientation that the only student who has ever returned early was expelled for threatening his host brother with a weapon.

'It was a butter knife, but we had to take action.'

I tell Abbu it is unlikely they'll let me fly anyway.

'What do you mean, let you?'

'Abbu, the nurse said I can't sit on the porch. You think they'll allow me to fly internationally?'

'No one can stop my daughter from coming home.'

Those platitudes. He's always used them, I will inherit them, they piss me off. It also rankles me that he has not once mentioned the doctor's call from the summer or alluded to his own role in the matter. The disease, to him, seems to have fallen out of the sky, an unexpected test of faith from God. Ammi has started using a singsong voice on the phone, making the same old jokes about Kelly's ineptitude as a host mother while I fume, wanting to snap back that Kelly isn't the only adult who has failed me. Faisal messages to say I should call Nana Ji, who has just returned from the hospital and says he wants to speak with me. I tell him I will, but later fail to recollect the Multan landline number from the shelves of memory.

February

I settle into a rhythm with disease. The nurse comes at 10 a.m., and the sound of tires churning on gravel or the doorbell ringing wakes me up. The medicine is too harsh on an empty stomach, so while she sits around, reading a book, I quickly eat a banana and pour myself apple juice. Then I take the three drugs my body has decided to accept. After she leaves, I turn the stove on and make myself two fried eggs and buttered toast. I eat as slowly as I can, partly to prolong purpose, partly because eating any faster might cue my guts to wring themselves out again. The plate empties, as it must. I wash it by hand instead of sticking it in the dishwasher, then dry it, wipe the stove, re-arrange the kitchen towels. I pick at each breadcrumb on the table with my fingertips and scrape them off into the sink. I put away the salt and pepper. I twist the bread tie. Then I give in to the long arms of the day.

It has been decided that I will quarantine at home. I thank Kelly profusely for this, and she waves me off, telling me she would be distraught if I left the house for a facility. It is an odd predicament, one I have never faced before – I am deathly sick, entirely reliant on others, and living with people who are not blood. Every time they care for me in ways that I would have taken entirely for granted back home, it feels like an enormous favor. Kelly is doing the best she can, and she is doing it in her matter-of-fact way, without any expectation of indebtedness from my side. But I cannot help thanking her and thanking her, and this posturing – gratitude and comfort rarely sit together – exhausts me as much as the physical ailment does.

Kelly and Ethan work till six on most days. Amy returns from school around three and we watch TV together for a couple of hours, before she leaves for Kyle's house or Crista's. Initially, I insist on sitting away from everyone and eating separately, but they all scoff at that, and the doctor confirms that since all three of them are taking preventative drugs, I do not need to quarantine from them. One afternoon, I start shivering uncontrollably and Amy bundles me up in the woolen throw that sits near the couch, tying my damp hair back with her hair tie. Afterwards, as I return from the bathroom, I see her stealthily toss the throw into the laundry hamper, and that one act – the kind quietness of it but also the accusation of filth in it – fills me with such shame I feel nauseous.

Ali calls and I half-heartedly ask him about the new semester. Our conversation dries up soon and I tell him perhaps we should not talk for a bit. Seeing Facebook pictures of him walking around Central Park or huddling with friends in restaurants pricks needles inside me. I don't wish to play pitiful love interest while he gallivants, able-bodied, through Manhattan.

Winston and I become friends. I can empathize with him better, feeling like a kept creature myself, bound by parameters I don't fully grasp. Now that I am always home, I am in charge of putting out his kibbles and letting him in and out of the house. This too I prolong, and it feels good to nourish another creature's body when my own is so broken. He often comes and sits quietly with me by the couch, sensing that something between us has shifted for the warmer.

Hamid comes to hang out once. We sit on the back porch and eat chocolate chip cookies his host mother has sent for me. He asks me if it's normal that his urine is orange, and I nod, realizing anew that there are people across the coast now – from Hamid to Hannah – who are on drugs because of me.

'It's not your fault, Hira,' he tells me, reading my face.

'Then whose is it?' I ask, frustrated. Nailing that down seems very important, because we are not in nineteenth-century Europe, no one I know has ever had the disease, and it's not a part of any collective imagination that I can attach myself to. Of the myths around the disease, of the old idea that tuberculosis was caused by depressing thoughts and melancholy, I am thankfully not yet aware.

'Why does it have to be anyone's fault?' Hamid counters.

I am seventeen, my moral universe is not very complex. There must be someone to blame.

'It's how God intended,' he says.

'You sound like my father.'

Kelly finds out about Hamid's visit. It's a small town, and someone has called her to complain.

'No one should be visiting the house.'

'He's taking the drugs,' I point out. 'We sat outside.'

'Others don't know that.'

'You heard what the doctor said. It's only contagious to people you're continuously exposed to.'

Her eyes widen.

'That doesn't matter,' she says, her voice shrill. 'You just attended a wedding full of old people. The entire community could have been at risk, so you understand why people might be paranoid.'

I stay quiet because she is obviously right.

'Look,' she continues, sighing. 'I know this is hard, but it's hard for all of us. I really need you to cooperate here. Quarantine has to mean quarantine.'

I want to be victim so badly. Only later will I realize the immensity of all Kelly is juggling – a sick exchange student whom the entire town probably hates, a teenager of her own, and a new husband who would have loved to simply send me off to a facility. To my face, Ethan cracks the usual jokes and avoids all talk of disease, so I forget to hold a grudge against him. Instead, I store up resentment only for Kelly, who is often brittle as she discusses doctor visits and quarantine rules with me. Women are penalized for all the noticing we do. Something about us makes it very hard to forgive us.

*

Weeks pass, but the only unit of time that matters is the day. There are some good days, on which I manage to cobble together a series of activities – a long breakfast, a caloric lunch like pasta Alfredo because the nurse says I need to regain weight, a phone call back home – and dusk arrives, harmless, and the calendar moves. Muslims believe in farz-al-kifayah, the concept of a communal obligation; if one person in a family or community fulfills it, everyone else benefits. My father believes in God, and I don't know if I do, but on tranquil days like this, I know that his faith, his constant belief that the shadow of Muhammad falls over him and his family, follows me oceans away. I feel unintimidated by this strange sickness inside of me and know that it will pass.

Other days, I sit in the living room and stare out the tall windows, because if I look at the sky long enough, I will notice a change in color. The arms of the clock crawl. The dust of hours accumulates over everything, and minutes move so slowly that I am horrified at it being my eighteenth year around the sun. Everything I did before the diagnosis seems cacophonous and overwhelming. I used to wake up and make breakfast and go to school and practice and do homework and have dinner, all on the same day. How? Now, every moment is a universe. Time is unmoving and solid, a humid town anticipating a storm. At the end of such a day, I can't recall what I thought of or did, what occupied me inside the vast canopy of dragging moments. At night, I will myself to sleep but my body, stationary and housebound, is never tired. I lie awake, my head propped up with pillows so I can breathe. Deep sleep often arrives only with the indigo winks of dawn.

I sit in such silence that my voice begins to surprise me. Every now and then, I clear my throat to make sure I haven't forgotten how to talk. Space, too, is an oddity. After sitting on the couch for a few hours, looking again and again at the clock, that cruel clock, I look forward to the prospect of moving to the kitchen for lunch. For the first time, I am grateful to have to cook, my weakened, failing body providing me with my only purpose. Sometimes, I go up to Amy's room, not to try on her clothes anymore, but for the change of scenery. During this year of supposed adventure, the limits of my universe become the pettiest they have ever been.

Zahra messages to ask how I'm doing, if I want to talk. I tell her I'm fine, and it's mostly true. I'm not miserable. I do miss Hamid, the weekly mac and cheese at school, the odd trip into Eugene with Sam and Alicia. I tell myself that once this passes, I will take more pleasure in the inane and ordinary – my daily walk, afternoons by the lake, the guiltless proximity of strangers. I have only three more months before I return home, and I resolve to make the most of them as soon as I can.

*

Then, the call. One day my parents ring me from Abbu's cell phone. Ammi and I make small talk, or rather, I tell her about the new pasta recipe Kelly has taught me, detailing the Parmesan that grates out like grains of rice, the roasted garlic and freshly crushed pepper. Suddenly, Faisal is on the phone instead.

'Hira, Ammi's been meaning to tell you,' he says, rushing into the words. 'We're in Multan right now. Nana Ji passed away last Friday.'

March

What do I tell you of the eve of despair?

*

A car rushes by on the highway down the hill. Winston jumps on the patio; his nails scratch the wood. The fridge hums. A red-winged blackbird sings from a perch on the maple tree. It's the bird Kelly has been looking out for because its arrival means spring is here.

I stare at the bird. What spring? Then I pinch the telephone plug out of the jack, disconnecting the call, because I'm seventeen, and this is my first time with death, and I don't know what one does with it. I walk back to my room and shut the door even though no one is home.

There is the moment right after receiving terrible news, when the tears haven't come yet, and everything is still, and nothing hurts, and you wonder if you are in fact a monster, incapable of grieving. I sit on the bed, waiting for my eyes to fill up. Even after they do, I cry silently, the tears making their way down without urgency. A river in dry season. I think back to July, when I saw him last – the white beard, the sly smile of someone sharing one joke with you and another private one with himself.

What happened? No one told me he was this sick. He had asthma and a smoker's lungs, and he was in and out of hospitals often, but that has been going on for years. Was it sudden?

How has my grandfather been dead for four nights without my knowledge?

Faisal did ask me to call him. 'He wants to speak with you,' he had written. I shudder and guilt achieves what grief could not – I let out a howl, then another, and another. I crush my head into the pillow. There is no one around, the world is deaf, I can scream till the hills echo.

I have been practicing for this moment for months. So many nights, I have worried myself into sleeplessness, fearing loss on that other continent. But of course, the final cruelty of loss is that it allows no preparation, comes every time with the freshness of new snow. I think to myself, the world will end. It can no longer go on.

After many days, my body feels needed. Its howl matters. I weep and weep, shaking with disbelief, because how can it be that he and I will only meet in my dreams from now? I cry until I grow tired, a long-lost fatigue washing over me, tasting almost like relief.

When I wake up, it is dark outside. The pillow cover is still wet. I reconnect the phone line and within five minutes Ammi calls again.

'Why did you wait four days to tell me?' I shout, even though I should know why. We are people who hide pain and disease.

'How do you tell your child that your father is dead?'

She doesn't sound rhetorical. She, my mother, is genuinely asking me – how does one do it? I feel envious of Faisal, who is there to shoulder that burden, be a son when she needs one. I tell Ammi to give the phone to my grandmother, whose voice sounds hoarse.

'Hira beta, assalamu alaikum.'

I freeze. What do you say? Condolence is the last frontier of language. So few of us do it well. Some years ago, Aliya's youngest brother, a lean teenager with dimples, had drowned in the Kallar Kahar lake, and when she returned from the funeral, I avoided her for hours, intimidated by her grief, before going to the kitchen and hugging her wordlessly, staying silent as she shuddered in my arms.

To my grandmother, I say the usual words, the ones I've heard Ammi and Abbu say on their afsos visits to the village. She tells me that he passed away in his sleep, deep inside Friday night. His children, spread throughout the country, left for Multan that same night, getting into their cars as dawn broke above. Before going to bed, Nana Ji had gone to check the locks on all doors, as he did each night. He twisted the knobs on the stoves to make sure no gas leaked, then sat at his bedside and took each of his countless pills, his inhaler, the steroids for his asthma. His last words to her, said in the dark after he had turned the light off: 'I think I'm healthy enough to go to the market tomorrow.'

What she is saying sounds rehearsed, undoubtedly because she has told the story many times. She emphasizes his self-sufficiency – he was up and about, dependent on only God till the last minute. When you condole with someone at home, they often recount what happened right before the death, going back to the moment in time before time stopped. The infrastructure does not allow for the long, protracted illness and hospice of richer nations, and so death often appears very suddenly. It seems even more important then, to commemorate a person's last moments, the cliff of grief. The final cup of tea, the last joke, which side of the bed.

Ammi's back on the phone, telling me that the third day of mourning just ended. Faisal and Abbu left an hour ago to go back to Pindi, but she will stay till the end of the week. I ask her who is preparing food for the guests, which room she is sleeping in, if they used marble or mud for the grave.

In the background, I hear women mourning. Their soft, constant moan is that of peacocks wandering a garden on a dewy morning. Every now and then, a loud wail punctuates the lull. The incessant prayer, the low humming, the stacks of Quran chapters to be read and blessed upon the deceased – all to give people something to do, a way to count losses. My mother, aunts, uncles, grandmother, that intimate circle of people, are gathered in Multan. The congregation of grief is there, and I am here.

'Ammi,' I say, 'I want to come home.'

*

'Absolutely not,' says the doctor.

'My grandfather just died,' I repeat into the phone.

'And I'm sorry for your loss,' he responds impatiently. 'But I believe you have been told this before. You cannot leave the confines of that house until you are no longer contagious.'

Kelly looks on helplessly as I repeat to the doctor that my grandfather is dead, he is dead and I am not there, and I must go. I can wear a mask on the flights. I will be careful to disinfect surfaces. I will try to get my own row of seats. He tells me flatly, robotically each time, that it is an impossibility.

'How can you be so cruel?' I cry out.

The line grows silent. Then he answers, his words clipped as if they are coming from behind clenched teeth.

'Ms Amjad, this country takes TB seriously. Yours clearly doesn't, or else you would not be in this predicament. I strongly advise you to stay put, because if you try to leave, we will intercept you. And rest assured, you will be moved to a quarantine facility, not your host mother's house.'

Hanging up, I turn to Kelly in anger.

'Can you believe him? There's no way he would find out. I'm sure if you dropped me off at the airport and . . .'

'Why would I do that?'

There is ice in her voice. I look at her eyes, hard as stones, her steely little mouth.

'Hira, I'm sorry about your grandfather, I really am,' she says. 'But you returning will not bring him back.'

I remember how ardently he had insisted I stay in Pakistan. 'While her elders are still sitting,' he had said.

'And you need to think beyond yourself,' Kelly continues. 'You've already put so many people at risk. Now you want to fly across the world, possibly infecting some compromised person who comes your way. Do you understand how unethical that is?'

'I just want to go home to my mother,' I say weakly.

She sinks into one of the dining chairs, her face full of pain.

'I'm so, so sorry. I can't imagine what she must be going through. But this is how it has to be.'

I don't yet know how to react to life – its sadness and disappointments – without blaming those around me, because I am only half formed and so it feels to me that I am nothing but the sum of other people's actions. I rush away to my room, hating Kelly. I pace next to the bed and plot. There must be a taxi company I can call. Perhaps Ammi can buy the ticket and send it to me over email. I can surreptitiously start packing at night. I can leave while Kelly and Ethan are at work.

I sink into the bed, weighed down by impossibility. It cannot be done. It would be wrong. I think of how ashamed Abbu would be if I were to leave in the dark like a thief. But it's more than just him. I know that I am no fugitive; I will never have it in me to abscond.

Instead, I boil ramen and eat it with the door shut. When Kelly knocks to ask for dinner, I tell her I'm not hungry. Before sleeping, I place an empty glass underneath my bed, repressed hope threatening to break my bones.

'Allah, please don't let this be here when I wake up,' I plead. 'Let this all be a dream.'

In the morning, the prayer is awake inside me even before I open my eyes. I raise myself from the pillow and immediately swing sideways. I pick up the glass and fling it at the wall, where it shatters upon impact. The room is set ablaze with the luster of broken rainbows.

There's the one about being an atheist until the plane starts falling. The flaw in the joke being, of course, that there is a fundamental difference in the believer who always believes and the one who turns to God only in the face of imminent death.

God begins to feature heavily in my life. Those that cannot meet Him in their hearts need to seek Him on the prayer mat, so I take my jaye nimaz from where it has been stowed away for seven months, the topmost shelf of the closet. Motes of dust shake out over the carpet as I unfold it and turn the mehrab eastwards. At first, I simply sit with my legs crossed, rocking myself and pleading to God that there might be some magical way I could return home while harming no one. I pray for lungs that don't heave and a body that doesn't blaze with fever each night. I heard somewhere that it's a prayer when it's for other people; for yourself, it's only a wish. I pray for my grandmother and for Ammi. I pray for Nana Ji's ascension to the Heaven I don't believe in.

The early twentieth-century artist Constantin Brâncuşi worked on several sculptures of birds during his career, moving from the mythical *Maiastra* with expansive plumage to the dramatically simplified *Bird in Space*, which sought to represent the essence of a bird rather than a bird itself. When the sculpture arrived at the harbor in New York, US Customs levied a tariff for manufactured metal goods, refusing to accept it as a work of art.

What I'm trying to say is that those of weak belief need well-defined ritual, something they can look at and say, *Ah, that looks like faith*. Sitting on the mat, I turn to Arabic.

Al-hamdu lillahi Rabb il-alamin. Ar-Rahman Ar-Raheem.

I still remember the fatiha, I note with relief. As I continue to recite, my words trample over one another. I can't tell if memory continues to serve or if I am indiscriminately skipping verses I have not recited in months, hiding what I forget even from myself.

I get up from the mat, tucking one corner in like a book, and go to the restroom. Rolling back my sleeves, I wash my hands and arms, my face, and my feet after pulling them up, one by one, into the sink. As I raise my leg, I feel the tug of plastic sticking to my inner thigh, reminding me that I'm bleeding, forbidden from worship. I stall with one leg inside the sink, staring at the water as it pours over my toes. How can God care about this? If I am making my own God, I will not color him petty. My God I will color red.

Returning to the prayer mat, I raise my hands in intention.

*

Next, I start bargaining with Him daily, the way my aunts do back home, promising Allah that if He grants their wishes – returns their sick husband to health, provides a windfall to pay off loans – they will finish the Quran, give five cauldrons of rice at the saint's shrine, fast every Thursday. Nicole told me her mother has been making a yearly pilgrimage to Santiago de Compostela for the past ten years, ever since her husband beat cancer.

I have little I can promise Allah, so I bargain with my loneliness. I keep count of the days that have passed since

I saw anyone except Kelly's family or the nurse. Sitting in the living room all day, I tally the number of hours I have spent silent. These figures I bring to God like a meticulous accountant.

Allah, it's been four weeks since I last saw people. Please heal me, so I can return home.

As children, Faisal and I were told that the more you laugh, the more you will cry, that the universe allots equitable portions of mirth and sorrow. Sometimes, after raucous bouts of laughter that sent us rolling in bed with our legs flung towards the sky, we would sober up. For the new few hours, we would stay somber and restrained, tiptoeing around fate and its landmines, hoping we could make it forget that it was our turn to cry. Now I keep count of my miseries and hope the universe will notice.

*

I expect Ammi to be devastated when I tell her I'm not allowed to return, but she remains calm, as if distracted by her own grief. That grief she also doesn't wish to talk about, as if it is too abstract and unwieldy a thing to approach. When I ask how she's doing, she says she's completely fine, then changes the subject to a research scholarship she is thinking of applying for.

But it doesn't matter that she doesn't care. It doesn't even matter about Nana Ji, who is long buried now. I had thought that without seeing him in a shroud, being carried away towards freshly shoveled mud on a charpai hung over my uncles' shoulders, I would never accept his death, but I do. I believe it, because if the human in us doubts that we all die, the animal in us knows, anticipates it at every turn. Ammi tells me that my grandmother is selling the house and moving in with my oldest uncle. The blue house is gone. My mother is an orphan. My grandfather is dead. I believe it all.

No, I am desperate to return because, although my disease lives deep within me, feeding on the hollow of my chest, all my pain and longing seem to radiate from far away. Home is where I have brought my illness from, the embers still glowing in its embrace. The past few months in Oregon feel like the snowflakes I eagerly lifted my fingers for in November, shimmery, ephemeral flecks that dissolved upon impact. The weight of my life is back there, the locus of grief is back there – and it pains me to write this because I will have to confront this over and over and over again my entire life – the mouth of the fall, the gleam of dawn, the spring of pain, it is all there, it will always be there.

*

At the end of March, Kelly and Ethan leave for Hawaii. Kelly asks me repeatedly if it's okay that she goes, and I tell her of course. Their honeymoon is already two months late because of me, and, in any case, my mourning is a private one. Grief is a strange, embarrassing thing. It's hard to share it with anyone, and how do I even begin to share it with people who have never met Nana Ji, seen him smile, heard him plead with my mother not to send me oceans away?

It touches me, however, that Kelly seems to have asked Hannah to check in on me, because the older woman calls every afternoon.

'You said home changed after your parents passed, right?' I ask her, the third day she calls.

'Yes,' she replies.

'Were you able to attend their funerals?'

'I went afterwards. I didn't want to see them dead.'

'But didn't you want closure?'

She laughs and laughs, until she is gasping for breath. Then she asks me what I had for lunch.

Later that day, Amy comes in from school with a pile of mail.

'Look who it is,' she says, winking. 'Hira's boyfriend.'

I take the package, heavier than a letter, with Ali's return address written in sharp block letters.

'How did he know our address?' I wonder out loud.

'He messaged me on Facebook,' Amy says. 'He's so sweet.'

Some remnants of that old thrill course in me as I tear open the envelope. A note falls out.

Hira—

Ammi told me about your grandfather. I'm so sorry for your loss. You are so brave, meri jan, although I wish you didn't have to be. I saw this at a bookstore in Queens and thought of you. Hope it helps with the pain.

Always thinking of you.

Ali.

Inside is a small book, tinier than my hand. It is a collection of poems by Faiz, the front cover showing him with a cigarette held loosely between two fingers. The title of the book is written in blood red. I crack open the spine to silky pages.

It is odd to read in Urdu again, my eyes roaming back and forth over characters that hug one another, twisting and shapeshifting to remain in embrace. Back home, Rabia and I would often complain about Urdu literature, how it was stilted, formal and over-embellished. We never realized that our discomfort reflected how low the bar was, how little we were expected to know of the language that its beauty sounded overwrought.

211

In the coming days, I start picking up the book more and more frequently. It is a homecoming to language and feeling. When the ceaselessness of time becomes too much, when my mind numbs to the monotony of quarantine, or worse, when it awakens to the fear of something even worse happening back home, I reach for Faiz. I flip to a random page and whisper verses to myself.

Why not give your desolation a pretty little name?
I counted the torments of this life today, I thought of you countless times today.
Who slit the veins, of your dawn and mine?

Faiz speaks of a loneliness that diffuses through each moment – the emptiness of evenings, timelessness that snuffs out the sun and moon, sadness that renders a desert out of a flowerbed.

'You're really enjoying that book,' Ethan notes upon his return, after seeing me read it all evening. He and Kelly are tan and brimming with stories about pristine water and volcanoes. I nod and don't tell him that I have taken to sleeping with the book in my hands, reading till my eyelids grow heavy and waking to its impressions on my face. Even after turning the lights off, I repeat the words over and over like the beads of a rosary.

Yeh gham jo is raat ne diya hai
Yeh gham sahar ka yaqeen bana hai

Faiz tells me to believe in the inevitability of dawn, and so I wait for it with him by my side.

*

212

Once every week, the nurse brings a test tube along with the medicine. She hands me the tube and I go out to the patio, making sure to keep in her line of sight. I pick up Amy's old skipping rope that hangs outside the garage and jump until my throat clogs. Then I uncap the tube and cough into it, trying to collect as much morning sputum as I can. The nurse gingerly takes it back and drives away. The next day, as soon as I open the door, she says without looking at me, as if it exhausts her to always bear the same news, 'Still contagious.' The doctor has told me the earliest I can leave the country is when the sputum tests come back showing no active bacteria.

I discover I can get books for as cheap as a cent through Ethan's Amazon. By the time I finish reading Faiz twice, I have received my first shipment. Again, there is the purpose of pages. After the nurse leaves, I sit down in the living room, picking a spot where the sun spools. I read until lunch, until dinner, until late into the night, the way Faisal and I used to do in the balm of Pindi summers. I keep note of how many pages I have left and hungrily order more before I run out. Sometimes, I hear Kelly's morning alarm go off and rush to bed before she comes down. She will worry about me, and it will be hard to explain how welcome it all is – voices in my head that are not mine.

April

April arrives, and my days don't turn. *The same corner of the cage, the same mourning of roses,* writes Faiz. It remains breathlessly cold. From the dining table, I see the sun cut a sliver of gold into the lake, but I know of its deception. Each time the door opens, a gust of chilling wind blows in. By this time back home, winter leaves must have shed, forming piles of crackling yellow in the yard. The air will be changing character, growing heavy with the promise of summer. Uncle Shafiq must be rolling open the car windows each morning. Faisal will have to take off his sleeveless uniform sweater during recess. Ammi will start drinking chai in the backyard again. The next time I talk to her though, she tells me they're getting the jamun tree felled. It's too unruly. I start weeping.

'What's wrong?' Ammi asks, and I can feel her awkwardness over the phone line. Ammi has never known what to do with tears, her own or others'.

'I'll never see the tree again,' I say, my voice wavering.

'Yes, the two of you should have said your goodbyes,' Ammi replies, laughing gently, because it's easier for both of us to pretend it's about the tree.

Abbu asks me each time we talk whether I have gotten another sputum test, what the results are.

'Abbu, wouldn't I tell you if I had good news?'

'Bus, Inshallah, next time. I have a good feeling about next time.'

Every time he says this, a claw draws over my heart. It frustrates children, the endless reservoirs of hope their parents have for them.

The tests continue to come back positive for contagion, and I learn to manage my disappointment. From the way the nurse gets out of the car and her slow gait as she approaches the house, I can tell. In fact, I know that if the news were any good, she would have called from the hospital.

*

Paola the nurse and I are learning to like each other. After I take the medicine, she sits out on the patio while I put on a pot of coffee for the two of us. She has taught me how to make coffee from the machine, something I have seen Kelly do but never trusted myself to do. She tells me tap water has too much taste of its own and insists I use spring water bottles from the garage. I pour out the coffee and then heat milk in a saucepan, scooping up the quivering skin into Paola's mug. I tell her how back home we save the cream on top until it is enough to turn into butter and ghee. She tells me that when she was a child in Oaxaca, her grandfather would mix the milk skin with coarse sugar and feed it to her in the mornings.

She shows me photos of her husband and two children, and describes her family's migration from Oaxaca to San Diego, where she saw jumbo tubs of strawberry ice cream for the first time and fell in love with America. She says this with a wry smile, so I ask her if she still loves America. She nods with emphasis.

'It's the best place in the world,' she insists. 'Anyone who comes here and then complains . . . I have no time for that. That's just ungrateful.'

Another time, she tells me she can't imagine why my parents sent me so far away, and to live with gringas too.

'Well, I hope I'll get to leave soon.'

She shakes her head.

'This country is cigar smoke. It never leaves.'

Every few days, she brings over a scale. I dutifully climb on top and read out the measurement, and she claps her hands and tells me, while checking a notepad, how much I have gained since the last time.

It's not just my weight that is improving. I notice one day that my lungs no longer feel weighed down as if by stones. I spend less and less time coughing, and when I do, it doesn't turn my entire body warm and fatigued. I can walk upstairs without taking a break on the landing. I close my eyes and try to remember what other symptoms have receded, but I can't conjure the feeling of being deathly sick anymore. Merely weeks into recovery, I can no longer access the archive of pain. What the body suffers, the body forgets.

*

Ali calls, and my heart flutters when I hear his voice. It's the most hopeful thing we do as a species – we lose love to death, and then we love again. I thank him for the book.

'I have a good chunk memorized by now.'

'I thought you'd like it. How are you doing?'

'You know . . . How are you?'

He tells me that he just got into a summer program in Dubrovnik and will leave for Croatia in May.

'Will you go home at all?'

'Yes, in August.'

I stay quiet, remembering his promise by the Hudson.

'I'll try to visit Pindi when I'm there,' he says. 'You'll be back by then, right?'

216

'Who even knows. Pray for me.'
'You think I don't every day?'

*

April 14th is the fifth Thursday of Nana Ji's passing, the final day of mourning. Ammi, Abbu, and Faisal are again in Multan, from where Faisal emails me a photo of the three of them with my grandmother. Abbu looks the same, but Ammi has lost weight, her cheeks thinner. Faisal bears the warning signs of someone about to shoot up several inches. I look at him and have that distinct sibling feeling. I want to hug this brother of mine, crush his bird bones with love, but I also want to scrub his face with soap.

In all these months of me sending photos of one humdrum event after another – my first volleyball game, a trip with Kelly and Amy to the McKenzie River, the mediocre meals I cooked – I did not once ask them to send pictures back. Now my eyes feast, sating a hunger I had not recognized.

In the picture, my grandmother wears white chiffon. Silver spins around her temples. How often did I see her during those summers in Multan, leaning into the bathroom mirror, applying henna to her scalp with a stained toothbrush? I can still smell the henna, the Imperial Leather soap by the sink, the musk of the eucalyptus tree in the courtyard entering through the gaps in the bathroom door, the smell of rust in the tap water. In the months following a man's death, the widow dresses simply, without vanity, and so my grandmother has stopped dyeing her hair. Now, it keeps time – I can tell how long he has been gone by how far the silver runs down her scalp.

There are other photos Faisal has scanned and sent with the email. One of Nana Ji and me on my fifth birthday party, for which he drove up to Pindi. He leans in as I blow the candles, his own mouth rounded in anticipation. Another one of him, Faisal, and me sitting in a giant teacup at an amusement park. We would beg him to twist the wheel round and round when the teacup started rotating, so that everything around us became a blur of color. When the ride ended, he would hold our hands as we stood up, asking us to tell him when the world had stopped spinning, so he could let go.

That afternoon, Paola calls.

'Didn't you say the mourning for your grandfather ends today?'

'Yes.'

'God works in funny ways. We just got back your test results. You're clean.'

O ur legs dangle into mossy green lake water.

'How does it feel?' Amy asks, sipping on wine that Kelly has allowed her in celebration.

We are sitting by the dock. Ethan brought down the grill in his car trunk, while the three of us walked down with wine and cutlery. I moved on the gravel like on ice, worried my legs might not remember what gravity felt like.

'I had forgotten how pretty the lake is,' I say, looking at the tall trees standing like sentinels on the hills surrounding the water, the cottages speckled among them with windows aflame in the waning sunlight. From the other side of the lake, I hear shouts of glee. A figure zips across the surface on a water ski.

'It's going to be gorgeous in a few weeks,' Kelly says, bringing over grilled hamburgers and sitting down next to us. 'We can start going on those walks again.'

A young couple loiters by the dock, the woman holding an infant in a chest carrier. I tense up before remembering that I am no longer a threat to them, the carrier of a strange disease. I am clean, free to be near the skin of strangers again. It feels like too much power to have.

'So, does this mean you can come back to school?' Amy asks.

At the thought of returning to Lakeview, my heart sinks. I have missed many things – walking on country roads, laughing with Hamid, even singing hymns at church. The inconsequential academy of Lakeview High, its hostile hallways, I haven't missed one bit.

'I'm going to be so far behind,' I say. 'There's no point.'

'I'm sure the teachers will be more than happy to have you back,' Kelly says, winking. 'I hear you're a star student.'

Amy must have said that to her, and probably not as a compliment. Even before I got sick, I was slacking at school in a way I had never done in my life, missing assignments and doing the bare minimum on essays. The fact that Kelly can't see how little I have tried frustrates me. I want to be back around people who expect things of me.

I put the plate down and take my sweater off. The sun presses on my shoulders, bare in a tank top. Kelly's jeans are rolled up to her knees as she swishes her feet around in the water. Amy is wearing basketball shorts. I wonder how much I will miss the giddiness of bare skin back in Pindi.

I think of telling Kelly that I want to return soon, but I worry how she will take it. Perhaps she will be more than glad to be rid of me.

'I could also leave for home sooner,' I say tentatively, and her face clouds over.

'No, don't do that. Early summer's the best time in Lakeview. Doesn't your program end in less than two months anyway?'

It's April 18th, and the program end date is May 30th. If I stayed, I would go home with Zahra and the rest of the cohort. We would all gather in DC for an end-of-year orientation and meet Mr Shahid again. We would share notes on America, and then board that Emirates flight to the homeland. It would be a neat bookend, the way it was meant to be.

*

'Absolutely not,' Abbu says, horrified, when I tell him Kelly wants me to stay. 'I'm going to call the travel agent right now.'

220

It chafes, in ways that it did not used to, that Abbu can make such unilateral decisions about my life. It feels like an affront to the independence I have earned over these past few months. Of course, it is messier than that; familial independence is a lifelong tug-of-war, not the bounty of a few months away from home.

'You got sick because she didn't care for you, and now she wants you to stay.'

'No, Abbu. I got sick because of your recklessness.'

The words are out before I can cage them.

'What are you talking about?'

Abbu sounds conciliatory, but I am child to the man, and even on the phone, I can tell that his voice sits right at the edge of anger. I decide, for once, not to hold my tongue in front of him.

'Abbu, you were the one who decided I shouldn't take the medicine. You sent me away without taking the right precautions. It was your fault.'

'I have no idea what you're talking about.'

Abbu can remember the patterns on the blanket he was swaddled in as a child – his memory terrifies us sometimes. I stay silent. After a while, he sighs.

'Beta, we can't live in constant fear of death and disaster. I did what I have always done. I put you in the hands of God, knowing He would take care of you.'

'Well. He didn't.'

Even before I hear the click, I know he will hang up. I stare at the receiver for a second, then run over to grab the international calling card, so I can call back and apologize. But apologize for what? I put away the card.

As a child, I had sometimes worried that we lived in a godless world. Each time, I went to Abbu, and each time, he sat with me for hours, telling me that it was natural to have doubts, and yet, how could one remain blind to the dead earth brought to life, the extraction of light from day so it turned into night, the moon obeying an ancient rhythm and turning from a luminous orb into the old stem of a palm tree? But I was a child then, and children are allowed doubt.

Years later, Abbu will ask me in a moment of frustration, 'When will you start praying, Hira? Are you waiting for me to die?' And it will take me aback, because I haven't realized it's that personal, but of course it is. A deep, abiding faith in God and a desperate love for Muhammad have helped my father through the darkest places man can tread, and he wants his children to have the same strength. It is such an integral part of his character that he considers my own faith an act of loyalty to him. What I need to apologize for, what I cannot find in myself to apologize for, is my failure to will filial obedience into divine faith, to lay my trust in Allah as blindly as my father does. If I could, Abbu, I would. And perhaps one day I will.

*

Kelly, Amy and I go to a nearby strawberry-picking farm. At home, we scrub the dirt off the fruit and hull it. Kelly chops half the strawberries into scarlet slivers and puts them aside to sweat in sugar. Then she teaches me how to make shortcake the way Hannah taught her years ago, reading out measurements from a worn-out recipe book.

Hamid, Sam, and Alicia visit, bringing tales from Lakeview High – the upcoming Prom, yearbook photos, the end of basketball season. A familiar boredom washes over me, along with its accompaniment of guilt. I am in America to learn about new things. I am so tired of new things.

Hamid stays after the other two have left, and we take our old seats on the patio.

'I'm thinking of going home early,' I tell him.

His eyebrows shoot up, but he quickly lowers them.

'I figured you would.'

He sounds resigned.

'What?'

'Nothing.'

'Say it.'

He looks up at the sky.

'You know, after you left school,' he says finally, 'I was so lonely. I felt sorry for myself, surrounded by all these Americans, without my only friend around.'

He pauses.

'I'm sorry, Hamid.'

'But then, I found out it was so much easier without you.'

He's not catching my eye.

'I started hanging out with people after school. I started listening to the music they were listening to, watching movies with my host dad, going fishing. And I realized I had never tried before. They're such great people once you get comfortable around them.'

I am unsure of what to say.

'So you regret being friends with me?'

He shakes his head, not with as much conviction as I would like.

'I just . . . don't think you really tried here. It's like coming to a country and not speaking the language. How are people supposed to understand you?'

'But I do speak their language,' I snap back. 'Better than them.'

'See? Right there. You can be arrogant. As if you're above changing yourself for anyone.'

He's saying this with hesitation, worried about offending me. And it's true that his words are drawing lines between us, fissures that form between friends at some point or another. But they are also giving me perverse pleasure. All these months,

I have been waiting to be accused of exactly this – that I haven't tried enough to placate America, that my loyalty remains undivided, that I am stubbornly holding on. Having left, I am so, so desperate to be someone who hasn't.

'Look, I don't mean to upset you,' he says, into my silence. 'It's just what I've learned. The more you assimilate, the easier it gets. We came here to be Americans for a year, not to stay Pakistani or Omani or whatever.'

'But that's not possible.'

'Then what's the point? Why move at all?'

'One can't escape the past,' I say.

'No one's telling you to do that,' he replies, frowning. 'You being open to people doesn't wipe away your history.'

Is there anything more enraging than a friend who has a point? I think back to my argument with Zahra.

'Look, you can do whatever you want,' he adds, leaning back in his chair to indicate he's done arguing. 'All I'm saying is, you don't have to roam the earth so defensively. Your existence doesn't require anyone else's acknowledgement.'

He leaves a little while later, as the sky turns the lurid pink of cotton candy and birds gather for the day's last pilgrimage. This is the last time I will ever see him. Hamid, my friend, it will take me years to understand what you mean.

*

I warily pick up the phone, wondering what my parents have to say now. It's Ammi.

'Your father's still angry at you.'

'Cool.'

She sighs. For seventeen years and counting, my mother has played emotional conduit between me and my father. Being a parent means translating the world to your child. Being a mother means getting punished for it.

'It's not easy for him to admit when he's wrong. You should know that, you're just like him.'

'Yes, I should empathize with the flaws he's kindly passed down.'

'Hira,' Ammi starts, then falters.

A few moments of silence pass. I resolve not to make it easier for her by talking.

'I didn't go to your room for weeks after you left.'

She is speaking faster now, as if the words, not let out, will be lost forever.

'I knew it even then. Your father didn't, but I did. We had let you go.'

A lost memory of Ammi arrives, like morning breeze in the desert. She's sitting under the jamun tree. Pindi rain. The magic of those green eyes.

'I learned of your sickness the same day your Nana Ji got very sick,' she says. 'Since he died, I've had so many nightmares. They're all about you.'

I swallow air, hoping she can't hear.

'Now would be a good time to have you back. Every night will be miserable for me until you return.'

Across the Potohar and the Hindu Kush, over ocean and mountain clay, her voice breaks.

'Hira jan. Come home.'

Later, I will think of it as a decision to pull away from America, to choose blood over all else, but in the moment, it doesn't feel like one. I am helpless, answering the most heartbreaking pull in the world. I hang up with my mind clear like the pilgrim's as she moves around the Kaabah, the Sufi's as she whirls in imitation of the planets.

Hira jan. Go home.

By the time Kelly returns, the program coordinator has emailed me an unconfirmed itinerary for May 1st.

'I've decided to go back early,' I blurt as soon as she walks in the door. She frowns, putting a bag of Trader Joe's groceries on the kitchen counter.

'Hira, it's literally an extra month.'

'My mother wants me back.'

She takes out bunches of kale.

'But you just recovered. You should spend this last month properly saying goodbyes instead of running away. Graduation and Prom are coming up. Your parents have done nine months without you, what's one more?'

My mother has lost her father and has been having recurrent nightmares in which she loses her daughter. Kelly has never been apart from Amy for more than a week; surely, she can understand why Ammi might want me back. But the thing one must keep in mind is that people will frequently forget the humanity of those you leave behind, and it's not because they're bad people, but because it's not their job to remember. It's yours, only yours.

'Yes, but my mother needs me back now,' I respond, helping her stack tiny tubs of yogurt in the fridge.

She stays silent, and I grow impatient. Why does she even want me to stay? Haven't I put her through enough? Perhaps it's the same reason I was considering staying. That attempt at a neat ending. The bow on top.

'Why would you do that?' she suddenly snaps. 'Why would you cut your program short, to return to a life you've always had?'

Returning to that life – comfortable and familiar, among people who have been shaped by the same biases, whose tongues rove the same way inside their mouths – seems very appealing.

'Kelly, you haven't left this highway town in fifteen years,' I shoot back. 'I'm not sure you know much about leaving a place.'

It's not strictly true, because Kelly's adolescence and youth were fairly itinerant. But I can sense her real question, which is – why would you go back *there* when you could be *here*? Her eyes flash.

'I haven't needed to leave. I'm happy with my life here.'

'And I'm happy to go back.'

'There's a reason you left. Didn't you want to come here? Didn't your parents make you apply?'

'Trust me, they regret it.'

Do they? I have never asked them, because – and this is also why I don't say anything else to Kelly, why I huff off to my room, why I end up leaving without a single complaint about the lack of food, the empty evenings, the small, silly things she said that hurt me – that's not how people speak to one another. Kelly also doesn't confront me about the judgment she must have seen in my eyes all year, my stubbornness, and my arrogance. Those are the endings of novels: the big blow-out, the climactic confrontation, the earnest question, the clear answer. In life, we either talk around one another, or then there's silence.

That Sunday, the pastor makes an announcement.

'As some of you know, a young member of our community has been very sick for the past few months. I'm happy to announce that she is back to health and here with us today. Do say hi when you can!'

After the service, some people keep their distance, throwing glances at me every now and then. Many more come over to shake my hand and tell me how happy they are to see me healthy. I smile back and wonder, for the hundredth time that year, at the casualness with which Americans can walk up to near strangers and wish them well. Such ease, such off-handed good will. Where does it come from, where can I get some?

*

I spend the next five days packing and getting gifts for my family. Amy takes me into town, where I buy chocolates and a music player for Faisal, dress shirts for Abbu, a sweater for Ammi. Ali confirms that he will visit Pindi in late summer, and it thrills me to think of us meeting in that familiar landscape. I obsess over home even more than I have these past months, allowing my mind access to memories I had stowed away all year. The runway at the airport, bumpier on impact than American touchdowns. The car ride home, the road lined with canteens and telecom offices. The old electric switchboards of home.

I will live in Urdu again, answer phone calls with salam and address shopkeepers with bhai, suniye ga. I will walk around, invisible again, because I will look the same as everyone else. Sundried shalwar kameez, the halcyon light of early summer, leaves floating around the backyard.

The last days move more slowly than ever, each moment alive with a different thought of home, each night dense with dreams. Ghazals play on my laptop as I sit by the lake. I pore over Faiz in the evenings, his verses painting my own yearning red.

The night before I leave, there's a knock on my door. I wake up, groggy, and look at the bedside clock. 2 a.m. Amy opens the door.

'Put on your coat,' she whispers. Soon, we are both outside and in Kelly's car. Amy turns on the engine, shushing at me to close the car door softly. We drive down the hill and onto the same side road where I used to take my walks. A few moments in, she brakes and turns to me.

'Ready?'

Not really, because I don't have a license and the only time I've ever spent in the driver's seat is when I was a child and Abbu would send me to grab something he left in the car and I would go and sit, simply sit and twirl the locked wheel and feel cool. But it's 2 a.m. and the road's empty and it's been a hard year. I switch with Amy. I settle into the seat and press the gas so timidly that she clucks with impatience. I press harder. She puts her hand in her coat pocket and retrieves two cigarettes.

'It's your mother's car,' I point out banally, because of course I'm going to do it.

'Good thing the windows were open in your fantasy,' she says and winks. She lights both and hands me one. The car sways as I take a drag. I bring my hand back to the wheel, the glowing ember unsteady between my fingers. We drive in silence for a minute.

'So,' she asks. 'Is it how you imagined it would be?'

When is it ever? In the fantasy, there was an audience – the audience was the fantasy. My heart is full because Amy has remembered.

'Yes,' I lie.

'I'm thinking of spending the summer at Hannah's,' she says.

'That'll be good for you.'

She nods, and I accelerate.

'What about Kyle?' I ask.

'Who ever ends up with their high school sweetheart?'

'A lot of people.'

'I don't wanna be those people.'

'Don't be, then,' I say, because no one needs permission, but we all need a blessing.

We drive in silence for a bit.

'Also, I thought about it more. It's not Prom Queen.'

'You just realized that?' I ask.

'No, a few months ago.'

'What is it then?'

'College, New York, my own apartment,' she says, looking out. 'Anywhere but here.'

The car is approaching a dead end. The hills are shadowy guards to the valley, dark and foreboding. I nod, and bite my lip to not utter the obvious, which is that no one ever leaves. No one has ever left.

*

The next day, Amy is back to her usual nonchalance. She makes me eggs for breakfast, then packs her night bag, gives me a big hug, and heads out the door to Kyle's. Ethan is visiting his mother in Eugene; he and I did not even say goodbye, but it's one of those goodbyes that don't matter. Kelly and I set out for the airport around noon, the bright May light rendering it a more pleasant journey than the dark-ridden one we made several months ago, on the night I arrived. Somehow, only nine months have passed.

Kelly is quiet as she drives, speaking only to ask me if I have made sure I have everything – laptop, passport, ticket, wallet. Then she gets out at an exit.

'Gas?' I ask.

We pull up at a McDonald's. She orders two Filet-o-Fish and fries at the drive-through.

'Figured you're not going to be eating these any time soon,' she says, winking.

230

We eat in the parking lot, to the sound of cars zooming by. I ask her to open the trunk, so I can take out the gift I bought while in town with Amy.

'I was going to give it to you at the airport, but since we're already stopped,' I say, handing Kelly a framed photo of the two of us from the wedding.

'This is lovely! Thank you so much.'

'Not at all.'

Then, as she is pulling out of the parking lot, she brakes and turns to me.

'Will you stay in touch? Don't be a stranger.'

'I would love to,' I say.

We will stay in touch for years, creating a steady archive of correspondence about life events and inside jokes and general musings. Once out of the bondage of our strange, unnatural relationship, we will flourish as friends, because I share with her something I don't with anyone back home – intimacy without history.

At the airport, I check in my luggage and gather my four boarding passes. EUG > SFO > JFK > DXB > ISB. Kelly stands with me until it's time to go. I make my way through the small security area. An announcement rings, the corridors echoing a final call for Heera Em-jad. After one final look back, I leap towards the plane, eager to return, there where they know my name.

May

I wake up to water. From the window, I see endless blue stretch out under the plane. Panicking, I look at the passengers around me, reading on their Kindles or toggling the entertainment screens. Why are we crossing an ocean on the way from San Francisco to New York? I touch the arm of the woman next to me.

'Why are we above the sea?'

She looks over, her surprise at being addressed quickly turning to delight.

'That's Lake Michigan!'

She glances at me again and seems to realize I'm not American, because she adds, 'It's one of the biggest lakes in the country.'

I nod, suddenly very stupid. Lakes.

'I went there as a child once,' she continues brightly. 'It's beautiful. You must visit.'

I thank her and continue to look down at the never-ending water, alight with small fires in the evening sun. How vast this country, with lakes that could be oceans from the sky.

At JFK, I transfer to the international terminal, walking through corridors that look out at the skyline. It is late, almost midnight, and the information screens are displaying flight information for Cairo, Nairobi, Abu Dhabi, Delhi. We are travelers to the Old World, moving in the direction of the Earth. Middle-aged men walk about with large trolleys stacked high with indiscriminate black suitcases. Brown girls

232

with American vowels wait to board planes to the mother-land, hair ironed and brows plucked for the relatives waiting on the other side. I smile at an aunty in a sari, who stares back. Alhumdulillah, it's time to stop smiling at strangers.

On my way to the departure gate, a large crowd stands near an overhead television. There is general applause, and I see a few people hug. The screen itself isn't visible. I reach the gate for the Dubai flight, where most awaiting passengers appear to be Indian families traveling home for the summer. When I get to the head of the queue, the woman checking boarding passes stalls and stares at the cover of my passport. She looks up at me, then turns to the man next to her and speaks in his ear. I catch the name of my country. That infuriating slant, the aspirated P; one last time, I tell myself. The man takes my document.

'Is something the matter?' I ask, feeling passport envy for the Indians zooming past in the adjacent line. The man notes down some information from my passport onto a piece of paper, then looks up and wordlessly hands it back to me. I shrug at the woman behind me and she grimaces in shared confusion. Buoyed by this solidarity, I walk onto the connecting bridge.

*

Sweat and cologne. The welcome announcement in Arabic, followed by a few words in halting English by the Norwegian head hostess. Bollywood beaming from TV screens. A sleek menu card that lists chicken machboos for dinner and falafel for breakfast. A halal sign on the back of the menu. I make note of every detail, welcoming any sign of America fading from my life.

In Dubai, I sit down at the same café where I tried to order an egg sandwich with a $100 bill. I use my few remaining dollars to buy a croissant and turn my laptop on. The Facebook message icon is red. Three new messages. The first image on my timeline is of Sumaira holding an American flag, standing in front of a crowd of people and smiling widely. 'WE GOT HIM!' reads the photo caption.

I open Amy's message.

'Hey, we heard about Osama bin Laden. I hope you get home safely. Mom and I are worried, let us know.'

Zahra's message reads, 'CAN YOU BELIEVE IT?!'

She's online, so I message her back.

'What happened?'

'You don't know??'

'Traveling.'

'Oh, right. Dude, they caught OBL. In Abbottabad.'

'OUR Abbottabad??'

'Nahi, Nigeria's Abbottabad, BC.'

I send back the gaping emoji. She types for a while. My parents and I have been to Abbottabad to visit family friends. Where did they catch him? I imagine a shootout in the main town market, where Abbu and I would walk in the evenings for fresh naan.

'The Americans conducted an operation in the middle of the night,' Zahra writes back. 'The Pakistani government had no clue, or so they say. Obama did a press conference last night. They killed him and buried the body at sea.'

Lake Michigan pours into my mind, its waters stretching to infinity.

'That's crazy,' I type.

'It's fucked up. It's going to get so much harder to travel to America from now.'

I can't help but admire my timing. It seems like an impeccable moment to be on the way out.

'Where is Sumaira's photo from?' I ask.

'She went to a celebration in New York. Wanted me to join, said it would look good if I told my friends at school about it.'

'You didn't go?'

'Screw that, dude. Mera uncle thori tha.'

'LOL,' I type, remembering when Kyle half believed me when I told him I was related to Osama. I zoom in on Sumaira's photo. A pink-faced man stands in the background with both fists up, mouth stretched into the same open smile she wears. The red of her scarf matches the flag. She looks like a parent who has shown up to dance at Prom.

'It's disgusting,' Zahra writes. 'All this apologizing we have to do. What for?'

Sumaira, who seldom leaves her house after dark and hates public transport, must have driven to Times Square to join the late-night celebration. Perhaps she and her Jersey friends went together, piling into a car, showing up with flags and unerring gratitude. I think of all my fellow exchange students, who will have lots of explaining to do at school. Are they from Abbottabad? Had they known where Osama was? Are they sad about it? I feel somewhat bad for them, but mostly very, very relieved.

Zahra writes back, as if she has read my mind across the Wi-Fi, 'Amma says things are going to get really bad in Pakistan. The terrorists will retaliate. Be careful at the airport.'

The third message is from Hamid, also asking to let him know how I am. I respond to him and Amy and then scroll down my timeline. Several people from Lakeview have updated their statuses, full of celebration. A woman from church writes, 'Those two-timing Pakistanis should be taught a lesson.' Americans are full of lessons to teach, but this particular woman was so tediously dull in my interactions with her that I'm genuinely impressed she spelled Pakistan right.

Amy has commented underneath.

'It's unfair to judge an entire country for its government. I can tell you that all the Pakistanis I have known have been wonderful people.'

235

I laugh out loud, knowing well how many Pakistanis Amy has known in her life. At the same time, my heart grows as I imagine her typing away at her keyboard, defending a place and people she knows only through me.

*

Every now and then, the crowd waiting to board attempts a queue, before reverting to a swarming congregation of women in sparkly dupattas and black abayas and men in well-worn shalwar kameez. The builders of Dubai, on whose shoulders the city heaves, are going home.

I stand by the gate and look hungrily at the passengers. These are my people. Not Kelly or Amy. Not the Indians at JFK. Not the New Jersey Pakistanis. It's these men and women, with tongues tangled in Shahpuri and Mirpuri and Pashto, who are plucking out sim trays and inserting Ufone and Telenor sims, who are counting out the flimsy, dirty notes of the State Bank, whose hair is the kind of black on which you can still see an ant move – these people are mine. I move to the start of the queue, say salam to the man checking documents, and walk onto the plane.

M y seat is next to a man whose mustache and short beard are starting to flirt with silver. I get to the row and nod towards the window seat. He gets up and starts looking around. A moment passes but he doesn't move.

'That's my seat, uncle.'

He doesn't speak to me. Instead, he addresses a young man in the middle aisle, sitting with women on either side of him.

'Is this your family?' he asks him.

'Yes.'

The older man nods in satisfaction, then turns to me.

'Beta, go sit with the ladies. Young man, come sit with me.'

What?

'Nahi,' I say. 'I have the window seat.'

He looks at me as if I were a fly on food.

'Beta, you should sit with the women. We'll both be more comfortable that way.'

Why do I have to give up a window seat because this man can't handle the slight possibility of his legs brushing against mine? The young man has left his seat and is now waiting for me to take it.

'No, I'll be most comfortable in my own seat.'

They both stare at me.

'Okay, as you wish,' the older man says, moving out to let me through. I see the two of them shrug in collective puzzlement. I pull down the armrest and lean against the window, thankful that it's only two hours to Pakistan.

237

We land in a Pindi awash in early morning light. I peer down, eager to recognize any landmark. All I can make out through the haze are flat roofs dotted with blue water tankies. The terrain itself is plain, devoid of gradient. As we near the runway, wild bushes appear on the side. Everything is yellow and not green like Oregon, dusty and not clean.

We touch down. A few shukar Alhumdulillahs go around the plane and several people get up.

'Please keep sitting,' the head hostess instructs in clipped British notes.

'Sir,' she continues condescendingly, to a man still tugging at his suitcase. 'Sit down, please.'

'Aih akhni payi eh zara beh julo,' another man translates for him, and he sits down. The air turns live with conversation, as everyone starts calling family members waiting at Arrivals.

'Bas panj dassan mintan ich milde aan.'

'Dasso manh kor kor aya eh?'

'Fir milde an.'

I lean against the headrest with my eyes closed, savoring each word and dialect until it is time to disembark. Climbing down the stairs that lead to the shuttle, I breathe in deeply, and the smell crushes me. Arid air that has forgotten rain. The capricious cool of a morning about to turn warm. Far off, someone is burning plastic.

The shuttle carries its own menagerie of smells. Flowery perfume. Nail polish. The mustiness of bodies pressed into a small space. As soon as we pull up by the Immigration building, people rush out. I try to politely wait my turn but am pushed out by the tide. The entrance is a narrow doorway, its glass chipped at one corner. From afar, I see Abbu waiting in a mud-colored shalwar kameez. He keeps staring as I approach him, then suddenly blinks and breaks out into a wide smile. We hug for a long time, my head buried in his shoulder. Ammi might not be

238

a hugger, but Abbu's hugs are pulverizing – I feel the beloved crush of each bone of his. On my back is the relentless pour of people.

An airport official stands next to Abbu, waiting patiently for us to pull apart. As soon as we do, he takes my hand luggage and wheels it to the front of the Immigration line, ahead of a family of five.

'I don't mind standing in line,' I say, and the officer looks at me dourly, as if to say, *What the fuck am I doing here then?* It's clear that he's been sent by a senior, someone Abbu must have called before coming to the airport.

'No problem, madam,' he replies, and hands my passport to the officer, barking at him to hurry up. The officer sets aside the family's passports and begins to flip through mine, as I resolutely avoid eye contact with the mother. She and I chatted while in line for the airplane toilet. Within half a minute, my passport is stamped and back in my hand.

'Not like America, huh,' Abbu says to me as we walk away from the snaking line of my fellow passengers, waiting their turn with documents in hand.

'In America, people wait their turn.'

We pass by a squadron of gun-wielding men on our way to baggage claim. Perhaps there had always been men with guns around the airport, and I'm only noticing it now because – and this will never cease to amaze me – I did not see a single gun during my nine months in America.

'Is the security because of Abbottabad?' I ask, and Abbu clicks his tongue.

'Same old rubbish. Don't worry about it.'

The one functioning carousel is circulating luggage from two arriving flights. Every few seconds, a bag falls off the overcrowded ramp and narrowly misses someone's feet. Abbu and I squeeze through the crowd, and I adjust a couple of the more precariously perched pieces on the carousel. On the other side of the ramp, a man in a creased shalwar kameez grabs my unmarked black suitcase. Abbu snaps at him.

'O bhai, what's your problem?'

'Sorry, sir, it was a mistake,' the man replies, and I feel such shame. Ammi and Abbu are never pleasant in public, not to anyone and especially not to men in creased shalwar kameez, but I feel it acutely in this moment. Why can't Abbu talk to strangers the way people in church talked to me, the way Kelly spoke with till managers at Walmart?

Next to us, two men greet each other. One of them has his arm in a sling.

'Shah ji, how are you? How was the flight?'

'Fit fat, sir. What happened to your arm?'

The man grins, patting the cast.

'Oh, this? Battle scars from Abbottabad.'

They both burst out laughing, holding on to each other's hands as they bend over. Abbu and I look at each other, and I can tell he's trying his hardest not to crack up.

*

Outside, men stand around in white ahram, garlands of marigold hanging around their necks. The arrivals board shows that a flight from Makkah landed an hour ago. As I pass by the pilgrims and their families, a few people turn to look. A woman whispers and points.

Ammi waits in the parking lot, as beautiful as she ever was. We hug and then she holds me at arm's length.

'You've lost so much weight!' she says. 'And why are you so dark?'

'I barely recognized her from the distance,' Abbu says as we get into the car.

All last week, I sat by the lake under the sun, my skin turning crisp and muddy. Amy noted everyday how well I tanned, without burning, and the next day, I returned to the dock with added fervor, thrilled to be outside after three months of quarantine, under a sun I had mistrusted all my life.

'Where is that shirt from?' Ammi asks, as we get into the car. 'Very stylish.'

It says 'American Sweetheart' in white lettering, with a red and blue heart underneath. I love the way it hugs me at the waist, its sleeves tight around biceps that still show residual tone from volleyball.

'I got it in Eugene.'

'It should have stayed in Eugene,' Abbu says, with sudden curtness. He looks at me in the rearview mirror, as if just noticing what I am wearing. 'Don't you have a single dupatta you could have worn?'

I sit, dumbfounded, as we merge onto the main road. This is what we'll talk about after nine months of separation. My dupatta.

'Funny thing is, they don't wear dupattay in America.'

'Who cares what they do in America?' Abbu snaps.

'Aray, let it go,' Ammi says hurriedly. 'Tell us, how was your flight?'

I plunge into details so we can glide past the sudden tenseness. I tell them about finding out the bin Laden news in Dubai, about the aloo paratha Emirates served. But I am thoroughly distracted by my body, in a way that feels too much like déjà vu. The nausea I associate with early girlhood is back, except now I wonder if the association is in fact with this place, this godforsaken place. I feel the familiar desire to do away, maybe chop off, my breasts, neck, arms, really, to be simply a face floating without the body, without its weight and shame. Dear country, would that suffice? I shrink into the car seat, angling myself so that no eye from outside can see me.

'This overly chivalrous man wanted me to give up my window seat and go sit with other women,' I tell my parents.

'I'm sure he meant well,' Abbu says. 'No need to overthink everything.'

'I hate it when they do that,' Ammi says, turning to me and nodding in agreement. 'Every man thinks he's a contractor for our honor.'

I sit in silence, somewhat vindicated. Ali has promised he will visit, but I had forgotten the rules of home, the limitations of my mobility here. What street do I know where I could walk with him – hand in hand, in broad daylight – like we did in Manhattan? Love here is either the thief or the poet, in the guise of night or verse.

'Where's Faisal?' I ask.

'At the neighbor's house,' Ammi replies.

'Why didn't he come with you?'

'They were finishing up some video game. He'll be back by the time we get home.'

Before I left, Faisal sometimes followed me around the house, pleading that we play a board game or watch a movie. Sometimes, when I had to study or call Rabia, I would lock my door on him, saying he should find friends his own age. My heart sinks in fear. Perhaps he has.

'Seema, tell her about Australia,' Abbu says.

'She just arrived. Give her a second to breathe.'

'What about Australia?' I ask.

'I'll tell you later.'

'What is it?'

'I got an email yesterday, from a university in Sydney. They want me to come research with them for the summer.'

'This summer?'

'Yes,' Abbu says proudly. 'It's Australia's best university. Fully paid. Lodging. Per diem.'

'And I'll work with two excellent professors.'

'They're even paying to fly her out.'

242

'Wait,' I say, shaking my head. 'So, you asked me to come back just so you could leave?'

They either don't notice the bite in my voice or pretend not to.

'Oho, you'll be with me and Faisal,' Abbu says. 'And it's only for two months.'

'But I came early at your behest, Ammi. That's not fair.'

No one speaks for a moment.

'So you needed a reason to come back?' Abbu asks. 'Isn't that what one does after leaving home?'

Ammi keeps her eyes ahead, and I say nothing else for the time being. Later that week, I will bring it up with her again in anger and her eyes will flash and her mouth will draw into a snarl almost cruel, almost because that mother of mine is many things but never, ever cruel, and she will ask, 'So you think only you can leave?' And I will recognize her hunger as my own because, well, where else could I have gotten it from? And I will think, Good Lord, we are all people who leave.

I look out the window, speckled with dried-up dust. Men on bikes climb onto narrow sidewalks to circumvent road traffic. The bikers, hawkers, walkers – all men. The only woman on foot is a young beggar at a traffic signal, moving from car to car with a child at her hip. A few others ride on the back of motorbikes, precariously perched in modest side saddles.

'Are you happy I'm back, Ammi?' I say, touching her shoulder.

'Of course,' she replies, and puts a gentle hand on mine. 'Your father said I shouldn't come to the airport, because of all the security issues after Abbottabad. But I told him there's no way I'm staying home.'

She squeezes my hand before pulling hers away.

'Thank God my daughter's back from that wretched place.'

243

I lean back into the seat. Ammi continues to talk, telling me we have to visit an aunt's house later today, but that we'll go home first so I can change into shalwar kameez.

'Let me call Aliya,' she says, holding out her hand for Abbu's cell phone. 'She'll come over to make your breakfast.'

'It's fine, I can make it myself,' I say. Kelly has promised she'll email me recipes that I can recreate at home – strawberry shortcake, baked fish, pasta. Ammi scoffs.

'You're not in America anymore, you have people here to take care of you.'

We slow down at a checkpoint. A policeman leans in to talk to the Toyota driver in front of us.

'Osama's corpse is going to line many pockets this week,' Abbu says, smirking.

I shudder at his cynicism. Maybe the policeman is doing a routine check for documents. A few moments pass. Then the two men shake hands and the Toyota rolls away. The policeman puts a folded note in his chest pocket and calls our car forward.

'Amjad Awan, Additional Collector, Customs,' Abbu introduces himself in the same brusque tone he used with the man at the baggage carousel, a tone he would never use with, say, Chief Collector, Customs. The police officer salutes him and pulls open the barrier.

My armpits are sticky with sweat, and I cannot wait to be out of this horrible shirt. Cars pass by, and a riksha bellows dark black clouds. A truck has somehow made it into the cantonment; on its back are painted flowers and verses.

Dilri lutti tain yar sajan
Kadein mor muharan te aa vatan

When we get to the house, I reach for the car door so I can open the gate.

244

'Nahi, nahi, he's coming,' Ammi says, and the colony guard comes running over from underneath a tree, where he is seeking shade from the cruelty of sun. He opens the gate we are parked in front of, and we drive in. Abbu raises his hand to him in greeting, then parks the car in the porch.

'My sweet child is home,' he says, opening the door to the backseat.

I look up at him, at those kind eyes and crow's feet I will wear one day, at the slouch of shoulders that Faisal will. Paint peels from the walls of the house – no American siding here, that magic vinyl that cowers to neither sun nor rain. The garden is full of leaves. The backyard must be as well. But wait. The tree is gone.

The windows are opaque with dust. Generators hum. A stray cat mewls.

What's the point, Hamid had asked? Why move if you do not wish for places to change you? But perhaps you leave to find out what doesn't change, the discontent and itch that are constant. You move only to discover, amidst the waiting and the hoping, and the dashing of that hope, that there is only one place the boat will dock. Wherever you go, there you are.

The tiredness of ages burrows inside of me. I take a deep breath, pumping air into scarred lungs that will permanently bear witness to disease. I wish to remain unmoving, still and static, as continents shift and rearrange themselves around me, as everything changes and nothing does.

I plead with my limbs to walk these final yards home.

Acknowledgements

Many thanks to my agent, Matthew Turner, who saw worth in a very early draft of *American Fever*, and to Francine Toon, Charlotte Humphery, Nico Parfitt, Louise Court, and the rest of the wonderful team at Sceptre. Thanks, also, to Lilly Golden, Kathleen Schmidt, and the Arcade team for bringing the book to life in the US.

Thanks to the writing community that has nurtured this novel, including the Helen Zell Writers' Program and the Hopwood Program at the University of Michigan. I will be forever grateful to my teachers and my brilliant MFA cohort. A special thanks to my friend Forrest Maddox, who was a bright light during my time in Ann Arbor.

So much of *American Fever* is about place, and so I thank all the places that have shaped it – the Pacific Northwest of America, the Potohar Valley, Multan, 6/4, the Old West Side of Ann Arbor, suburban New Jersey, the streets of New York, the vistas of Hanoi, Phnom Penh, and Bali.

Thanks to my early readers Haider Shahbaz and Danish Shabbir, whose confidence in the book made all the difference. Thanks to Linda and Larry, my generous hosts in beautiful Blachly. Thanks to my in-laws, who have supported me at every turn. Thanks to my brothers, Hateem and Ahmed, for the love, humor, and babysitting hours they have provided over the writing of this book. Thanks to my parents, Jamila and Tanvir – where do I begin? Thanks to my son Ameer, who leaves this writer wordless with love every day. Thanks, finally, to Bryan. Todas as minhas palavras são tuas.